POETIC JUSTICE

POETIC JUSTICE

ANDREA J. JOHNSON

TORONTO • NEW YORK • LONDON
AMSTERDAM • PARIS • SYDNEY • HAMBURG
STOCKHOLM • ATHENS • TOKYO • MILAN
MADRID • WARSAW • BUDAPEST • AUCKLAND

W🌐RLDWIDE™

ISBN-13: 978-1-335-73653-6

Poetic Justice

First published in 2020 by Agora Books, an imprint of
Polis Books, LLC.
This edition published in 2022.

Copyright © 2020 by Andrea J. Johnson

This edition published by arrangement with Harlequin Books S.A.

For questions and comments about the quality of this book,
please contact us at CustomerService@Harlequin.com.

Harlequin Enterprises ULC
22 Adelaide St. West, 41st Floor
Toronto, Ontario M5H 4E3, Canada
www.ReaderService.com

Printed in U.S.A.

"Vox audita perit, litera scripta manet."

The spoken word perishes, the written word remains.

ONE

I HADN'T SEEN Langley Dean in ten years.

When we'd last spoken, she'd pushed me into the pool while I was wearing Bickerton High's Scrappy the Seabird mascot uniform. The useless velvet wings and doughy web-footed moon boots wilted under the weight of the water and dragged me below the surface faster than a battleship anchor.

Sometimes I dreamt about the valiant escape that might have happened if I hadn't been strapped into the helmeted shoulder harness that held the Seabird's head on. That clownish costume with its gratuitous layers of felt and silk was my temporary tomb. If EMTs hadn't been onsite for the homecoming football game, I would have died.

And yet, I didn't recognize Langley until after the trial fell apart.

Maybe the self-protective portion of my brain didn't want to dredge up the past. Maybe time had turned the svelte beauty into a paunchy broad who lived in a troubled world lightyears from my own. Maybe I was simply too far away.

What I knew for sure was when her trial began, I sat a full courtroom's length apart from her and her defense counsel. My stenography station was a tiny Formica table located at the base of a raised platform reserved for witnesses. All my focus was on the grizzled jury clerk who stood in the gap between us. He droned through felony drug charges and asked a series of questions meant to determine if anyone had previous knowledge of the case or any prejudice that could lead to bias against the defendant.

Those standard little voir dire inquiries should have been a red flag.

The truth of the matter was my job as the trial's stenographer was to listen, not analyze. As far as I was concerned, at that point, she was just another face in the long line of hardened criminals I'd seen in my five years as a court reporter in the Trident County Superior Courthouse, where the residents of Bickerton, Delaware, tried their most heinous crimes.

"Victoria?" the judge called from her elevated position at the front of the courtroom. "Excuse me, Ms. Justice, do you need a break before we continue with opening statements?"

"No, ma'am." My words emerged as a whisper.

The other aspect of my job was to be seen, not heard, but I appreciated Ms.—I mean Judge—Freddie's concern for my well-being. Writing a word-for-word account of the proceedings was no small task.

"Call out the time when you do." She switched her focus to the recently selected jury. "Good morning, ladies and gentlemen. This is Mulligan versus the State of Delaware. My name is Frederica Scott Wannamaker. I'll be presiding over the case. We ask that you give the attorneys your undivided attention."

The jurors' eyes grew wide as she spoke. I'd have found it amusing if I hadn't seen it a million times. Civilians expected a *Law & Order* episode come to life, but they'd soon experience the mundane reality of small-town justice. No cutthroat attorneys tricking witnesses into confessing. No camera flashes from the rabid media. No distraught family members begging for the judge's mercy.

Like ninety-five percent of our drug cases, the gallery sat empty—except for the state chemist, who quietly occupied the front row, and a state trooper, who I assumed was the arresting officer. He sat in the back with his arm draped over the pew, while he drummed an impatient rhythm against the oak. The light thumpity-thump echoed into the recently restored rafters designed to mimic the courthouse's original antebellum-era architecture.

I smoothed the collar of my gray pantsuit as the jury rose for their oath. *Showtime.* A crackle of static underscored their call and response as the bailiff used her shoulder mic to radio the criminal unit for Ms. Freddie's trial clerk. The prosecutor, Deputy Attorney General Spencer James Stevenson—a recent Vanderbilt grad who apparently bathed in a bottle of Drakkar Noir cologne—strutted over to the podium, where he'd address the jury for opening statements.

He straightened his Armani tie and gave me a wink. Stevenson couldn't have been more than a decade older than my twenty-five years, but he was too cocky to take seriously. He was being playful and overconfident for the jury's benefit, not mine.

I stared at the attorney's big, bald head and prayed my dark eyes remained impassive. The job required neutrality at all times—Stevenson knew that—and I refused to cosign on his good-ol'-boy-doing-the-will-of-the-people act. Granted, Delaware wasn't southern, but our seaside hamlet clung to all of The South's worst tendencies—and he loved to wield those values in his favor.

I placed my hands on the steno machine's keys and stiffened my petite frame to emphasize a commitment to impartiality. All I was willing to give Stevenson was a curt nod as a signal to begin his opening remarks. The movement also caused a bushy crop of brown ringlets to fall across my eyes and obscure his smarmy face from view. Perfect. All distractions cleared away to make room for the words that flowed through my fingers.

After the attorneys finished their opening statements, Ms. Freddie said, "You may call your first witness, Mr. Stevenson."

"Your Honor, the State calls Corporal Ashton North of the Delaware State Police."

A split second after the corporal, a hulking figure in dress blues, marched forward to recite the oath, the attorney fired off a round of questions about the cop's qualifications. Dang. Stevenson was fast, but I was faster.

My steno machine, a pentagon-shaped apparatus no larger than a child's lunchbox and just as light, held twenty-two unmarked keys that allowed me to write well over 240 words per minute. The excessive speed lulled me into a trance for the first half-hour, but as the testimony found its groove, my awareness blossomed.

"What happened once you established probable cause to search the defendant's vehicle?" asked Stevenson.

"I seized a brick of suspicious powder from the front passenger seat," Corporal North replied in a hoarse bass. "This led to a full-vehicle search, whereupon I opened the trunk to find scales, baggies, three cell phones, and five thousand dollars in cash. I identified the powdered substance as cocaine."

"Once you had all those items in your possession, what did you do?"

"I placed the items in separate evidence envelopes provided by the Delaware State Police and labeled each with the defendant's name, a description, and the complaint number. I used blue evidence tape to seal the envelopes and signed my name on those seals."

The corporal responded with authority but tossed anxious glances my way prior to each answer—like he was unsure whether to talk to me as the record taker or to the attorney. A giggle formed in my throat as his lashes fluttered and his bright blue eyes ping-ponged between the prosecutor and me. I stared at the stenograph machine to keep the laughter at bay.

Blocks of shorthand welcomed me from the miniature screen above the steno keyboard. Denoted by a collection of letters read from left to right, all of the words were in a language of briefs, AKA abbreviations, or shortened word forms that helped me capture every sentence with a ninety-eight percent degree of accuracy. I couldn't afford to let anything affect my proficiency, and that awareness sobered me into submission.

I looked up to discover Stevenson had left his podium and struck a meditative pose in front of the jury box. He leaned one hand on the delicate oak rail, the other rested in the pocket of his slacks while he addressed his next set of questions into the ether.

"What happened then, Corporal?"

"I returned to the station to file a report and submit the materials to the evidence sergeant. He entered them into Troop Eleven's log. The drug envelope would have stayed in our evidence locker to await pick up by the Controlled Substance Lab, but I got clearance to hand-deliver that item for testing."

"You *personally* dropped off the drug evidence at the lab that same day?"

"Yes, sir. I was lucky enough to get there within four hours of arrest."

"Was the envelope still sealed when you dropped it off?"

"Yes, sir."

"Did that evidence envelope ever leave your sight prior to arriving at the lab?"

"No, sir. The drug envelope stayed in my possession."

For a moment, I struggled with the word "possession." I couldn't remember the brief. Was it POGS or POEGS? Not wanting to waste another nanosecond on debate, I wrote it out phonetically. I depressed the keys in three quick strokes, one chord of letters for each syllable. The movement gave me three lines of text, POE/SES/SOGS. I perked up my ears. The extra strokes had caused me to fall behind.

"Your Honor, I believe we've established chain of custody. I'd like to enter the drug envelope for identification." Stevenson's mouth spread into an obsequious smile meant to reassure the jury, but they looked as bored as I felt.

"Any objection, Mr. Harriston?" Ms. Freddie asked defense counsel.

My gaze followed her voice over to Beau Harriston, Trident County's finest criminal defense attorney in private practice. He was sitting at counsel's table with his shoes off and his eyes closed, hands pressed to his mouth as if in silent prayer. He responded with a loud grunt that caused his jowls to shake and waved a hand in the airspace above his receding hairline as if to say—*get on with it*.

I gritted my teeth. Harriston's inconsiderate gesture and its implied meaning weren't things I could officially capture with my steno machine. I fell even further behind while I debated the accuracy of writing "no objection," as his reply, versus "shaking head in the negative" as a parenthetical for the unspoken implication. My dislike of the old defense attorney rose with every keystroke.

Mr. Stevenson handed the trial clerk a tan catalog envelope covered with writing on the front, lined along the left side with white masking tape, and sealed at the flap with neon blue tape. The clerk placed a thumbprint-sized sticker on the lower right-hand corner of the envelope and passed it back to the prosecutor.

Everyone leaned forward as the attorney placed the evidence in front of Corporal North, who thoroughly examined the package.

"Is this the envelope transported on the day of arrest?"

"Yes, sir. This bears my signature on the blue evidence tape, which is still intact. The case information is clearly visible and matches my notes. The only difference is this white tape, which I know from experience and can see from the words printed here…" The corporal pointed to the left edge of each envelope. "That's the tape used by the Controlled Substance Lab to reseal the evidence after the chemist runs a test. Otherwise, the envelope is identical to the one I dropped at the lab."

"To be clear, what did you put in that envelope on the day of the arrest?"

"A brick of cocaine weighing two point two five pounds." Corporal North held up the envelope.

"Did you receive a copy of the chemist's report confirming cocaine in the quantity noted?"

"Yes, sir."

"And is this that report?" Stevenson handed the corporal three pages.

While the witness perused the document, I glanced at the computer-aided transcription program open on my laptop—otherwise known as CAT—to see if my usage of the steno machine's numbering system had translated. I always used the number bar across the top of the steno keyboard during drug trials due to the constant references to milligrams, ounces, pounds, and dollars. My earlier use of 5/THOU/-DZ translated beautifully as $5,000. All the other numbers were garbage. Good thing I'd turned on my AudioSync microphone to catch inconsistencies.

As my attention drifted back to the trial, I caught Corporal North setting down the lab report with a nod of his head. Nothing more annoying than a witness who failed to speak up.

"Please respond verbally for the record." My words slipped out as a murmur. A quiet moment of confidence between the two of us, carefully constructed to convey no emotion, but I couldn't help but return the embarrassed grin he gave in response.

He was quickly becoming my favorite person in the courtroom.

"Yes, sir." He peeked at me for approval. "This is a

copy of the report from the Controlled Substance Lab confirming my observations."

"And with the exception of the state chemist's white tape," said Stevenson, "has this item been tampered with in any way?"

"No, sir."

"Your Honor, I ask the envelope be admitted as a numbered exhibit." The prosecutor handed the package to the trial clerk.

"Any objection?" Ms. Freddie's plump face peered over the bench at Harriston.

The arrogant defense attorney gave a noncommittal shrug, and she let out a slight growl. I could tell she wanted to admonish him for failing to respect the court.

"Admitted as State's Exhibit One," she bellowed. "Madam Clerk, mark the evidence and give it to Corporal North. You may expose the item for the jury."

Once Corporal North received the envelope, he tugged at the blue tape and ripped it open. As his hands worked to remove the contents, I scanned his fingers for a wedding ring.

Desperate much? Stay focused.

I pried my attention away from the witness stand and fixated on the letters filling the steno machine's view screen.

STKPWHR/SKPS/THAT/KOE/KAEUPB/-U/
SAOEZ/-D/OPBT/DAEUT/-F/ARS
STPHO-FRPBLGTS/T-S/TPHOT

The word gage on the left showed 43,378 and counting. A green meter on the right, representing the machine's battery life, flickered and faded to yellow—a clear sign we'd been in trial for about three hours.

Time for a break.

I tapped the touch screen so the view changed from shorthand to English with the hour illuminated underneath. My gaze sought Ms. Freddie's. She'd told me to call out the time the moment I needed a break. I opened my mouth to do so but stopped short at the wide-eyed astonishment etched on her ebony skin.

Had I done something wrong? My breath grew shallow, and I dropped my attention back to the trusty steno screen, a source of strength when I needed to gather my wits, and reread the last Q&A my hands had transcribed without really hearing.

> MR. STEVENSON: And is that the cocaine you seized on the date of arrest?
>
> CORPORAL NORTH: No, sir, it is not.
> *Monday, November 2—11:08 a.m.*

The whole courtroom had gone dead silent.

TWO

THE JURORS' JAWS hung open. Maggie the clerk stood up from her desk at the front of the bench and craned her neck toward the witness. Stevenson, who'd been pacing, froze midstride so he looked like the silhouette on a crosswalk sign. Even Grace the bailiff dropped her guard, head tilted to the side in disbelief.

Only defense counsel and his client remained unfazed.

Corporal Ashton North sat motionless, his eyes and nose scrunched in confusion. He clutched the empty evidence envelope to his chest and did not appear to breathe. On the table in front of him sat a two-pound bag of C&H Pure Cane Powdered Confectioner's Sugar that was still in the original packaging, complete with the $2.08 price tag courtesy of our local Redner's Supermarket.

Something had definitely gone awry.

Soon nervous laughter trickled from the jury, but the cackle from the defendant made my lungs clench.

I remembered that sound from school. That was the last sound I'd heard before my head sank below the surface of Bickerton High's pool. Anxiety, like shards of chilled glass, ripped through my chest. I lifted my head and locked stares with the face that had been the ominous backdrop to an otherwise routine trial.

Harriston slipped on his loafers and hopped up.

"Your Honor, a bag of powdered sugar is not sufficient evidence. I move the charges against Langley Dean Mulligan be dismissed on all counts."

In that moment, everything blurred. *Langley Dean.* She was The Lovely Lady D when we clashed our senior year of high school. What once was a pale, auburn-haired ingénue with thin pink lips, upturned nose, and fiendish eyes so cold they registered as silver, was now a pudgy, sunburned woman with crow's-feet and a bad orange dye-job. The Lovely Lady D was barely recognizable, but her affect lingered.

I took a deep breath and parted my lips to ask for a break, but five sharp raps of the gavel against the solid oak of Ms. Freddie's massive desk created a thick smacking sound that called the room to order. She rose. Her stocky frame radiated the authority of a colossus. Coarse black strands tumbled out of her bun, and the double strand of pearls around her neck rattled out a warning.

"I'd like to see the attorneys at sidebar." She pointed the gavel at me. "You, too, Victoria."

Langley's head turned and an uncomfortable flash of recognition bounced between us. Her eyes tracked my movements as if she couldn't believe I was real.

Oh, no. Not here. Not at work.

I closed my laptop and grabbed the steno machine by its tripod so I could walk across the well of the courtroom to the judge's position on the bench. I could feel Langley's icy gaze follow me as I climbed the steps of the rostrum to the sanctity of Ms. Freddie's gigantic platform. I couldn't afford to succumb to Langley's intimidation tactics. I had a job to do.

Besides, she'd be out of sight the moment I took my place on the bench. Thank goodness. My heart settled.

For the first time in my career, I was happy to be at sidebar—until Stevenson's frat boy cologne invaded my nostrils.

Scratch that. Sidebars sucked.

The environment wasn't conducive to creating a verbatim record. Ms. Freddie occupied a chair the size of a recliner, while I sat on a footstool to her right. The attorneys stood on the steps to the bench and leaned over my head to speak with her. We were all huddled so close, I could smell of stale coffee on Harriston's breath.

Everyone radiated tension, especially once the white noise surrounded us. The bailiff switched on the annoying static to protect our confidential conversation from the jurors' ears—a little detail that reduced my cognition by fifty percent. To make up the difference, I stared at each person's lips as they spoke.

The process was like watching mimes act out a scene between an umpire and an unruly baseball manager. Stevenson was, of course, the manager as he flailed his arms and insisted Corporal North possessed sufficient authority to vouch for the narcotics. He even demanded we put the state chemist on the stand to verify the report, since the docket had her testifying anyway. Harriston disagreed and took the role of umpire. He remained cool and dignified as he campaigned to dismiss the felony drug charges.

I tried to keep up, but my thoughts clouded over with the memory of Langley's eyes. The way the silver glinted as she'd lured me from the locker room toward the school pool. She had told me to put on the mascot costume early so we could get a yearbook photo. I could barely see out of the mini eyehole ridiculously positioned under Scrappy the Seabird's beak. I didn't realize she'd led me to the edge. A swift kick in the gut and down I went.

"Enough!"

The judge held up her palm to cut both attorneys off mid-rant. She leaned away from our huddle and signaled the bailiff to take the jurors to the jury room. As soon as they were gone, Ms. Freddie switched off the white noise and motioned for Harriston to proceed.

"Your Honor, loss or destruction of evidence by the prosecution deprives the defendant due process and runs contrary to the Fourteenth Amendment." Harriston swept his arm toward the witness stand, where Corporal North still sat. "Chain of custody law requires the State authenticate the evidence and eliminate the possibility of misidentification."

"That statute doesn't require I authenticate evidence to a degree of absolute certainty," Stevenson's voice grew frantic, "just a reasonable probability. The lab report gives us that."

"Wrong. How can the State prove the authenticity of a substance if the evidence in the envelope doesn't match the description on the report?" Harriston flashed his veneers at the judge and swooped in for the kill. "Mr. Stevenson has failed to prove, beyond a reasonable doubt, that my client was in possession of narcotics on the day in question. Even if the chemist's report reveals a controlled substance, the door is open for the jury to infer tampering or false arrest. At the very least, we have a gap in the chain of custody."

The universe clearly loved screwing with me. Did he just imply Langley might have legal grounds for getting away with *another* crime? Tears formed at the thought, and my hands shook with rage. No one had believed what she'd done to me. Why should anything have changed?

"I call B.S." Corporal North burst to life on the witness stand, and everyone jumped at the sound of his fierce rebuttal. "Are you implying I don't know how to do my job?"

"Corporal, calm down," said Ms. Freddie. "No one has drawn a conclusion. What we need to do first is clarify the chain of custody." She turned her attention to the deputy attorney general. Her broad facial features twisted into a dark mask of disgust. "Mr. Stevenson, you have to overcome the presumption of innocence. Where do the drugs go after they are tested and the lab report completed?"

"I can answer that." Corporal North raised a hand and reached for her arm, even though he was out of range. He looked desperate and frustrated, and I wanted to let him know he wasn't the only collateral damage in this case. "Typically, our evidence sergeant retrieves the tested substances from the CSL and stores them at the troop until trial. In this case, the envelope never returned. Our people received word the lab did an internal audit, and the evidence transfer was put on hold. So, everything stayed at the CSL until this morning."

"I appreciate your candor, Corporal." Ms. Freddie then raised her voice to prompt the bailiff. "Could we get the chemist, Phyllis Dodd, up here at sidebar?" When Phyllis was absorbed into our circle, the judge started her examination. "Tell us why your office held this evidence."

Phyllis, a freckled-face brunette, who was slim, trim, and oh-so prim, spoke as if the answer was obvious. "As the person fiscally and administratively responsible for the lab, I do random inspections to ensure everyone follows procedure and our documentation matches the inventory. This deters theft and dry-labbing. We held the prosecution's evidence for such an audit. Everything cleared."

"Dry-labbing?" I asked. My mind was so preoccupied, I was afraid I'd misunderstood. I hadn't heard the term before, and I certainly didn't know how to spell it on my steno machine.

"Yes. Recording results for substances that were never tested." Phyllis bowed her head and smoothed the lines of her French twist in a nervous way that alerted me to my mistake in highlighting her lab's possible weakness.

"Your Honor," Harriston pounced, "I think she's essentially admitting knowledge of suspicious activity at the lab, which is sufficient grounds for a mistrial—"

"Excuse me, Counselor." Phyllis's voice was acidic. "Audits, spot checks, and dual testing are all part of the standard safeguards required to maintain our certification. The fact that we ran additional tests—"

"Your Honor," said Corporal North, "may I add that the envelope transferred over from the lab this morning got put in your criminal unit's evidence closet for safekeeping until trial. I watched your clerk store the item."

"Madam Clerk, is that accurate?" Ms. Freddie squinted over the bench at Maggie, her trial clerk and one of the employees in the criminal unit. "Was the evidence intact when you received it?"

"Yes, Judge." Maggie's face collapsed as if she couldn't believe they'd dragged her into the conversation.

I imagined she was grappling with the same option that cycled through my brain—cut off a limb and run screaming from this bear trap of a trial.

Maggie elaborated, "I received that delivery at seven thirty this morning and locked it in our evidence room, along with the other confiscated items in this case. That bundle came out of storage a little after nine—right after jury selection. The log didn't indicate anyone else had been in the evidence."

Ms. Freddie held up three fingers. "Corporal. Lab. Courthouse. What say you, Mr. Stevenson? This is your indictment. You bear the responsibility to maintain the integrity of the evidence."

"But, the officer assured me—"

"Stop there, Mr. Stevenson. We've already heard from the corporal. What did you do to follow up on this timeline?"

Ms. Freddie shuffled through her paperwork while every eye in the courtroom bore into the prosecutor's skull.

Every eye except mine.

I stretched my torso from side to side and dared to catch a glimpse of Langley's face. Did she understand where this could lead? Stevenson was sinking fast, and she'd once again get to enjoy seeing someone out of his depth. Her face appeared beyond the huddle, and she waggled her fingers at me—one brow raised above a chilling silver eye. The movement was subtle, so as not to arouse suspicion from the bailiff, who stood nearby, but it was enough. I snapped back into place under the cloak of bodies.

"What else could I have done?" Stevenson was almost whining now. He tugged at the knot in his tie as if it was the cause of his discomfort. "Everything followed standard procedure. I move to exclude Exhibit One and—"

"The jury has already seen the evidence." Ms. Freddie rattled her pearls. "You can't unring a bell, Mr. Stevenson."

"And you can't conceal exculpatory material that may exonerate my client." Harriston bared his teeth. "That goes right back to the defendant's right to due process. So say it with me, Your Honor, *case dismissed.*"

Ms. Freddie cut her gaze at Harriston's cheeky play to force her hand. "Well, Mr. Stevenson? Last chance to say something intelligent."

His silence stretched for several seconds and beads of sweat formed at his temples.

"All right, Mr. Stevenson. I don't doubt the lab report corroborates cocaine, but it's obvious that's not what we have." She snapped her fingers. "Wake up. A dangerous substance is missing. This situation points to a breach. A major breach. One that might have statewide implications. I advise all of you to launch an investigation within your offices. But more importantly, I recommend the Delaware Department of Justice examine the retention practices of the Controlled Substance Lab and the State Police."

She picked up the indictment that listed the charges for the case. "I am inclined to grant Mr. Harriston's motion to dismiss the felony counts of possession and distribution due to a lack of evidence."

I ventured another glance at Langley. Her head was down. She'd taken a pen and started carving into the wood of defense counsel's table, like she didn't have a care in the world.

"The misdemeanor paraphernalia charge," Ms. Freddie's voice rumbled on, "regarding the scales, baggies, cash, and cell phones still stands. I'll give counsel thirty minutes to work on a plea, or we can go to trial on the solo charge."

"But—but—Your Honor." Mr. Stevenson stamped his foot.

I could tell he wanted to argue, throw some foul words at the judge—or, heck, to throw a punch at Mr. Harriston, but he couldn't get the words out. After several uncomfortable seconds of wrenching at his neckwear and sputtering an incoherent torrent of curses, the prosecutor yanked the striped indigo tie from his neck and slammed it onto the desk in front of Ms. Freddie so his palm thwacked against the wood.

"A plea?" screeched Stevenson. "Why don't you give her a key to the city while you're at it?"

The sound of his mocking hung in the air. Ms. Freddie was the toughest judge in Trident County and the only female Superior Court judge of color in the state—two facts that often led to pushback from pompous men of privilege, like Stevenson. Rather than play into his game, she locked her jaw, folded her arms, and lowered her brow until her dark eyes formed the slits that marked her famous iron stare. Game over.

Stevenson's ignorant display soured into embarrassment when it became clear his protest was futile. With a faint whimper, he hunched his shoulders and backed away from the bench. The musk of defeat wafted off him in waves. Phyllis, almost as sullen, followed and took a seat in the gallery.

Beau Harriston, who could barely contain his amusement, inclined his head at Ms. Freddie. "Sounds like we'll be working on a plea." He then plucked Mr. Stevenson's tie from the judge's desk and drifted after the deputy attorney general to begin plea negotiations.

My face must have shown signs of worry because, once they departed, Ms. Freddie turned to me and whispered, "Are you all right? You look tired."

I pressed my lips together in a halfhearted attempt at a smile. Ms. Freddie was my mother's oldest friend and Kappa Mu sorority sister. She'd watched me grow up. When I graduated from Delaware State University six years ago, she'd suggested her office as a place to intern while I figured out what I wanted to do with my life. She and my mother prayed I'd get attorney fever and apply to law school, but I astonished everyone that summer and fell in love with court reporting. Learning a secret language to capture, transform, and transcribe the spoken word into verbatim transcripts was tantamount to magic.

"What about Langley?" I asked.

"They'll probably recommend a plea of probation or time served. With the heavy counts dropped and the defendant already out on bail, the misdemeanor won't be enough to hold her. She'll walk today."

"Is that safe?"

I could hear snippets of Langley bossing around her lawyer as they filled out paperwork at counsel's table. Each cackle made me wince. I shifted on the footstool where I sat at the judge's knee.

"Her file says these are her first drug charges, so all we can do is hope. The rest of her record is clean, except for a DUI last year and an underage drinking charge from more than a decade ago."

I lowered my head and blew out a loud breath. As far as Langley was concerned, that underage drinking charge was my fault. Nothing could be further from the truth.

"Is something wrong, Victoria?"

What could I say? Telling Ms. Freddie about my relationship with Langley wouldn't make a bit of difference in the trial's outcome, but I needed to say something in order to clear my conscience. As a sworn officer of the court, I had a responsibility to disclose any relationship that compromised my ability to remain impartial.

"Did Ma ever explain why I didn't go to Princeton?"

Ms. Freddie furrowed her brow. "Not exactly. She asked me for some legal advice because of that accident your senior year." She bit her lip. "She was reluctant to share the full story, so I never asked outright—but I assumed passing on Princeton had to do with your illness." Her hand touched mine in a moment of solidarity. "Weren't you in the hospital for pneumonia that year? My goodness, you were so young. Getting into college at fifteen is hard for anyone. No one blamed you for staying home." Her dark eyes searched mine. "What does any of that have to do with this?"

"Everything."

This wasn't the place to share the details of such an intimate story, but I needed her to understand why I couldn't continue with the trial.

"The pneumonia was the result of a drowning attempt perpetrated by Langley Dean—Langley Mulligan—the defendant. Her version of payback. She assumed I had gotten her busted for having alcohol on school grounds, but it wasn't me." I leaned forward on the stool to lend more privacy to my words. "I would have told you before trial, but I didn't recognize her. For what it's worth, Langley is guilty. If not for this, then something far more sinister."

And I still have the scars to prove it.

"Victoria, I'm so sorry." She squeezed my hand. Based on the tears in her eyes, I sensed she meant the gesture as a hug. "I can't imagine how you feel. You were brave to have shared this, but you know I can't do anything."

"I know. I didn't mean to suggest that you should." I swallowed my anger. "I had to share the truth so you'd understand why I plan to call in another court reporter to take the plea. I can't handle this."

"I understand. Do whatever it takes." She gave my hand another squeeze and blinked away her tears. "Go talk to your colleagues. I need to do the same. The law prohibits me from spearheading an investigation, but I'll need to report a few things about this case to President Judge Yaris. Get me a copy of the transcript as soon as you can, okay?"

She lifted her head and announced to the near-empty courtroom. "We're in a thirty-minute recess while the attorneys conduct their plea negotiations."

The bailiff cried out, "All rise."

I rose from my footstool and moved out of Ms. Freddie's path.

As she stepped down from the bench, she turned to me and whispered, "Give me ten minutes. I'll meet you in the kitchen for tea. We can have a real conversation. You can tell me the whole story…uncensored." She pressed a finger to her lips to let me know that our teatime would be as friends, not coworkers.

Just knowing she'd taken an interest in my story made me feel better. I was lucky to have someone at work watching my back. I didn't know how I'd survive without her guidance, so I pressed a finger to my lips in return and watched her go.

THREE

"THAT'S THE FIRST TIME I've seen anything like that," said Grace Tisdale, Trident County Superior Court's chief bailiff and head of security.

Grace had a matronly face and a Peter Pan haircut gone prematurely white, but her body was as lithe and nimble as a professional athlete's. She climbed onto the bench, where I was still standing after Ms. Freddie's recent departure, and squatted beside my footstool for a private conversation. "You hear whispers about this stuff happening all the time upstate, but I never thought it would happen down here."

"Me neither." I plopped back onto the footstool so we could gossip face to face. "I can't believe she dismissed the felony charges."

Grace made a clucking sound. "This has Old Beau Harriston's name written all over it."

"You think so?"

"I know so. You haven't been around long enough to see how cutthroat he can be. I'm never surprised at some of the crazy things he says or, better yet, does— especially when a juror or someone from the media is within earshot. He loves swaying the public with alternative *facts*." She mimed sarcastic air quotes.

I raised an eyebrow.

"Of course, if he's feeling gracious," she rolled her eyes, "he'll simply show up late to court or flood the clerk with evidence or demand dozens of sidebars to wear out the jury."

"That stuff never works."

"Sure it does. Check it out." Grace handed me a navy-blue business card with bold gold letters. "Oh, and Old Beau says he wants a copy of the trial transcript. Give him a ring when you're ready for payment."

I skimmed the contact information and flipped the card over to find Harriston's picture and a tagline.

BEAUREGARD MONROE HARRISTON, Attorney at Law—*Don't dare plea, we'll set you free!* OVER 200 CONSECUTIVE WINS AND COUNTING—licensed in Delaware for 40+ years.

"Okay. Point taken. He knows how to win." I plucked the business card with my middle finger. "Still, you can't blame the man for taking pride in his work—but what you're suggesting is evidence tampering. That's illegal and a whole lot different than blabbing to the press."

"True. But take a second to consider why he's won so much. Either he's only accepting cases he thinks he can win, or he's dancing with the devil to make those wins happen."

We eyeballed each other.

Grace was the oldest and sharpest bailiff on staff. She'd worked in the courthouse for over twenty years. If anyone's opinion was worth considering, it was definitely hers. But was it realistic to think a prominent attorney would be willing to risk his career for a witch like Langley?

I slipped Harriston's card into the pocket of my suit and looked over at the balding attorney. He was resting his backside against the edge of Stevenson's table with his legs crossed at the ankle and his arms folded. Based on the twitch of Harriston's bulbous nose and heavy jowls, he appeared completely dissatisfied with the words of the frenzied prosecutor. I wanted to see if I could eavesdrop on their conversation from my perch, but Grace interrupted my thoughts.

"Think about it. This is the kind of publicity his business needs. Getting clients acquitted after winning a trial is one thing. But getting the charges dismissed during trial makes him a demi-god, especially when all the big law firms from upstate have shaved his business down to nothing."

"So, you think…" my lips puckered on a seed of doubt, "Mr. Harriston needs to win this case because he's losing clients?"

"Exactly. Don't you ever walk The Quad? Old Beau has a 'for lease' sign in his window. I mean, come on— his office has been there since I was a kid."

Even though I lived less than two miles from Bickerton Square, where the courthouse was located, I never walked to work and didn't spend time hanging around the building. Bail bond agencies, the drug lab, and the county's government offices crowded most of the area. To my mind, nothing in the center of town was worth exploring except Cake & Kettle, a local teashop that had become my lunchtime hideout.

"For all you know, he could be leasing his office space and moving to a better one."

Grace shook her head. "He's on the verge of eviction for late payments. Maggie says he's constantly in and out of the Prothonotary's Office asking for favors because his secretary and law clerk quit eight months ago. Their paychecks kept bouncing."

"Paralegal. The true definition of a law clerk is one who works for a judge."

I didn't mean to correct Grace. The words came out as absentminded filler because I didn't know how to respond. Her theory was pure hearsay, but the idea made sense. Harriston had been awfully smug at sidebar.

"Sorry, Grace. Can we talk about this later?" I lifted my steno machine and stood. "I'm going to send in another reporter right after I check my laptop. I've already cleared the switch with the judge."

"Everything okay?" Her voice grew serious.

"For now." I fixed my lips into what I hoped was a carefree grin. "Just be mindful of the switch, will you?"

"Whatever you say, boss." Grace unfolded from her crouch and adjusted the long sleeves of her starchy polyester uniform. "If I didn't have to get back to those jurors, I'd make you talk."

"Excuse me, ladies." Phyllis Dodd's high-pitched voice pierced our conversational bubble.

The chemist's willowy frame and flawless posture placed her freckled face at eye level, despite our elevated position on the bench.

"My time is valuable. I'm due to give testimony upstate in less than two hours. Is my presence still required here? If the judge dismissed the drug charges, shouldn't the trial be—"

"Yes, ma'am," Grace said, "but we still have a plea on the table. She likes to hold the jury and witnesses until the final disposition. But if you come with me, I'll walk you through to chambers. We can ask the judge's secretary if it's okay for you to leave."

And with that, Grace climbed down from the bench and escorted Phyllis out of the courtroom through the side door that led to the judges' collection of private offices.

As I strolled back to my workstation, I focused my sights on Harriston and Stevenson. Their discussion was loud enough to hear from my desk, but I missed my opportunity to eavesdrop when I bumped into the back of Maggie Swinson, the judge's trial clerk. She'd perched on my desk shamelessly flirting with Corporal North, who still sat on the witness stand.

"You know, most of us clerks hang out at Cooper's on Wednesday nights for karaoke. You should stop by for a drink," Maggie said in her southern Delaware drawl where U's were elongated and G's barely exist. "We could do a duet together. 'Endless Love' is one of my particular favorites." She emphasized the statement by leaning her medically enhanced bosom close to the corporal's face.

"Seriously, Maggs? Can you park your rear somewhere else?"

Rude? Yes, but I feared her enormous rump was going to knock my water cup onto the laptop I'd left running. Besides, Corporal North had a white-knuckle grip on the edge of the witness stand—a sure sign he needed saving. Maggie was a full-figured country queen with a honey-blonde bouffant, a brilliant smile, and a notorious reputation as a man-eater.

"Excuse me, darlin'." She snapped at me. "I wasn't in the middle of a conversation or nothing."

Maggie slid off the desk, and her genteel façade slipped for a second as she narrowed her eyes at me. She then twirled back to the corporal, reached into her bra, pulled out a slip of paper, and handed it to him.

"Here's my number, in case you want to come." She

rocked her hips like a pendulum, pivoted, and sashayed over to the attorneys, who were still deep in debate.

I sat down and plugged the charger cable into my steno machine. Then I scrolled through the transcription software to make sure the Bluetooth connection had successfully transferred all the notes from sidebar to the laptop. I even checked the mini-microphones I kept running during trials in case of emergencies. When I paused to reach for my Styrofoam water cup, Corporal North stared at me.

"You spent a long time talking to the judge and bailiff." His voice was higher and tighter than the coarse bass he'd used during testimony—the strained voice of a man trying to hold back his anger. "What's going on? Is the judge planning something?"

Did he really expect me to answer that? Sure, he was the investigating officer on the case, but he was also a witness. My goal was to maintain neutrality or silence when confronted by witnesses.

"The judge?" I sipped my water and conjured up a generic reply. "She clarified a few issues for the record. Criminal trials can be rough on stenographers."

No exaggeration there.

"Rough on witnesses, too." He gave a derisive snort. "At least you didn't embarrass yourself in front of the jury." He cleared his throat and muttered to himself, "Damn that Mulligan chick. Should've gone with alcohol. I bet those charges would have stuck."

Not likely.

The words danced on the edge of my tongue. Sarcasm wasn't going to help his situation, but nothing else seemed appropriate in the face of watching Langley's unfathomable luck claim another victim.

North banged the top of the witness stand with his fist and glared into the distance. Unsure whether he was waiting for a response, my gaze went to the jurors who filed out of the jury room, into the gallery, and through the double doors at the back of the courtroom.

"You know, Corporal, we're in recess. You don't have to sit here if you need to report to your superiors." I widened my eyes and hoped he'd take the hint. All I wanted to do was archive my notes and escape to the kitchen to meet Ms. Freddie. People didn't usually notice me in my little nook—a fact I enjoyed—and I hated how his lingering presence highlighted my position, not an ideal scenario with Langley just a few yards away.

"Yeah, you're right." North gave a resigned huff. He gripped his campaign hat and stood. Then he stuck the powdered sugar inside the corresponding evidence envelope and handed the bundle to me with his hand still inside. "Your clerk forgot to collect these."

I shrugged. This wasn't the first time Maggie had left items unattended during a recess. I accepted the moot evidence by wrapping my hands around the length of the envelope, where the white evidence tape concealed the left side. Heat tickled my palm as I clasped the package. When North removed his hand, the warmth disappeared.

"That's funny," I mumbled as I set the materials on Maggie's desk, which was catty-corner to mine.

"What's funny?" Corporal North paused while stepping down from the witness stand.

"I thought I felt your hand through the envelope, but that's impossible…isn't it?"

"Not unless…" He rotated toward me at a slow burn,

as if realizing something for the first time, "...there's a hole. Try it again."

He set down his hat and reclaimed his seat so we could reenact our exchange. His hand inside, my hand outside. We lingered mid-clench.

"Do you feel something, or are we playing the world's weirdest game of handsies?" He relaxed his jaw into a dopey grin that almost made me forget he was a witness.

Almost.

I lowered my gaze and let a bushel of curls conceal my embarrassment over happily groping a state trooper's hand. I moved to slide away. But, as I did so, my palm rubbed against something scratchy. A flash of heat and...nothing.

"There it is again," I whispered. "Hold still."

I grabbed a pen from the desk with my unoccupied hand and placed a dot on the envelope under the area of my palm, where I felt the flash.

When I disengaged from the package, I poked at the marked target with my fingernail. It was a small flap of white tape concealing a jagged hole the length and width of a large paper clip, through which protruded North's flesh.

"What the..." I rubbed my thumb across his skin through the slit. "Did you do this when you opened the evidence, or has this been there the whole time?"

"What? No." North took his hand out of the envelope. "No way. I only made one rip—right along the blue edge near my signature."

"Who do you think—"

"I don't know." He grabbed the envelope and held the

hidden flap up to the light. "But there are several layers of tape here…and it's not all from the lab."

He angled the envelope for my inspection. Sure enough. Strips of clear packing tape were visible over the lab's white masking tape, as if someone had opened and resealed the envelope a second time.

"Should I call the judge?" I turned to make sure our antics hadn't caught the attention of the attorneys… and Langley.

"I'd rather talk to the chemist first," he said. "I don't want to jump to conclusions. This could be from the audit. Do you know if Phyllis Dodd is still around? I thought I saw her a few moments ago."

"She left with Grace, the bailiff. They were headed to chambers."

"You've made my day." He handed the envelope back to me with a twinkle in his eyes. "Thanks for playing handsies with me. I owe you one."

Despite my reluctance to succumb to his flirtation, I watched him leave the courtroom. Tall as a Redwood and just as sturdy, his body gave the navy-blue and gold Delaware State Police uniform superhero dimensions. But, as he sauntered across the well toward the gallery, I noticed he stopped by the defendant's table and glared. The corporal attempted to mask the eye contact from the rest of the room as he donned his hat, but the unspoken interaction was unmistakable.

"He's quite the barnyard stud, ain't he?" Maggie stepped into place behind her desk, having finished gathering paperwork from the attorneys, and joined me in admiring Corporal North's rear view.

I faced her and dropped the suspicious evidence envelope on her desk. "He thinks he may have found tampering on the evidence packaging."

"Well, he should have said something to Mr. Stevenson." Maggie cocked her hip and placed a hand on her waist. "He better not try to blame this on the clerks in the Prothonotary's Office. We didn't have anything to do with it. You court reporters and bailiffs are the ones who keep asking to rifle through the evidence closet every five minutes."

"Whoa, Maggs. Cool it. He's not interested in throwing around blame. He wants to hear what the chemist has to say before...." I don't know why I bothered trying to talk to Maggie. If it didn't involve a man fawning over her, she wasn't interested.

"Well, whatever. As long as he leaves my name out of it." She snatched the case file and evidence from her desk and stormed out of the courtroom, with Mr. Stevenson in tow.

I shook off her remarks and hunched over my equipment to do a final save when a sinister voice, an edgy vocal fry reminiscent of the Kardashians, drew my attention.

"What up, Sooty? Been swimming lately?" Langley's clownish orange hair and ruddy skin gave the already contemptible statement an eerie bite. She was wearing black combat boots with a long-sleeved jean jacket over a black Lycra dress, whose hem clung above her knees. When she'd gotten my attention, she leaned back in the chair beside her attorney.

"Watch it, Langley. You'd have my head if I walked into your workplace and called you a Mick or a Paddy." I should have ignored her, but I was determined to stand my ground. Trash was the only language Langley spoke.

"You know each other?" Harriston was pouring himself a drink from the water pitcher residing on counsel's table.

"Oh, yes." Langley raked her ruby red talons across the wood surface.

The low-pitched scraping sound sent prickles along the scars on my shoulders. The ones I'd received when I struggled under the weight of the mascot's head harness.

"We were on the Pep Squad together our senior year," Langley crooned. "She was our sacrificial lamb—I mean, mascot, Sooty the Seabird."

"That's Scrappy the Seabird. And boy, you sure made me feel welcome. Almost seemed like you were trying to kill me with kindness." I clenched my jaw and gradually rose. "It's amazing one person could get away with being so sweet."

Langley ignored my comments. We were in a public forum, and I was cutting too close to the truth.

Instead, she spoke to her attorney as if I wasn't there. "Sooty was a wonder kid. Jumped right over seventh and eighth grades to become our high school's math champion, literary geek, and resident nark—all that fuss about her brain made her a little too big for her britches, if you ask me."

"Look, Langley." I stood arms akimbo to show her she held no power over me. "I'm not going to engage in some clichéd *Mean Girls*-style showdown with you. We were never friends and seeing you today is nothing but a bad roll of the dice." I abandoned my equipment and took two steps toward the exit located at the rear of the courtroom. "Congratulations on your case. You seem to have an infinite number of ways of getting out of trouble. Now, if you'll excuse me, I have an appointment."

Langley jumped out of her chair and slammed her hands on the table. I stumbled backward.

She spat out a maniacal cackle apparently satisfied by my reaction. "Still a mouthy little brat, aren't you? Always quick to condemn someone with your goody-two-shoes act."

"I never condemned you, lied about you, or narked on you. That's what you choose to believe. Find someone else to blame for your problems."

My temper flared. I'd finally found peace, and Langley's presence threatened that harmony.

"Mr. Harriston, I believe your client is out of line. Do I need to call a guard?" I raised my voice and, as if on cue, one of the enormous corrections officers who monitor the holding cell next door stepped into the courtroom from a side entrance.

"She has a point, Ms. Mulligan." Harriston's jowls wobbled. "You're out on bail. The court expects you to conduct yourself as a responsible citizen. We shouldn't hurl insults and accusations at a state official." He tapped two fingers on her wrist. "Let's not press our luck."

"Take it easy, everybody. We're just talking." She cautiously inched around to the front of counsel's table with her hands raised in surrender and her sights on the corrections officer. "I'm innocent. I never had any drugs. The whole thing was a setup. Although, why would I expect a nark like you to believe anything I say? I saw the way you were cozying up to the judge and that cop. Did you tell them about us?"

"Wow. In ten years, nothing's changed. Listen, not everything is about you. It's called doing my job."

"Is that so? Well, I'm glad to hear that because now I know exactly where to find you whenever I want to… play."

As the last word slipped from her lips, she twisted her body, grabbed the water pitcher from the table, and flung the contents at me.

Everything slowed to the tempo of a dirge as the fat wave of frosty liquid crashed against my face. Darkness enveloped me. I was fifteen again and back in that pool.

Water thrust its way past my nostrils. Droplets seared the back of my throat. Panic-stricken heartbeats hammered so loud it muted all other sound. Pressure threatened to collapse my lungs until I recognized I was holding my breath in anticipation of a more treacherous onslaught.

Gasping for air, I groped at my bowtie blouse—the soggy clumps of fabric an unnerving reminder of my watery tomb. Voices clamored from all directions.

"Not so high and mighty now, eh, Sooty?"

I opened my eyes to find Langley speaking to me from the ground. She thrashed against the burly prison guard who kneed her in the back and shouted submission instructions as he pressed on a set of handcuffs. Mr. Harriston stood by my side, with his handkerchief, dabbed at my face, and issued rapid-fire apologies. I gripped his arm to steady myself.

"Forgive me," Harriston said. "That shouldn't have happened. I blame myself. If I'd had any inkling she was capable of this, I would have—I should have taken her outside as soon as she made it clear you knew each other."

"Ma'am, would you like to press assault charges?" The guard's voice echoed in my head. "We could ask for the surveillance video to support your claim, ma'am. Ma'am?"

My heart raced and my thoughts swirled. The emotions of the moment—fear, sorrow, hate, panic—combined with the adrenaline to create an elixir that left me dizzy.

"Please, please. Let's all be rational." Harriston's words came out in a jumble. "This is just a misunderstanding. I assure you Ms. Mulligan meant no harm. This has been a stressful day for everyone."

"Assault?" I struggled to find my voice. The word seemed foreign but right.

"This is your call, ma'am. I can put her in a holding cell and contact Bickerton P.D." The guard rolled a handcuffed Langley over into a sitting position while I remained mute. "They'd have an officer here to take your statement within the hour. I could give your office a call when they arrive."

"Yes…assault. I'd love to press charges." My vision zeroed in on Langley's fiendish silver eyes as the fight drained out of them. "Well, Langley, you know what they say about karma."

FOUR

I PUSHED THROUGH the double-doored antechamber at the back of the courthouse and squinted as the stark noon-day sun and crisp autumn breeze cut across my eyes.

Free at last.

Fresh air and sunlight were exactly what I needed in the wake of Langley's attack. Gulls mewed over-head as they flew south. Traffic moved steadily along the narrow streets, and a few townsfolk roamed the pavement for a lunchtime stroll. To my right, beyond the County Administration Building, a cacophony of voices floated over from the town center as municipal workers argued over the fastest way to construct the bandstand and lighting scaffold for Wednesday's Post-Election Festival.

My drenched clothing, trembling hands, swollen eyes, and spastic breathing didn't belong in this idyllic setting. I needed a fresh shirt from my gym bag and a private place to regroup before Bickerton P.D. arrived to take my statement, so I hurried across the courthouse parking lot toward my Mustang. A few jabs at the key-less entry pad and the car became my fortress of soli-tude, where I proceeded to talk myself down from the panic attack and impending hyperventilation.

I reminded myself that water was an essential part of how Bickerton thrived. With the town lying four miles inland from where the Delaware Bay met the Atlantic Ocean, the expectation was that the average resident had a healthy relationship with the sea. Some folks were seafarers reveling in their bounty of blue crabs and shrimp, while others were cutthroat sales clerks determined to cash in on the clams and oysters caught by the local watermen. During the summer, fancy restaurants boasted fresh sea fare with an ocean view, eager teenagers hauled surfboards along the beach route, ferries shuttled people across the bay, and thousands of tourists sunned themselves on the sands of the Atlantic.

I'd lived in Bickerton my entire life, so I loved all of those things about our town. Yet, my relationship with water remained distant and crippling.

Several moments passed before I could breathe normally. I pawed at the damp folds of my white bowtie blouse only to find a stress rash forming on my chest. I needed to remove the shirt or risk inducing another panic attack. As I struggled to pull the drenched fabric over my massive crown of hair, I caught the shape of a fast-moving, tweed-clad figure out of the corner of my eye. Phyllis Dodd, the state chemist, hurried past my vehicle as I ripped off the wet shirt.

Slouching low in my seat to avoid exposing my camisole, I peeked over the dash to get a better look. Phyllis appeared to be fleeing from Spencer Stevenson and Corporal North, who were following her through the parking lot. The trio stopped one row over from mine and started arguing. Dodd, whose height nearly matched the corporal's, prodded at North's chest while he straightened his back against the force of her onslaught. Spencer Stevenson settled between the two titans with his arms crossed and his shirtsleeves rolled up to the elbow, amused by the unfolding mayhem.

I found that if I didn't wriggle against the leather of my driver's-side hideaway, I could hear Phyllis Dodd's shrill voice fending off the commanding tones of Corporal North.

"I don't like what you're suggesting, Corporal. If you indeed found a suspicious entry point on that evidence envelope, any number of factors could have caused something like that. You can't expect me to respond to something I haven't seen."

"Ma'am, calm down," said North. "I'm trying to explore all of our—"

"Playing dumb isn't going to fly, Phyllis." Spencer Stevenson's frigid tenor cut into the conversation.

"You're out of line, Stevenson," said North. "I can handle this."

"Can you?" Stevenson gave the corporal a dismissive look and stepped in front of the officer so he could stand nose to freckled nose with the chemist. "I got read the riot act in court, and I'll be damned if I let anyone embarrass me like that again. Someone has to take the blame for what happened. If you don't give us a straight answer about the envelope, it will be you."

"Don't you dare strong-arm me, Spencer, especially when all you're doing is following orders from that old windbag." Phyllis Dodd's voice grew louder. "What neither of you seem to understand is an investigation will shut down the lab. Drug testing for every case will require outsourcing—that alone could cost the state millions of dollars, along with dozens of jobs neutralized and a backlog in the system. On top of it all, we could lose our accreditation. You're being irresponsible if you follow through on this without proof—"

"Well, if that's your only battle cry, consider the

damage done." Stevenson's smirk shone across the parking lot. "I already put a call into the Delaware Department of Justice and the State Police. Missing drugs are all the proof I need. If you have a problem with it, take your concerns to Judge—"

Wannamaker. An alarm sounded in my head. I was supposed to meet her during the break, and I was nearly thirty minutes late.

Remorseful and breathless, I raced into the courthouse kitchen with my gym bag and apologies at the ready. Ms. Freddie, however, was nowhere in sight.

Her robe was neatly folded over a chair by the refrigerator. The settled kettle was still steaming, and she'd pulled the metal tea caddy out of the cupboard, along with two ceramic mugs.

Ashamed as I was to admit it, her absence was a relief. I needed a few moments to change since my camisole was the only garment underneath the suit jacket I'd hastily buttoned over my bare chest when I ditched the wet blouse and raced out of the car.

Taking advantage of the moment, I walked through the kitchen into the stunted passageway that contained the unisex bathroom. The plan was to pull a T-shirt and towel out of my gym bag and undo as much damage from my argument with Langley as possible.

But when I pushed down the oblong handle, the wooden door smacked against something hard and ricocheted shut. I retreated, mumbling words of regret for invading someone's privacy, but something seemed off. No frantic scrambles or angry rumblings of objection came in response to my flustered apology.

I dropped my duffel and carefully reopened the door. The room was dark and had a tinny odor like copper pennies left out in the rain. I reached inside and groped for the light. This time the wood thunked against what I recognized as a pair of legs splayed across the linoleum.

"Is everything okay in there?" My voice bounced off the tile walls in a shallow echo.

Slowly, I poked my head beyond the threshold to find the top half of Ms. Freddie's body draped across the toilet seat. She was face down in the water, a purple tie around her neck. The vicious knot replaced the double string of pearls she always wore in court—the strands now sat broken, beads scattered across her back. Blood pooled around a wound nestled in the tangled mass of jet-black hair that snaked its way along the surface of the water.

Her body didn't move.

I sank to my knees in the doorway, the air knocked out of me. The pit of my stomach tightened and churned as my mind reeled, unable to make sense of the scene.

Grace told me later that I had screamed and passed out.

What I remember is opening my mouth to breathe and finding my throat had clamped shut as the bile, hot as lava, clogged my airway.

I clawed at my neck, desperate to release myself from the creeping darkness that swallowed me.

FIVE

"THEY SAID YOU two were close," said Detective Connor Daniels of the Delaware State Police Homicide Division. "I'm sorry for your loss."

He directed the statement to the top of my bowed head and pushed a box of off-brand tissues toward me from across Jury Room Four's conference table.

"I should have ignored Langley and gone straight to the kitchen." Each syllable came out as a moan, mangled by heavy sobs. Yet, I uttered the sentence, repeatedly, like a Buddhist chant. I believed if I said those words enough times, I could change things. I could turn back the clock.

"Ms. Justice, I know you've been through a lot today, but I still have a few more questions."

Detective Daniels was a paragon of patience. I'd already broken down twice during our hour-long session and each time he'd pulled me back with a gentle pat of the table. His way of consoling me without making contact—as if the sorrow was contagious. When I looked up, his hound-dog eyes surveyed me. He offered a coffee-stained, snaggletoothed smile.

"Right now, the best way for you to help Judge Wannamaker is to tell me everything you can remember about today." Detective Daniels scratched the hairs of his graying mustache and flattened his nonexistent lips into a grim line. "We can't change what happened, but we can find a way to put things right. I need your help to do that, okay?"

"Okay." I took a handful of tissues from the box and swallowed a few times to slow my breathing.

"Rest assured. Bickerton P.D. has already booked Ms. Mulligan on your assault claims, so what we need to do is focus on the judge." He placed his elbows on the table and leaned toward me. "Finish telling me about your meeting with Frederica Wannamaker. If you'd already revealed your history with the defendant and recused yourself from trial, why go meet her for tea?"

"We wanted to talk as friends. I've known Ms. Freddie since I was a kid. She knew there was more to the Langley story than what I told her on the bench."

"You knew the deceased before you started working here?"

Deceased. I flinched and forced myself not to tear up again. "Yes. Ms. Freddie has been like a second mother to me. She and my mom went to college together."

"You've known the judge your whole life?"

I nodded but didn't respond. I'd observed enough testimony to know he wasn't asking a real question. Detective Daniels didn't want to lose momentum while he checked his mini-recorder and reached for the legal pad he'd shoved under his corduroy blazer during my recent crying jag.

"You said you are—how old?"

"Twenty-five."

He clicked the top of his pen and scribbled down the number. "How long have you worked here?"

"Five years. Six if you count the year I interned for Judge Wannamaker while I was training online for stenography. Once I got my court reporter's certification, I applied for a full-time state job."

"In all that time, did the judge ever confide in you about feeling threatened at work?"

"No."

The day had, however, revealed a number of people who didn't like her, and that thought worried me.

"Do you know of anyone, personally or professionally, who wished to do her harm?"

"No. But if you guys are thinking this has something to do with—"

"If you've seen or heard something unusual, that's the information I need to know. Don't focus on the investigation, and don't volunteer theories."

"What do you want me to say?" I flapped my arms, exasperated, and shredded the tissue I had clutched in my hand. "She's a judge. I imagine everyone she sentences wants to do her harm."

"Ms. Justice, relax and take your time." The detective put down his pen. The weathered lines of his olive skin grew deep as his voice took on a solemn tone.

"No one who actually knows Judge Wannamaker would do this." The words came out more like a plea and less like a declaration because... I wasn't quite sure.

Stevenson, Harriston, and Phyllis Dodd had disrespected her throughout the trial. I leaned back and started to link my hands at the top of my head so I could stare at the ceiling and think, but I stopped when the gesture exposed the skimpy camisole under my suit jacket.

Thanks for drenching my blouse, Langley.

Another sob erupted as I wondered how different

things could have been if I'd gone straight to the bathroom to change—

Bathroom.

An image of Ms. Freddie's mutilated form flashed across my mind. What kind of monster strangled a sixty-five-year-old woman with a tie?

An indigo tie.

I straightened my back and stared at the faded red tie around the detective's leathery neck until the truth came to me.

"I think the purple tie I saw in the bathroom is the same one Mr. Stevenson wore during the trial. He slammed it down in front of the judge during an argument at sidebar, but Mr. Harriston picked it up."

"I need you to think carefully before answering this next question." Detective Daniels narrowed his droopy eyelids and ran a hand across his mouth. "We're not a hundred percent sure about the cause of death at this point, but signs point to asphyxiation, either from drowning or from the restraint around her neck." He inspected my face, probably to gauge whether or not I'd fall apart again. "Do you remember seeing Mr. Harriston or Mr. Stevenson or anyone else leave the courtroom with that tie?"

A sharp pain ran through my head as the day's images sped through my brain.

Nothing.

"I didn't see the tie again until I found Ms. Freddie."

"Can you tell me who was in the courtroom the last time you saw that purple tie?"

"Harriston, Stevenson, Langley, Corporal North, Maggie the trial clerk, me, the judge, and Grace—actually, the bailiff had been asked to remove the jury, so Grace might not have been there. Phyllis Dodd, the state chemist, was in the gallery waiting to testify."

"Did any of them know you planned to meet Judge Wannamaker in the kitchen?"

"Maybe." I folded my hands in my lap unsure of how to answer. "We made the arrangements while she was leaving the bench. I suppose anyone in the courtroom could have overheard."

He jotted down some notes and read them over before he spoke again. "Okay. Let's establish a timeline." He flipped to a blank page and drew a horizontal line across the center. "About what time did the judge leave the bench?"

"Eleven twenty-seven. I always write the judge's departure and arrival times as part of the record. The trial clerk should be able to verify that. She usually writes down the time too."

"How long did you hang around the courtroom after the judge left?"

"Fifteen or twenty minutes. I could give you a better answer if I had my laptop. I remember saving my trial notes right before Langley started harassing me."

"That's good enough for now. I'll have you follow up on that when we finish." He absentmindedly tapped his pen on the notepad in time with the tick of the wall clock. "Did you go straight outside after you left the courtroom, or did you make a stop first?"

"Straight outside. I didn't want people seeing me cry. I went through the judges' hallway and out the employee doors because that was the quickest way to my car. I sat there for five or ten minutes before I realized I was supposed to be in the kitchen."

"That would put us at eleven fifty-seven. It's lunchtime. I would think the courthouse would be busy. Did you see anyone on your way to the kitchen or after you arrived?"

"No." My voice cracked at his reminder that I'd arrived too late, so I clenched my fists until the nails dug into my palm. The pain distracted me enough to continue.

"I wasn't in the kind of physical state where I wanted to be seen. Besides, I came through the employee entrance, which dumped me out into a hallway a few feet from the kitchen. The hall and the kitchen were empty when I got there—although, Ms. Freddie must have waited around for at least ten minutes because the kettle had boiled and the stove was off."

"Back up a second." Detective Daniels squinted at the notepad and thumbed through his notes. "You mentioned a 'judges' hallway,' what is that?"

"It's the hallway judges use to move from courtroom to chambers without being seen."

"How'd you gain access to the hallway?"

"Keycard." I pulled out the laminated pass I kept clipped to the waistband of my pants and showed it to him. "Every employee has one, but we don't all have the same level of access. The card only provides entry to the spaces where you're authorized to work."

I returned the keycard to my waistband. "Court reporters have access to the judges' hallway so we can follow the judges from courtroom to courtroom throughout the day—but, we don't have access to chambers, and we don't have access to the private entrance the judges use to get in and out of the courthouse. Our cards aren't programmed for those doors."

"Who programs the cards?"

"The chief bailiff, Grace Tisdale. She's head of security."

"Who else has access to the judges' hallway?"

"All the bailiffs and the judges' secretaries. They all have the same level of access as the judges. They can go everywhere. But folks try not to use the hallway... out of respect."

"Do the attorneys or clerks have access to that back hallway?"

"Clerks don't have access, and attorneys don't get issued keycards, not even the state-appointed ones."

"Can you access the kitchen from the judges' hallway?"

"I can't, but it is possible." I held up my hands and pointed in opposite directions. "One end of the judges' hallway leads to their private entrance. The opposite end has two doors, one is an exit-only door that connects to the antechamber of the employee entrance, and the other leads into the kitchen. Only a person with an all-access keycard can open the door between the judges' hallway and the kitchen."

"Does Judge Wannamaker have an all-access keycard?"

"Of course."

"We didn't find one on her. Would she be able to move through the courthouse without it?"

"No." A bit of worry seeped into my bones. "We're supposed to keep them on us at all times."

Detective Daniels grunted and circled something on his legal pad. What was he thinking?

"All right. Let's talk kitchen access." He reached for his twenty-four ounces of Royal Farms coffee and the hazelnut smell filled the confines of the narrow deliberation room. "Who has it? Who doesn't?"

"Well, everyone who has a keycard has access to the kitchen because it's located in the middle of a hallway that leads to a bunch of personnel offices: the civil unit, the court administrator's office, the court reporters' office, the non-public portions of the jury services office, and the Prothonotary's Office."

"Prothonotary's Office?" he asked before draining his to-go cup.

"The formal name for the criminal clerks' office."

"Have civilians ever slipped into any of those offices you mentioned?"

"We've had occasions when a member of the public hanging around the lobby follows an employee through the personnel doors thinking it's the restroom. But everyone knows everyone here, so folks don't get very far."

"Do you need a keycard to get around once you're in the personnel area?"

"Just for the court reporters' office. Otherwise, once you've swiped into the personnel area, you're good to go to the kitchen or any office."

"What about the evidence closet?"

His non-sequitur sobered me, and I stared blankly at him from across the conference table. "What about it?"

"Do you need a keycard to access the evidence closet?"

"Not really." I wiped my eyes. They itched as my tears dried. "The evidence closet is in the criminal clerks' office, and it has its own electronic lock activated by a keypad. Only the clerks have the code, but anyone requiring access to the closet can ask to have it opened. They keep a log sheet inside to record what goes in and out."

"Have you ever asked for entry?"

"Sure. The transcripts court reporters provide are the official record. Part of our job is to review the evidence and make sure we've properly identified all the marked exhibits."

"Okay. But if *you're* the official record, why does the court reporters' office have its own keycard access? Aren't trial transcripts part of the public record?"

"Yes, but we're not a lending library." I gripped the sides of my chair and searched for the best way to explain without getting defensive. People never grasped a court reporter's dual role and often challenged the idea. "Even though we're state employees tasked to capture court proceedings and guard the record, transcripts aren't created unless requested. Producing one is a separate billing process."

"Let me get this straight." He massaged his temples. "If someone wants a copy of the trial transcript, they have to pay for it?"

"Right. We're independent contractors in that respect. The materials used to create each transcript— steno machines, laptops, printing supplies—come out of our pockets. Transcript fees defray those costs. Basically, our door is locked to protect our investments."

"Fine." He sighed and reached for his blazer, pulled out a business card, and slapped it on the table. "Put me down for a copy of the Mulligan trial."

By the time I finished with the detective and gathered my equipment from the courtroom, it was five, a solid hour past closing time. Dimmed lights and empty halls triumphed over the day's chaos. Finally, I was alone and grateful for the silence. As I walked toward the court reporters' office, misery pressed against my heart and zapped all of my energy. What little pep I had left went to juggling the tiny steno machine and laptop, which I almost dropped as I stumbled through the office door.

The shared space had only one window that bathed the room in the sepia haze of the setting sun. The waning light made our three workstations look like an abandoned maze. The sharp right angles of each L-shaped desk cast long shadows across the floor. I switched on the overhead fluorescents to spoil the illusion and carried my equipment to the far-left corner where I stored them away.

The papers on my desk beckoned to me, but I ignored the call of responsibility and headed for the door with my leather jacket, my messenger bag slung across my back. As I locked the door, I checked the mailbox mounted outside our office and noticed a letter with my name on it.

I grabbed the envelope, pressed my back against the door, and ripped the letter open on the spot. After all, it could have been a check. What I found, though, was much more valuable than money—a recommendation letter from Ms. Freddie for law school.

Ma had spent most of my adulthood trying to persuade me to apply to law school. Over the summer, due to a do-it-or-move-out-of-my-house ultimatum from my mom, Ms. Freddie helped me start the arduous process of studying for the LSAT. I was reluctant because I didn't think my reserved nature was suitable for work as an attorney, but both women insisted my aptitude for analysis and logical thinking was too impressive to ignore. Ms. Freddie promised if I didn't score well on the test, she'd convince Ma to let her dream go.

To no one's surprise but mine, my score was nearly perfect, 179. Ms. Freddie had recommended a ton of law schools and insisted I use her as a reference. I had no idea she'd already written a letter.

I slid to the floor with the folded piece of fine linen paper clutched in my hand. Tears streamed down my face and fell onto the page, leaving translucent splotches on the final words to me from my fallen friend.

SIX

"MA, I'M HOME!"

I stood in the doorway of our two-story colonial and waited for an answer. We lived a mile and a half west of the courthouse off Route 9 in the part of Bickerton farthest from the beach. Ma despised the raised prices and clogged streets that plagued the seaside, so she was happy to oblige my desire to stay as far away from the ocean as possible. Trident County's coastline boasted the cleanest water and best boardwalks on the eastern seaboard, so it wasn't uncommon for tourists to descend upon our tiny town and balloon the population from 3,000 to 33,000 during the summer. This meant our secluded four-bedroom wasn't as fancy as the homes closer to the water, but we had room to spread out.

I raised my voice to a holler in case my mother was in her office upstairs. "Ma, I need to talk to you."

Nothing but the hum of the refrigerator in response, so I kicked off my pumps and sank my toes into the carpet. The plush fabric cradled my feet and provided a small sense of comfort.

My mother, Corinne Justice, was rarely home before dark. During her forty-four years as an employee of the Trident County School System—twenty-three years as an English teacher, sixteen years as a guidance counselor, and five years as an elementary school principal—she'd earned a master's degree, adopted me, and obtained a doctorate in education, all while directing the church choir and presiding over her Kappa Mu chapter.

She'd recently retired, but decided to pursue politics by running for mayor of our humble hamlet. With Election Day less than twelve hours away, I figured she could still be on the campaign trail.

"Back here, Angel." Ma shouted to my surprise. The volume of her voice made it clear she was sitting on the sun porch. "I came home as soon as I heard about Freddie."

"How'd you hear?" I hurried across the family room and through the kitchen to the open sliding glass door.

Ma sat cross-legged on a cushioned chaise with the cordless in one hand and a bottle of Moscato in the other. A heavy knit blanket draped across her shoulders. She wore a navy-blue dress suit with an American flag pin clipped to her lapel. Smears of plum lipstick and heavy black mascara stained her sienna skin from where she'd rubbed at tears and a leaky nose. Her tawny pageboy, which was usually flawless, was in disarray from where she'd tugged at the ends.

"WSYS already picked up the story. I saw it on the four o'clock news." She took a sip of sweet liquid courage straight from the bottle. "They said a courthouse employee found Freddie murdered sometime around noon and the small window of opportunity points to a suspect who works in the building." She yanked a strand of her hair and twisted it around her index finger. "Grace called about twenty minutes ago and asked if you were okay because you didn't answer your cell. She told me you found Freddie. Is it true?" Her bloodshot eyes watered as she waited for my answer.

I knitted my brows in quiet confirmation and sat

on the floorboards beside her lounge chair. "Grace shouldn't have told you."

"Oh, no." Thick droplets fell from her eyes. "Was it bad?"

I didn't answer.

"Call in sick tomorrow. I don't want you going back there with a killer on the loose."

"Ma—"

"Do not argue with me, Victoria. You can't possibly be safe in a place where a judge is murdered under the nose of the law. I will not put my only child at risk."

I picked at the hardwood floor to hide my disappointment. Ma had always been overprotective—even before Langley's attempt on my life…although that issue intensified things.

In answer to my silence, Ma reached out and lifted my chin. "I am yours, you are mine, and together we'll be fine."

Her favorite saying. One she uttered whenever I questioned her love for me, which had happened daily after I learned of my adoption. She broke the news just as I skipped over middle school and entered high school hell. Ma always used the phrase to remind me how she chose me, despite the odds. After losing her parents to old age, she decided at the age of forty to build a new family and took the risk of adopting from a pregnant teen hooked on drugs.

She could have been signing up for a host of problems, but I came out healthy—a victory, a Victoria—so she was determined to raise me in the most pristine environment possible. Some of her methods were sensible, like no dating until sixteen. But most of them, like insisting I get off the bus at a daycare center even though I was fifteen and a senior in high school, were…extreme.

This request fell into the latter category.

"Ma, I'm going to work tomorrow." I shoved my hand into my bag and handed her the letter. "I don't think Ms. Freddie would have wanted me to sit around and mope."

"'In life we are given two choices,'" Ma read aloud from the opening paragraph, "'rise up or fall by the wayside. Victoria has chosen the third option—the one rarely spoken of due to its inherent difficulty—rise above and forge your own path.'"

Ma held the letter against her heart, exhaled, and took another generous swig from her wine bottle. "I get it. You're old enough to know what's best for you." She handed the paper back to me and slouched against the cushions of the chaise. "But I think you should give a copy of that letter to Russell. I've been trying to get him on the phone to see if there's anything we can do for him, but I can't get through. If he picks up this time, offer your condolences. Read him the letter. He may find solace in those words."

Ma dialed and handed me the cordless. Her puffy eyes mirrored the same dull sorrow that gnawed at my soul. I clicked off the phone, placed it on the floor, and climbed onto the chaise beside her. She needed my comfort just as much as Mr. Russell did. Besides, I couldn't talk to Ms. Freddie's husband. The truth of the matter was his wife's death was gruesome, foul, and undeserved. I wouldn't be the one to remind him of that.

I spread out Ma's knit blanket, and we huddled beneath its scratchy folds. She nursed her Moscato while the day's events rolled over in my mind.

"Did the newscast mention this all started with Langley Dean's drug trial?"

Ma froze mid-swallow with the bottle still tucked between her lips.

Even though I wore the physical scars of Langley's wrath, Ma bore the mental ones. When they rushed me to the emergency room after the incident, the thought of losing her only child enraged her. She had gone after Langley with everything she had.

Despite numerous protests to Bickerton High's principal, the Trident County School Board, and the Bickerton Police, she was never able to press charges because no one had witnessed Langley push me into the pool. My word was worthless against the head cheerleader and the teammates who'd given her a solid alibi. "Langley was nowhere near the pool. She was serving drinks at the concession stand."

The county did offer a settlement for medical bills and damages, but Ma had always thought she'd failed to protect me.

"Langley wiggled her way out of felony drug possession today," I said when Ma didn't respond. "She threw a pitcher of water at me just as I was trying to leave the courtroom to go meet Ms. Freddie. I'm filing assault and menacing charges, but if I'd gotten away from Langley sooner—if I hadn't let her get under my skin—maybe I would have been there in time, and the murderer wouldn't have attacked…"

Ma's body reanimated at the word "murderer." She put down the bottle, swung her chubby legs over the edge of the chaise, and turned to face me.

"Don't you blame yourself, Angel. I love Freddie. I want her back just as much as you do, but don't put yourself through the agony of thinking you could have stopped it. You're not responsible. Blaming yourself is not going to change things." Tears fell from her eyes again. She pulled me into her arms. "Everyone in this community loved Freddie. Believe me, justice will be swift."

For both our sakes, I hoped she was right.

SEVEN

GETTING UP THE next morning was rough. Pain lit across my body like wildfire—a torturous dread so intense my bones ached. The thought of going to work without Ms. Freddie left me hollow.

I curled up in the middle of my queen-size bed, the downy fabric of the comforter pulled up over my nose, while sunlight streaked across the headboard and obliterated all chances of sleep. I rolled from the mattress onto the carpet to shield myself from the rays and listened to Ma in the next room. She was up at her usual time, 7:00 a.m., but absent were the cheerful songs she usually sang to start the day.

Her silence left me to stare at the walls covered with award-winning essays and plaques from regional Math Maven competitions. Each one prompted a memory of Ms. Freddie coming backstage to offer advice. She became better than Ma at dispensing encouragement because she never treated me like a fragile doll, and she always told me the truth.

Don't let them underestimate you because of your skin color.

Rise above and forge your own path.

Simple words, but they sparked me to action. I got dressed and made sure her recommendation letter had a prominent place on the wall alongside the other memories.

"Angel?" Ma pushed open the door and leaned into

the room. She wore a white version of the fitted Ashley Stewart suit she'd sported the day before. Her lips formed a tight pout.

"If you insist on going to work, hit the polls first. I don't want you using that as an excuse to miss my results party." Her mouth softened, and she blew me a kiss. "Just…be careful today. Remember, you're all I've got."

SITTING IN THE courthouse parking lot, I pressed an *I voted* sticker onto my cowl-neck sweater and mentally prepared for my first day of work without Ms. Freddie.

Thump. Thump. Thump.

My head snapped toward the sound.

Grace Tisdale stood at the passenger window, her fist poised to pound on the glass again. "Let me in."

I hit the power locks, and she climbed inside.

The seat creaked as she shifted to make room for her gun belt. "You can't go in that way."

"What?"

"I was hoping you'd get here a little earlier when there were only a few of them, but now there's no way you're getting inside the courthouse without a hassle."

"What are you talking about?"

"The press. They've been badgering everyone who goes in the building. They've latched onto this theory that a courthouse employee committed the judge's murder." She peered out the windshield like she thought people were watching us. "I asked Capitol Police—you know, Jim and those guys who do perimeter security for all the state facilities—to hang around out back a bit and keep the reporters off the workers, but all the nosey buzzards do is wander around the parking lot and come right back."

"Don't you think you're overreacting? We have media around here all the time."

"Don't you think you're *underreacting* based on what happened here yesterday?"

I frowned. She had a point, but the concept of the courthouse as a dangerous place wasn't something I wanted to consider.

"I appreciate the warning, but I'm pretty sure I can ignore a few desperate reporters." I put my hand on the door latch.

Grace reached over to stop me. "Do me a favor. Come around to the side of the building. We can use the judges' entrance. The media hasn't discovered that doorway yet."

I studied her for a moment. Despite the twenty-year age difference, Grace and I had formed a strong friendship inside and outside the courthouse because we didn't play the catty mind games so frequently displayed by our female coworkers.

"Is there something you're not telling me?" I asked. "You're not seriously buying into their killer employee theory, are you?"

"Magistrate Murderer is what they're calling them." She scratched at the bulletproof vest that bulged under her long-sleeved polyester uniform. "Maybe. Even the worst rumors start with a grain of truth. But even if it isn't true, do you want to spend your morning answering questions about it?"

"You're right." I grabbed my shoulder bag. "Lead the way."

We stepped out of the Mustang and headed straight for the sidewalk that ran parallel to the rear of the parking lot. Thanks to my stop at the polls, I'd had to park about as far from the employee entrance as one could park without using one of the meters on Merchant Street. From our vantage point, we could see the entire intricate puzzle that was the back of the courthouse.

Eight columns of cars stretched out from the rear of the structure. On one side, York Road flanked the building. This area marked the street entrance people used when called to jury duty. There weren't any people standing on the sidewalk by that entrance. No trials. The other side marked our destination and bordered the rear of the County Administration Building on Bickerton Boulevard.

At the head of the parking lot lay a gated loading bay and the half-glass double doors of the employee entrance. An army of reporters and four mobile camera crews milled about, blocking our safe passage.

Grace held up her hand for me to wait while she took a moment to speak into the walkie-talkie mic attached to the shoulder of her uniform.

"Tango Charlie Delta one two zero six, do you copy?"

Static popped on the mic and a raspy male voice sounded. "Copy."

"Pull out the van. I'm trying to deliver a package. Over."

"Roger that."

No sooner than Grace's mic went silent, a large blue and white striped van, with metal mesh lining the windows and the official Delaware State seal decorating the sides, backed out of the heavily gated loading bay that Trident County's Corrections Department used to transport inmates between the prison and the courthouse. The sea of reporters I'd spotted earlier reluctantly parted to make room for the vehicle.

"Let's go," Grace said once the diversionary tactic had been set into motion.

We raced our way to the far side of the courthouse—the portion closest to The Quad, where the sides of the County Administration Building and the Superior Court facilities met at a right angle to create a small area recessed from the parking lot. Prominent town officials parked their cars in this area, which marked the super-secret location of the side door our judges used to enter the courthouse from the street.

Ms. Freddie's empty parking space caught my eye as we dashed toward a nondescript navy-blue door at the side of the building. I broke pace as my thoughts drifted toward the judge's fate, but I soon snapped back to reality at the sound of my name.

"Victoria, is it true you found Judge Wannamaker's body?"

"Ms. Justice, is there a message you'd like to send the Magistrate Murderer?"

"Is there anything you can share with us about the crime scene?"

One moment of hesitation was all it took for the media to spot us and attack. The shock of the sudden onslaught turned my legs to lead. Grace gripped my wrist, dragged me the last few feet toward the door, and hauled me over its threshold. A violent slam and the click of the lock blocked out the voices that assaulted us.

Once I caught my breath, I turned to Grace. "How did they get my name?"

"Not from me. I'm a vault. You know this," Grace said over her shoulder as she swiped through a second door that led us out of the claustrophobic antechamber into a stark white hallway with dingy blue industrial carpet. I'd never been through the judges' entrance, but it was no more glamorous than the regular one.

"I suppose they could have gotten your name from anyone who came to work today. Half of those reporters have been here since I drove up at seven to meet Detective Daniels. He came by early to collect all the keycard records and surveillance footage I pulled from Courtroom Four last night. When he left, the parking lot was full of those vultures."

"Did you get a chance to look at any of the footage?"

"Nope. Just pulled and packaged it. I was too wiped to go poring through video feed. That's his job. He knew exactly what he was looking for. His request was pretty specific."

We were both silent as we walked the private hallway that ran behind chambers and the four courtrooms. Once we arrived at the two doors that marked the end of the hall, Grace used her keycard to buzz open the exit-only door that led to the antechamber of the employee entrance. She held it open for me. "They've cordoned off the kitchen for the next couple of days, so I have to send you this way."

"Right. I couldn't handle walking through there anyhow." I hung my head. "Thanks for this. You didn't have to—"

"I did, and I'm sorry you had to experience that out there. Judge Wannamaker deserves more respect than they're giving her. She was a decent person. We started here at about the same time, and she never questioned my ability to do a man's job." Grace clapped me on the back so hard I had to shift the weight of my shoulder bag to accommodate the force. "I miss her too. Keep your head up. Maybe we'll all learn something from this tragedy."

EIGHT

No TRIALS MEANT my day started at 9:00. Despite a trip to the polls and a run-in with the press, I swiped into the office with six minutes to spare.

"I didn't expect to see you today." Candace Fontaine, my supervisor and the courthouse's chief court reporter, rummaged through the filing cabinets near the window.

Candace was fiftyish and plump with strawberry blonde hair, flat features, and wire-rimmed glasses. She was the annoyingly perky kind of person who signed her name with a smiley face and loved the color pink, but Candace's enthusiasm was sincere.

"You must have had a difficult night." She gave me a dour look with drawn brows, which I assumed was her version of sympathy. "I waited for you after work, but those detectives kept you forever. How are you making out?"

"Not great, but being here is better than stewing at home. Work will help. Thanks for asking, though." I lifted my chin and moved farther into the cramped space. "Morning, James."

My coworker replied with a preoccupied nod. James Brandenkamp was busy scoping—changing untranslated steno into English when the computer failed to do so—the constant pastime of the busy court reporter. Candi once considered hiring a dedicated scopist so we could outsource the work, but nobody wanted to give up part of his or her earnings.

I flopped into the swivel chair behind my desk, slid off my coat, dropped my messenger bag on the floor, and pulled out my laptop from the bottom drawer as was my normal routine. I wasn't crazy about preparing the transcript from Langley Mulligan's trial, but it was the only project on my to-do pile, and the requests were mounting. Aside from the moot one from Ms. Freddie, I already had interest from Harriston and Detective Daniels. Plus, Candi had placed a transcript request from Stevenson on my desk, along with an order from *The Bickerton Bugle*. Dang it. A press copy would surely add more fuel to the fire already brewing outside.

"Eyes up, everyone." We both turned an ear toward Candi, although James never stopped typing. "Before you get too busy, let's divvy up the work on today's calendar. We only have two proceedings today. Victoria, you were in that—that, uh—trial yesterday, so you take your pick."

This was why I loved Candi. Because of everything that happened, she wanted me to choose first, which allowed me to decline without ticking off James. *Well played, Candi.*

"Do you mind if I pass on this one? One of the things Detective Daniels asked for last night was a copy of the transcript from the Mulligan trial. I'd like to work on it so I can get copies out today, if possible. That is, if you don't mind."

"That's fine," Candi chirped before James could open his mouth to protest. "That leaves case review with Judge Radnor or the 11:00 a.m. office conference with Maddox. Pick your poison, James."

I grabbed the papers Candi had piled on my desk the night before and shuffled through them while James worked out the math. On the heels of Candi's gung-ho attitude, James would look lazy selecting the office conference, which wouldn't take more than fifteen minutes. But if he chose case review, he'd be in court all afternoon and wouldn't be able to whittle away the hours on Instagram.

Candi drummed her magenta fingernails on the desk when James failed to reply. He was about to miss his window of opportunity.

"I'll take case review?" James said with a note of uncertainty in his voice.

Staying in Candi's good graces had won out. A fine choice.

I sat around for the next two hours and scoped my transcript while the others waited for their call to court.

At 10:55 a.m., Grace swung open the door and stuck her head inside. "We need a court reporter for the office conference in chambers."

"That's me." Candi collapsed the tripod of her fuchsia steno machine and hurried out.

Ten seconds after the door closed, Maggie buzzed her way into the room. She promptly positioned herself behind Candi's desk so she sat across the aisle from James. I don't know how Maggie managed to arrive the exact moment Candi departed, but it happened every day with the same precision. Best I could figure, James was texting Maggie for scheduled visits with the hope of hiding his slackerly indulgence from Candi.

However, I wasn't given the same courtesy. The right side of my L-shaped desk abutted James's. No matter where I chose to work, I'd always have a front row seat to their flirtation flybys. I busied myself with the task of printing and collating pages for the Mulligan transcript. I needed an original and four copies for distribution.

"Can you believe those reporters outside? It's insane," Maggie said to James in her thick drawl that hung in the air long after she stopped speaking.

She leaned over the desk, letting the mounds of her bosom bulge out of the tight V-neck T-shirt she wore underneath her bolero jacket. Maggie should have been ashamed. James was spitting distance from the legal drinking age. She had at least a decade on him.

"I know, right?" James said. "Grace was telling me Capitol Police are in the process of rethinking the entire security system to make sure nothing like this happens again. I told her they should close down the courthouse while they do it."

"I was thinking the same thing. I mean, first, I have to stand by and watch the State Police rummage through our evidence closet and seize half its contents. Then I spend all night answering a bunch of questions from some pushy detective. I could definitely use a few days off to recover. I'm traumatized."

Maggie was always prone to theatrics, but this last bit of overstatement piqued my interest. Time to join the conversation.

"They questioned you, too?" I asked. "Who'd you talk to?"

"A real crotchety fella named Dan—Danny—Daniels?" Maggie struggled.

I couldn't tell if her attempts were real or manufactured.

"Detective Daniels?" James asked. "Hey, isn't that the same guy you had, Victoria?"

"Sure was. He seemed pretty reasonable to me."

"Yeah, well, you didn't have to answer a slew of silly questions about the trial evidence or where you went during the recess. Everybody knows you were sitting in a corner somewhere fiddling on that funny little machine of yours." Maggie giggled and winked at James.

I ignored their love fest and shoved pages into the three-pronged report covers that would bind my transcripts. "Couldn't have been too traumatizing, Maggs, or you wouldn't be falling all over yourself trying to tell us everything."

"I'm getting there, darlin', but I'm having trouble concentrating." She gave James a coquettish smile and toyed with a strand of hair that had fallen from her bouffant. "You know, the odd thing is he kept asking me over and over whether or not I'd seen anyone walking around in the kitchen—which is a dumb question because everybody goes to the kitchen during recess to get coffee and snacks and whatnot. I even saw that hot cop and Phyllis Dodd heading back there at one point."

James was slowly nodding his curly red head, but I wasn't sure if he was agreeing with Maggie or admiring the rise and fall of her breasts as she spoke.

Maggie droned on, "That was obviously a trick question designed to catch me in a lie."

"Obviously." Yup, James was enjoying the free show.

"Then he asked what I did during the break. I told him I was helping Mr. Stevenson, who'd insisted on following me into the clerk's office to make sure we had a proper safety system in place for storing evidence. I agreed because I couldn't have my office blamed for missing evidence after that stunt you and the corporal tried to pull." Maggie spun her chair to face me.

"Oh, no." James's voice came out dazed. Maggie had removed her chest from his view.

"What stunt?" I paused my work to bore straight into her eyes. "Are you saying the tampering he found on the evidence envelope was a stunt? Corporal North was trying to help—"

"Well," she drawled, "Mr. Stevenson didn't seem to think it was helpful or polite that Corporal North told you and not him. He was on his phone in a heartbeat calling the State Police about North. I would have hung around and gathered an earful, but I had to run back to the courtroom to talk with Mr. Harriston about his—"

"Maggs, none of this sounds stressful, and I can't imagine you didn't have fun telling Detective Daniels every detail." I inclined my head toward my coworker. "You definitely managed to make things entertaining for James."

James jumped to attention and averted his gaze from Maggie's chest, but his incoherent response and the scarlet hue of his normally paper white skin made it clear he hadn't been listening.

"Now, I hate to play the ace in a game of misery poker, but I had to spend my evening rehashing a friend's death," I said.

Maggie avoided my gaze, so I stared at James until he pulled himself together.

"Someone we loved died within the walls of our workplace. I think that's worth us enduring any inconveniences that might come our way. You don't see me complaining."

"Oh, hush up. I know you're used to walking on water around here, but you'd be well advised to keep that self-righteous attitude to yourself now." Maggie's comely features formed the same flirtatious smile she'd given James earlier, but the pleasantness didn't reach her eyes—those clouded over with something wrathful.

"Ain't nobody saying they don't feel bad about what happened," she cooed. "I was just trying to make a point about how my integrity is being called into question, but here you come, as usual, trying to steal the spotlight by flashing around your relationship with the judge."

"Really, Maggs? You're quibbling over friendships?" My voice grew taut to cover my frustration. If anything, I'd always downplayed my relationship with Ms. Freddie to avoid reactions like hers. "Judge Wannamaker loved all of us and treated everyone here as her equal. We should be willing to do whatever it takes, regardless of the consequences, to help the police figure out what happened and why."

I swiveled my chair away from her in an attempt to end the conversation and resume binding pages, but her words stopped me.

"Easy for you to say, Little Miss First on the Scene." She didn't raise her voice, but the timbre carried enough bravado that James gasped.

"What's that supposed to mean? How did you know I found—" I gaped at Maggie and James, who was sitting in a desk chair between us.

Surely he could see the storm brewing and would jump in to back me up. But no. He poked out his lips like a nervous duck and rolled himself out of the line of fire.

"Darling, I'm just saying maybe you should take a good hard look at yourself because you're not the innocent lamb you claim to be. I wouldn't try to play that pity card if I were you."

My jaw tightened as my anger swelled. "Where do you come off telling me how to behave?"

At that moment, the door to the office flew open, and Candi backed her way into the room. Her hands were full with two thick files and her steno machine.

Maggie must have seen this as an opportunity to make me look bad in front of my supervisor because she jumped to her feet, ramped up the sweetness, and poured on the drama. "I'm just saying. You were the only one in there with the judge's body. Folks might take that the wrong way…or at least that's how those news reporters wanted to spin things when I was out there with them this morning."

I was speechless.

But, to my surprise, James was the one who spoke for me. "You've crossed the line, Maggie." The bass in his voice meant business. "I think you need to leave."

Maggie shimmied her shoulders at James and shot me a priggish pout. I fired a look of contempt back at her and remained frozen in my seat until she was out the door.

An antsy quietness descended as if we were all waiting for the room to decompress.

Candi stood in the middle of the office juggling her things. She looked from me to the door to James. "You know what? I totally didn't mean to pick up these files." She put down her steno machine and hit herself in the forehead like a ditz. "Could you return them, please? Thanks."

James shuffled toward her and reached for the folders.

"The top one goes to the civil unit and the other goes back to the criminal file room."

She was being diplomatic again, and this time James had to have known it. I turned to stare at the file cabinet and fax machine by the window. I wanted to hide my face for fear it would betray my relief for the rescue and my embarrassment for needing it.

"Do people really think I had something to do with all this?"

"Of course not." Candi sat on the edge of my desk and put her hand on my shoulder. "Maggie didn't mean those things."

"I wouldn't be so sure about that."

"Listen, we all know Judge Wannamaker meant a lot to you…to all of us." She gave me an encouraging smile. "But not everyone is willing to openly express their grief. I'm not excusing Maggie's behavior, and I don't condone it. But for her—for many of us—what happened here yesterday is hard to understand. We spend our lives telling each other death doesn't exist, but now we have to cope with a murder too horrible to imagine. For someone trying to stick their head back in the sand, your involvement is a reminder that Wannamaker's death is real."

"What are you saying?" I stretched the sleeves of my sweater over my hands and wrapped my arms around myself like a security blanket. "This is *my* fault?"

"Not even close." She stood up from her perch. "What I'm saying is that, despite our best intentions, there are going to be times in life when people lash out and say things to get under our skin, but you have to learn to rise above it."

Learn to rise above it. Candi's advice sounded like the words in Ms. Freddie's recommendation letter. *Rise above and forge your own path.* I'd failed to live up to those words.

"Why don't you take the rest of the week off? You're not missing anything today. You'd be off tomorrow anyway for the Post-Election Festival. Then you can take Thursday and Friday to reflect without distraction. Come back Monday willing and able to take the high road."

Candi was practically channeling Ms. Freddie and, as much as it pained me to hear my mentor's words reborn, Candi was right. They both were.

NINE

BEFORE SUCCUMBING TO the leave of absence, I gave Candi the original printout of the Mulligan transcript to have docketed and placed into the defendant's file in the Prothonotary's Office. Then I slipped out through the jurors' side entrance on York Road with my laptop and four transcript copies in tow. My plan was to avoid the reporters trolling behind the courthouse so I could spend the morning walking around town delivering documents.

I might have been better off mailing or emailing them, but I'd run the risk of not receiving payment. More to the point, since I was now the reluctant owner of tons of free time, hand-delivering each transcript seemed like a practical way to spend the day. But first, I headed across the street to Cake & Kettle, my favorite lunchtime hangout, for a little R & R.

Most of the restaurants in Bickerton were flashy fast-food chains with sports themes, flair, or all-you-can eat buffets—the familiar discount grub that appealed to our summer tourists. In that respect, Cake & Kettle was an anomaly. The British fare was authentic, the teas were imported, and the narrow glass storefront, with its gray and gold striped awning, was about as flashy as Grandma's Sunday shoes. I loved the place because crossing the threshold was like stepping into a 1920s English drawing room laced with the essence of cinnamon.

"This is the earliest lunch I've seen you take in six years," Jillian Galbraith shouted over the jingle of the door chime. She was sitting alone on a stool behind a row of squat bookshelves that marked the eatery's order area. As I moved toward her, she folded her newspaper and stood. Her tiny hands whirled in the air and beckoned me into an embrace. "I read about Judge Wannamaker in *The Bugle*. I'm terribly sorry, love. How are you making out?"

"Not so good." When we parted, I moved toward the pastry display.

Jillian's scones, golden domes of buttery perfection, were a lifesaver.

"Long story, but I'll give you the thirty-second version. Ma warns me not to go to work. I go anyway. A meltdown ensues with Motormouth Maggs—"

"Don't even say her name." Jillian said the words with civility, but I wouldn't have blamed her for losing her cool.

Just four months prior, Maggie'd had an affair with Jillian's husband and business partner, Shaun. She'd spared me the details since I had to work with Maggie, but the situation involved Jillian walking in on the two of them in the restaurant's kitchen, buck-naked and covered in flour. Jillian said she'd scoured the kitchen after that—tossing out all the dry goods—to put to rest any mystery whose hands…or other appendages had seasoned the mix.

"Forgive me." I squeezed her shoulder. "She-Whose-Name-Means-Shame starts shooting off at the mouth. Boss lady shows up in time to witness the aftermath and tells me—wait, no—she *asks* me to take the week off because, unlike me, Candi knows how to defuse a messy situation."

Jillian let out a nasally squeak I could only assume was meant to be a giggle. The recent separation from her husband had put her back on the market. The laugh, along with the bleached-blonde pixie cut, jungle red lipstick, and green contacts in lieu of her usual tortoise shell glasses, were all part of Jillian's mid-thirties makeover.

"You're the only person I know who'd be put off by a holiday from work. Don't let that witch get to you. She isn't happy unless she's wrecking hearts. She stole my man, but she won't steal my joy. Yours either." Jillian always knew how to pull me back when I began to whine about my job and my coworkers since many of them were familiar to her as customers.

"Candace might have done you a favor." She returned to her stool. "You look stressed. Let me make you some black tea with a nice Irish whiskey."

"I had a bad day. I didn't catch pneumonia." I rolled my eyes and made a gagging noise. "When have you ever seen me drink whiskey? I'll stick to the usual, a pot of lemon ginger tea and—oh, wow, did you make this lemon cake?"

I leaned over the four-tiered glass pastry case to get a closer look. The cake had been baked in a Bundt pan, and the sides oozed with a lemon sugar glaze that gave it a volcanic appearance. I inhaled and drew in the heavenly duo of vanilla and honey.

"No. That's Shaun's final contribution to the shop. It'll probably give you rabies. The lying sack of tripe. Purchase at your own risk."

The doorbell chimed, and Jillian gave the incoming customer a little wave. I concentrated on the confectionaries. The scones were a staple, but the lemon cake was a decadent departure from the norm. The day felt like the kind of day where I needed to make a change.

"Sorry, Jillian. You know I live and die by your scones, but my mouth needs a double helping of that lemon cake."

"Traitor." She gave me a look so dry I was surprised we didn't catch fire. "Do you plan to order any real food? I made a lamb soup that will change your life."

"Sorry, babe. In America, cake heals all wounds."

While Jillian busied herself filling the stainless-steel tea infuser with the aromatic blend of ginger root and lemon grass, I walked over to the wall of decorative teapots and pulled my favorite from the shelf, a stout white elephant whose tail was the handle and whose nose was the spout. I placed the container on the counter for Jillian, who was helping the next customer, and strolled into the empty sitting area and ensconced myself in a secluded nook. I shucked off my coat, pulled out my smartphone, and decided to send an invoice to the four parties who had ordered the Mulligan transcript. Just as I pressed send, a presence loomed over me.

"Cake for brunch? Kind of a bold choice. That's more of a supper or dinner entrée if you ask me."

Corporal North, in plainclothes, towered above me, holding a metal tea tray with a chunk of lemon cake, the elephant teapot, linen napkins, two rose-patterned china teacups and their requisite saucers as well as— get this—two forks. I glanced over at Jillian, who was wiggling her hips in some bastardized cross-version of a cha-cha and a humping gesture. Just because she was on the prowl for a man didn't mean I needed to be as well.

"I didn't think Jillian was the type to put her customers to work." I raised my voice so she'd overhear. "You didn't have to bring this."

"Not a problem. I recognized you from the courthouse and thought it would be nice to come say hello. I'm Ashton, by the way." He set the tray down on the coffee table stationed in front of the overstuffed armchair I occupied. His hand shot out toward me. "I don't think we introduced ourselves officially yesterday."

I made a reluctant reach for his gigantic palm, and he engulfed mine in a gentle caress reminiscent of our impromptu game of courtroom handsies.

"Victoria Justice." I snatched my hand back.

"Victoria, wow. I'm surprised to run into you here, you know, with the judge and everything that happened at the courthouse. I imagine things are pretty busy over there, with all the detectives and reporters running around."

"The courthouse is a busy place." My answer was deliberately vague.

He was clearly fishing, angling to sit down and ask why I wasn't at work. But after the previous day's interrogation with Detective Daniels, I wasn't in the mood to be in the presence of another cop—even if this one had the soulful blue eyes and wide, welcoming grin of a soap star.

"Do you mind?" I fiddled with my cell phone. "I'm waiting for a call."

"The lady at the counter said you'd say something like that." He sat in the chair across from mine and crossed his legs by positioning ankle over knee. "I don't blame you for wanting to be alone. It's tough losing a coworker. Trust me, I've been there."

I stole another glance over at Jillian, who was back on her stool peeking over the edge of her paper. She wiggled her eyebrows at me.

"Corporal North, forgive my rudeness, but I don't want to talk."

"Please, call me Ashton. I'm not on duty today." He slipped off his fleece North Face jacket to reveal a charcoal gray button-down shirt and an *I voted* sticker stuck to his neck.

I debated whether to tell him about the tiny paper oval but decided against it because the rogue sticker made his über good looks less intimidating.

"Actually," he said, "depending on what the DSP's investigative team decides to do about the evidence debacle in the Mulligan case, I might not be on duty for quite some time."

"They let you go?" My apathy turned to interest. I laid my phone beside the tray on the coffee table and gave him my full attention.

I'd misread him. He'd hoped to commiserate.

"C'mon, you're a state employee. You should know by now they rarely fire anyone. You just get shuffled off to another department." He ran a hand through the shag of his copper-colored crew cut. Ashy blond highlights flashed through his fingers. "I've been put on administrative leave, which is code for suspended until further notice."

"Ouch. What are you doing *here*?"

"I figured I'd lick my wounds by treating myself to the best breakfast in town." This time Ashton was the one who raised his voice so Jillian could overhear. He must have also been aware she was spying on us.

"Sounds like great minds think alike. Tea?" I reached for the tray, poured a cup, and pushed the saucer toward him. His confession had earned him a drink and a chat but nothing more. "You're on your own if you want milk and sugar. I don't use them, so Jillian never puts them on the tray."

"This is fine."

Lifting the cup by its saucer, Ashton gripped the handle with the thumb and first two digits of his opposite hand. His fingers were too thick to fit through the ear of the cup—an endearing and dainty gesture for such a mountain of a man. I couldn't help but chuckle at his debonair brand of awkwardness, and he surprised me by laughing too.

Ashton tipped his cup as if to say *touché* and took a polite sip. "What about you? Why aren't you in trial?"

"Funny story." I spread a linen napkin across my lap and reached for the cake. My hand hovered over both forks, and a twinkle flashed in his eyes. Screw sharing. A debonair man in any form could still be dangerous. "I was asked to stay home today too. Being witness to a crime scene has made me a bit of a pariah."

"You're the courthouse employee who found the judge?" He set down the teacup. Lines of concern riddled his forehead.

Oops. I'd assumed with all the media swarming around the courthouse everyone had known. A forkful of the sinfully moist cake gave me an excuse not to reply. I'd gotten too comfortable too quickly. I needed to be smarter with my next answer.

"Now I feel foolish bothering you," he said. "The

fellas at the troop can be huge gossips, and we definitely share case information when it's relevant but—those aren't the kind of details my guys would get on the Drug Task Force. Although, I suspected it was you after I interviewed with Daniels this morning."

"Detective Daniels called you in?"

"Oh, yeah. He claimed he needed to know the pre- and post-trial whereabouts of everyone in Judge Wannamaker's courtroom yesterday, but the only thing he seemed curious about was the color of Stevenson's and Harriston's ties."

"Ties?" The word came out muffled through a mouthful of buttery morsels.

He was fishing again.

I decided to play dumb. "What did you tell him?"

"Nothing, since I was too wrapped up in my own mess to remember for sure. But I've done enough investigations to know, if he's asking about a random item, there's something to it. If I had to guess, I'd say the murder weapon is a tie." He sat stone-faced, daring me to break the silence and confirm his suspicions.

Instead, I batted my eyelashes, flashed my pearly whites, and made him work for it. "Well, if that's your theory, do you also have one for the murderer?"

"Of course not. I'd have a difficult time making an assessment without viewing the crime scene." He gave me a conspiratorial look and went for broke. "Do you have a theory?"

"No." I poured myself a cup of tea while I decided if I wanted to elaborate on my answer. "But you're right. The suspected murder weapon is a purple tie, which I believe belongs to Mr. Stevenson."

"Did you tell Detective Daniels?"

"Naturally."

"But you don't believe Stevenson is the murderer?"

"I don't know what to believe." I sipped my tea and waited for the peppery notes of ginger to explode along the length of my throat. "For all I know, it could have been...*you*." I was kidding, but he did leave the court-room not too long after the judge. Maybe I wasn't the only one playing coy. "What did you tell Detective Daniels about your post-trial whereabouts?"

"I just came from the kitchen," Jillian approached our nook, "and they had everything waiting for me. One Big Ben Breakfast and a large coffee."

She set down a metal tray containing a gigantic mug, condiments, a roll of silverware, and a plate brimming with poached eggs, Irish back bacon, sausage, grilled tomatoes, mushrooms, hash browns, baked beans, and toast.

"Is there anything else I can get you two?" Jillian asked.

"No thanks, ma'am. This looks amazing." Ashton flashed a smile so radiant the skin around his eyes crin-kled. "What we could really use right now is a little space."

Jillian did another one of her high-pitched giggles—a sign she was all too willing to give us our privacy for the sake of a love connection. Before I could prompt Ashton to continue our conversation, the debonair of-ficer slipped a piece of his toast in my direction then used the rest to sop up his runny eggs.

Embarrassed by his call back to my cop-out over the cake, I pretended to miss the gesture and resumed my questions. "What did you tell Detective Daniels about the trial?"

"Exactly what you'd have expected. I was pissed by the end of things because I thought I was being set up, I mean, with that whole missing evidence scenario and getting yelled at." He put down his plate and took a big gulp of coffee. "Things only got worse after I left the courtroom and went looking for Phyllis Dodd. I caught her coming from back there where you guys work—"

"Really? Were Maggie and Mr. Stevenson with her?"

"Not at first." He scrunched his eyebrows together. "How'd you know?"

"I was talking to Maggie earlier—I guess it was an argument really—and she said she went back to her desk with Mr. Stevenson. I thought maybe they were all together."

"No. Maggie came along after I'd started talking to Ms. Dodd. She kept trying to flirt and horn in on our conversation, so the chemist and I slipped past Maggie into the personnel area and took refuge in the kitchen. Turns out Stevenson was already in there practically spitting fire."

"Was he alone? Did he have his tie with him?"

"Yeah, he was alone. No tie. I remember that much because he was in his shirtsleeves, pacing around and cursing into his cell. When he caught sight of us, he insisted on standing by while I asked Ms. Dodd a few questions about how they reseal the envelopes." Ashton returned to his plate and inhaled the grilled veggies. "When I hit her with your intel about the hidden opening under the tape used by her lab, she was as shocked as I was about the whole thing. I can spot a liar, and my gut told me her reaction was genuine."

"Did the judge come in while you were there?"

"No. We weren't in there very long. Somebody must

have complained about all the noise we were making because your bailiff came in and escorted us out through the back door."

That must have been when I saw the three of them arguing in the parking lot. I set my teacup and cake plate on the coffee table then sank back into the cushions of my chair. I'd expected Ashton to tell me something that would confirm the police had a lead on the killer, but all he did was open up more questions. At least three individuals—North, Stevenson, and Phyllis—had been through the kitchen around the time of the murder. With all those people hanging out where they weren't supposed to be, why hadn't anyone seen Ms. Freddie?

"Are you okay?" Ashton stopped chewing and his eyes grew narrow as he scanned my face.

"No…yes. I'm fine." I hunched over, placed elbows to knees, and buried my face in my hands. "I was just trying to make sense out of all this. I couldn't have been the only person who went into the bathroom yesterday." I lifted my head. "Did you know it's been leaked I discovered the crime scene? The press hounded me about that this morning. Of course, I didn't say anything. Heck, I wouldn't have known what to say even if I thought it would make a difference."

I shook my head until hair covered my face. I'd already betrayed too much emotion. "Now, *The Bugle* wants a copy of the trial transcript. I can't imagine what kind of crazy stories they'll come up with once they've read it. They already have a theory the murderer is a courthouse employee."

"That's not so far-fetched. Isn't that the group of people most likely to have the motive and the opportunity?"

"Not really. I think that distinction goes to you, Stevenson, and Phyllis. I heard you guys arguing in the parking lot yesterday." I lifted the hair out of my eyes so I could examine his face. "Sounded like all three of you have pretty strong motives."

Ashton dropped his fork. Picked up his ceramic coffee mug and held it pressed against his chest, sipping occasionally. We sat like that long enough for me to think through the steno alphabet six times, but he never looked annoyed or offended.

He looked bemused. "Is that supposed to be a test?"

"Yes." Though not intentionally. I didn't mean to accuse him, but the pain I'd felt the night before had festered into blunt anger. I needed answers.

"What's my motive for killing the judge?" he asked.

"You said it yourself. She embarrassed you on the witness stand and forced an investigation into your conduct."

"All right. I don't know if that's enough motive to kill, but I see your line of thinking. I had reason to be angry. I was in the right place at the right time. However, I didn't have access to the murder weapon. I didn't even know about Stevenson's tie until you confirmed it."

He had a point. "I suppose there's some truth to that."

"Look, I should have said this earlier. I'm sorry for your loss. You're obviously upset. You may even feel responsible, but you don't have to make me the enemy. I wouldn't have sat down here if I wasn't trying to help."

"Thanks." I leaned forward and reached for my cell phone. I clicked the power button to check the time: 12:02. "I should get going. I have to deliver a bunch of transcripts before I head home."

"Do you want some company? I could use some. Nothing to do today except worry about my fate."

I hesitated. The idea of dragging Corporal Ashton North around town as I did my drop-offs didn't appeal to me. I'd had enough of people for one day, particularly nosey people and cops—he was both.

"Let me make it up to you." His lips curved into a boyish smile that probably charmed the skirts off most women. "You said reporters were hounding you. I can help with that. Consider me your personal security for the day."

I bit my tongue to stop myself from speaking my mind. Ma always told me, *A man expecting to hit a home run his first time at bat is up to no good.*

TEN

ASHTON AND I braced ourselves against the chilly edge of the afternoon as we trudged east along Oceanside Drive away from Cake & Kettle toward the corner of York Road. We were still a block south of our destination, a large office complex that held several medical and dental providers, the WSYS news studios, the WGDT radio station, and *The Bickerton Bugle*. I walked in silence as we covered the distance. Based on the way the press had ambushed me earlier that morning, I found myself brooding over what we'd find upon arrival.

Things looked quiet as we approached the series of brick and glass structures. I steered us toward *The Bugle* and hoped the chances of having a microphone shoved in my face were less likely at a print news outlet.

The lobby stood deserted, except for a small information kiosk located in the center. Our footfalls echoed as the two of us moved across the marble expanse of the austere space.

"Hi. I'm here to drop off a trial transcript and pick up payment. My office was contacted by—" I pulled out Candi's phone message to refresh my recollection "Mike Slocum."

"Your name?" The receptionist seemed a bit annoyed we'd caught her lunching on a bag of cheese curls.

"Victoria Justice."

The woman spent an absurd amount of time wiping

the cheddar dust from her thumb and forefinger before dialing the digits for Mike's extension. When she realized we planned to hover, she shifted her bulk toward us and pointed a pudgy orange-stained finger toward a row of benches by the elevator.

"Wait over there. He rarely answers on the first ring."

Turned out we didn't have to wait. Before we made it to the bench, Mike Slocum came striding through the automatic front doors carrying a topless paper box filled with a large bag of fries and a couple of sandwiches.

"Excuse me, Mr. Slocum. You have some visitors." The amber-haired receptionist flapped one arm in our general direction and went back to her cheese-flavored lunch.

I hustled forward, glad she'd excluded my name from our meager introduction. Mike didn't seem to recognize me, and I was more than happy to keep it that way.

"I came to pick up payment for the Langley Mulligan trial transcript." I reached into my bag and pulled out the document. "I emailed you a copy of the invoice about a half hour ago."

"Oh, right. You must be from the courthouse." Mike skidded to a halt in front of us. He was tall and wiry, with dark skin and even darker eyes. "I don't think we're going to need that anymore—"

"Doesn't matter. I'm running a business." I straightened my five-foot frame. Usually, I didn't start a transcript without an upfront deposit, but with the murder investigation looming, it seemed like an unavoidable evil. "You requested it. That's a verbal contract to start the work."

"Listen, Missy," Mike's voice took on an irritated edge, "word on the street is the police are already kicking around a prime suspect. Seems one of the state's attorneys shows up on the surveillance footage right after the judge is spotted walking toward the scene of the murder." He thumbed through his fries and nonchalantly pulled out a thick one like murders were a common occurrence in our tiny town. "With a lead like that, the chance of me finding a bigger scoop in that transcript is slim." Mike moved to push between us toward the elevator.

Ashton and I exchanged shocked glances, but the corporal was quick enough to take action. He reached out a hand the size of a catcher's mitt and planted it at the center of Mike's plaid shirt, stopping the reporter's forward momentum.

"Like the lady said. Doesn't matter. She delivered. You pay." Ashton's voice boomed, and even though he wasn't wearing his uniform, his shoulders struck the commanding pose of a cop.

I peeked over at the receptionist to see if we'd attracted her notice, but she'd moved her attention from cheese curls to ginger ale, her smartphone glued to the non-carbonated hand.

"Hey, man. Cut me some slack." Mike's machismo withered in the presence of the much broader and heavier man. "I'm just trying to save *The Bugle* a few bucks. Wait here. I'll download your invoice and get accounting to cut you a check."

As soon as Mike was out of earshot, I turned to Ashton. "He's probably talking about Spencer Stevenson. Between the surveillance video and the tie, would that be enough to make an arrest?"

"Depends. The wise move would be to wait for fingerprints or some DNA." Ashton put his hands on his hips and looked around the vacant lobby. "But the bigger question is why would Stevenson take that kind of risk? Any number of people could have walked in on him at any moment."

"You're right." I set Mike's transcript on a bench and rummaged through my messenger bag until I found the phone message that contained Stevenson's transcript request. I held it up for Ashton's examination. "But if he's in his office today, we certainly have an excuse to go ask him."

ELEVEN

"SPECULATION IS ENOUGH to ruin a reputation." Stevenson took a long draw from a pink paper cup that reeked of alcohol.

We sat across from him in the clutter of his office. Stacks of files spilled over onto every surface, dozens of notecards littered the floor around his desk, and a bottle of cognac peeked out from behind a set of law books haphazardly piled on a shelf. The attorney slouched in his high-backed desk chair in a pinstriped Armani suit, a mere shell of the brash lawyer from the trial.

"Media speculation aside." Ashton leaned forward, chin in hand. "Why do you think it's being leaked you're a suspect? Our boys wouldn't put a name out there if they didn't have concrete evidence to support the claim."

Stevenson didn't seem to be listening. He stared out the window, which overlooked the tiny gravel parking lot reserved for Trident County's branch of the Attorney General's Office.

I glared at Ashton to let him know he wasn't exactly helping to create a safe space for Stevenson to open up. I'd given the lawyer his transcript, but I still needed him in a good mood so he'd remember to forward payment approval to the State Comptroller's Office. I used a softer tactic.

"The fact they didn't retain you after questioning is a good sign."

"Big deal. The damage is done." Stevenson's voice grew scratchy as the effects of the day drinking emerged. "They're saying my tie contributed to the cause of death. Do you actually think I'd be stupid enough to kill a judge?" He didn't wait for my answer, and I didn't attempt a response. "The truth is I have no idea where that tie went after I took it off."

"Mr. Harriston didn't hand it back to you?" I asked.

"No." His reply shot out like a bark. The first signs of life from him since we'd arrived. "I didn't realize I'd left the tie behind until I sat down at Maggie's desk and took off my jacket. Trust me. I went over this a thousand times with Detective Daniels." He exhaled his frustration. "Maggie escorted me back to her cubicle because I wanted to look at where she stored the drug evidence for trial. We only needed a couple of minutes to go through the log in the evidence closet and confirm she was the only one in and out that day. She stored that bogus trial evidence and went to get us some coffee while I waited at her desk."

Maggie went into the kitchen? Why didn't she say anything when we talked? She'd been so gossipy with the details—or maybe that was all an attempt to mask her involvement.

"Is that the only thing you and Maggie did?" I raised my voice because Stevenson had spun his chair toward the bookshelf to pour himself another drink. Ashton cleared his throat to get the attorney's attention.

Stevenson swiveled back around in a lazy arc, refreshed drink in hand. "We sat around her desk and talked about you two discovering that hole in the evidence envelope," he cut his eyes to the corporal, "which got me thinking I should call the Department of Justice. Put a bug in their ear about auditing all the drug evidence housed at the Controlled Substance Lab, the police troops, and any other law enforcement agencies with narcotics stored on the premises."

"Thanks a lot for that, by the way." Ashton's nostrils flared. "Your little phone-a-thon may cost me my job."

"If you're clean, you shouldn't have anything to worry about." Stevenson raised his cup to toast the corporal then drained the contents.

"I could say the same about you," countered Ashton.

"Can you? You know, I think it's funny that after three solid years of attempting to bust Langley's husband, you arrest her on similar charges only to botch that job too. Sounds like maybe *you* should be worried."

The two men scowled at each other.

I broke the stalemate. "We're all on the same side here, guys. Let's stay on point."

"Whatever." Stevenson rubbed the back of his shaved head and returned to his story. "After a while, Maggie left to help Mr. Harriston with something, so I sat at her desk and made a few more calls. I wanted to see if I could get support for a motion requesting all state courts suspend drug trials for sixty days pending investigation of the lab. You know, hopefully, save somebody else the embarrassment."

He crumpled his cup and threw it on the floor. Then he toyed with the silver nameplate on his desk so Deputy Attorney General Spencer James Stevenson winked at us several times, disappearing and reappearing.

"Doesn't add up." Ashton crossed his arms with such

force, his biceps bulged through his jacket. "You were in the kitchen when I found you."

"That's right. After a couple of calls, I was shooed away by one of the other clerks, so I ducked into the kitchen." He ignored Ashton and appealed to me. "The cops say they have surveillance video showing Judge Wannamaker walking out of the kitchen, turning around, and stepping back inside moments before I arrive. If that's true—and I doubt it is—I didn't see her, and she sure as hell wasn't in there once I got inside."

"Well, what do you think happened?" I asked.

"I think I'm being framed—like with the drugs at trial. You said yourself you saw Harriston with my tie. I bet this all boils down to him."

"Why would it?" Ashton leaned back. "Harriston had nothing to gain from Wannamaker's death. He'd just won his case. You were the one being disruptive. You were the one who weaseled his way into the personnel area. You were the one who lost." Ashton didn't bother to hide the snide undertones in his voice. "Seems pretty reckless to throw around accusations based on a hunch."

"Well, isn't that exactly what you and the person who leaked my name are doing?"

ASHTON AND I cut across the gravel parking lot behind Stevenson's office and walked over to Merchant Street, where an outrageous number of law firms lined the road—all plastered from door to floor with a different laundry list of exhausting surnames. Merchant Street ran parallel to Oceanside Drive, so we were only a block away from the rear of the courthouse and two blocks southeast of Bickerton Square, where the County Administration Building, the Controlled Substance Lab,

City Hall, and all the other state and local agencies resided.

When we reached the sidewalk, we merged into a stream of municipal workers bustling toward the center of town, where I hoped to drop off a transcript for Beau Harriston, whose private practice was old enough and prominent enough to hold a distinguished place on The Quad.

"Do you believe Stevenson?" Ashton asked. "Do you think he's being framed?"

"Doesn't sound like *you* do." I looked at him and attempted to keep pace with his long stride. "He definitely has motive and opportunity, but he seemed more focused on the drug thing."

"Maybe he's a multitasker."

"Maybe he's hiding something. Did you notice how quick he was to dismiss the tie issue?"

"Yeah, and how quickly he threw Harriston under the bus."

"That too, but I was more interested in what he had to say about Maggie. Earlier today, she mentioned she took Stevenson back to her desk, but she didn't tell me she got them both coffee. That puts a fourth person near the scene of the crime." I shivered against the chill in the air...or maybe at the thought? "Maggie could have been in the kitchen at the time of the murder. Heck, she could have done it. The way she was talking this morning, it didn't sound like she was too fond of Ms. Freddie."

"What are you saying?" His paced slowed until we found ourselves jostled among passersby. "She grabbed the tie before she left the courtroom. Took him back to her office, went to the kitchen, waited for the judge, sprang a trap, made two coffees, and headed back to her desk like nothing happened?"

"It's possible." My voice came out sharp. I didn't like that he was making light of my theory.

"Possible, but not probable. She was too busy being a flirt," Ashton said as we stopped at a crosswalk. His jaw was set and his eyebrows pinched. He fingered the zipper on his jacket as he stared into traffic. The light changed, but he didn't move.

"What's up?" I tapped his forearm. "You have a different theory?"

"No, no. Sorry. I didn't mean to space out there. I just—I was replaying our conversation with Stevenson." He looked over at me and smiled, but the effort lacked the charisma from earlier. "This has gotten much more serious than I thought—the drug thing, I mean. If they're doing statewide audits, I think—I think Stevenson might peg me as the fall guy. I've only worked with him on a few cases and our relationship has never been buddy-buddy, but I've seen enough to know he always goes down swinging. I think I should do some damage control."

"Like what?" I brushed my hand across the portion of his chest that would have held his badge if he were still an active duty officer. "What happened to licking your wounds until things blow over? You've already been put on administrative leave, so hasn't the damage been done?"

"True. But, I'd be a fool if I didn't stay on top of things." He put his hands in his pockets and shifted his weight from to side-to-side. "I should head off and see if I can make up an excuse to talk to the evidence sergeant at the troop."

"How about I go with you?"

If he'd been using me up to this point, the time had come for me to use him right back. Maybe he could help me shake some information out of the detective who was overseeing Ms. Freddie's case.

"I have a transcript for Detective Daniels I was going to drop off on my way home, but we can drive over now if you need an excuse to go back inside the troop."

"Not a bad idea." His face brightened. "We can take my truck. Shall we?"

Ashton bowed low and held out his arm but froze when his eyes latched onto something over my shoulder.

TWELVE

I TURNED TO find an impeccably tailored Phyllis Dodd barreling down the sidewalk toward us, carrying a file box, her teeth bared and her lips poised in a snarl.

"I told you this would happen, but you wouldn't listen," Phyllis shouted. "They've thrown us out, shut us down, and put a padlock on the drug lab. Now they're digging through my personal history like I'm some terrorist. Did you know I'm under investigation for criminal misconduct and evidence tampering? I blame *you*." She shifted the box to her right hip so she could position her statuesque frame directly in front of Ashton's towering one. "Based on what they're doing to me, I can only hope they decimate you...because, believe me, they're coming after you next."

"Please, Ms. Dodd, relax." I reasoned with her while Ashton clenched his fists and chewed his lower lip. "I think there's been a misunderstanding."

"And who, pray tell, are you?" Phyllis looked at me from her ginormous height.

"Victoria Justice. I'm the stenographer from the Langley Mulligan case."

"Well, take this down, *Vicki*." Phyllis directed her wrath toward me. "Wannamaker lied to my face. That old mule promised me this would be an internal matter handled discreetly among the various government agencies. Instead, I have the State Police and the Department of Justice conducting a painfully public investigation of my lab."

"Leave Victoria out of this, Ms. Dodd." Ashton jumped in, not that I needed his help. "You have a problem. You address me."

"Don't get snippy with me, North. Your little envelope trick got me kicked out of my office. They've seized our records and accused me of inadequate security measures simply because our building doesn't have video monitoring, even though they've ignored my requests to update the facility. We follow every protocol to make sure only authorized personnel—"

"With all due respect, ma'am," Ashton crossed his arms and stood his ground, "those are problems you'd have to deal with regardless of the Mulligan outcome. You should have gotten your house in order. You knew Stevenson was coming for you. Don't expect my pity. Remember, you're not the only one under scrutiny."

"Screw you, Corporal."

Ashton winced but bit his lip rather than reply with the venom I could see coursing through his taut neck muscles.

Faced with his caustic silence, Phyllis switched her box to the opposite hip, whirled around, and marched to the other side of the road—the clomping of her heels against the asphalt almost overpowered her final words. "I should have grabbed the phone from Frederica and told the President Judge my version of this mess."

"Hold on." I evaded the arm Ashton threw out to stop me and dashed after her. Maybe Phyllis knew something we didn't. "You talked to Ms. Freddie before she died?"

"Unfortunately. I made the mistake of going back to chambers before I left court yesterday. I wish I hadn't.

The last thing I need is to be part of a murder investigation on top of everything else."

"Seriously, Phyllis?" I gasped. "I assumed you and Ms. Freddie were friends."

She stopped when we reached the curb and fussed with the edges of her box as the tension fizzled. Red splotches popped up around her freckles. "Forgive me. You worked with her. I meant no offense. We were sorority sisters once, but I wasn't a fan."

"Uh, forgiven? I guess?" I couldn't imagine anyone disliking Ms. Freddie, and the fact Phyllis did made me wonder about her role in this whole affair. "Did you happen to hear or see anything that would indicate she was in trouble?"

"Heavens, no. When the bailiff led me back to chambers, Frederica was on the phone with the President Judge—Judge Yaris. I waited, and she invited me to have a cup of tea with her to discuss the ramifications of trial. I stayed the extra minute or two out of politeness, but I didn't have a lot of time to linger. She showed me a shortcut to the lobby, where I was cornered by that brute."

She pointed to the opposite sidewalk where Ashton stood with his arms across his chest. Recalling his presence seemed to set her ablaze, and she attempted to eviscerate him with a glare before trotting away. I called out to her, but a Volkswagen honked me into silence.

After a brief game of Frogger, I retreated to the sidewalk with Ashton and relayed the conversation.

A look of irritation dragged his features downward. "Strange thing is," he stroked his chin, "I never saw her with the judge. When I ran into her, she was alone."

THIRTEEN

TROOP ELEVEN WAS a remodeled plantation house that sat on a back road a quarter mile from where the Trident County Correctional Facility spread out along the south side of Route 1. The surrounding farmland was arid and barren, which made the troop feel far more imposing than it would have in a vibrant setting.

Once inside, the memory of the building's regal white columns, ornate balconies, and imposing black shutters faded in favor of utilitarian fixtures and furnishings arranged so every nook and cranny spoke to efficient service over comfort. Evidently, this also held true for Detective Daniels' office, which he claimed spared no room for visitors. Instead, the detective escorted us into a cramped conference room while he went back to his desk for some paperwork.

"What's our game plan?" I leaned toward Ashton in my molded plastic chair.

"Not ours. Mine," Ashton murmured. "I don't want to involve you in this issue any more than I have already."

"Fine." I rotated my hands in a couple of quick circles to encourage him to continue. "What's *your* game plan?"

"Give him the transcript upfront. We can use that to get him talking. Once he's rolling, I'll excuse myself. You stall 'til I get back."

"That's it?"

"That's it. I'll grab a few documents from my desk and have a quick chat with the evidence sarge—"

"Does your lieutenant know you're here, Corporal?" barked Detective Connor Daniels. His voice caused us both to straighten in our chairs. "I thought you were supposed to be on administrative leave."

"Uh, no, Detective. He doesn't know…." Ashton's eyes widened with surprise as Daniels and his wrinkled corduroy suit moved through the doorway. "And yes, I'm on leave, but you see—"

"That's a shame. Last I heard, you were on the fast track to make detective for the undercover narcotics unit." Daniels took a seat at the head of the oval conference table and narrowed his eyes.

Ashton faltered, "I don't believe the LOA will diminish my ability to—"

"Actually," I patted Ashton's arm and addressed Detective Daniels, "the corporal's quick thinking and initiative are the reason we're here."

Ashton's glare nearly melted the skin off my face. He didn't know it, but he needed saving. If there was one lesson I'd learned from years of watching people tell their stories on the witness stand, it was that a variation of the truth always worked better than an outright lie. Besides, I had a few questions that required answers, and I knew how to play my cards. I dropped my tone to a whisper and let my voice tremble.

"Someone must have leaked my name in conjunction with the crime scene because I was accosted by the press on my way into work this morning. Ashton, a trusted family friend, came to the rescue and offered to escort me around town while I dropped off these transcripts." I reached into my messenger bag and pulled out the document for the detective. "Good thing he did. When I made my first delivery at *The Bugle*, I was blindsided again. This time the reporters demanded information that would confirm your office's claims of Spencer Stevenson as the prime suspect." I closed my eyes and tried to summon a few tears. "They said he followed Ms. Freddie to the scene of the crime."

Ashton reached out to hold my hand.

Nailed it.

"Ms. Justice." Daniels tapped the laminate surface of the table, as he'd done in our interview, probably to distract me from my tears. "These reporters are quick to pick up one idea and run with it. I can assure you we haven't released any information."

I acted choked up while Ashton responded. "With all due respect, Detective, these reporters had details. They mentioned there's suspicious surveillance footage of Stevenson at the crime scene."

"We have suspicious video of a lot of people." Daniels rubbed a hand across his mustache and exhaled heavily. "You. Phyllis Dodd. In fact, Beau Harriston disappears off the feed altogether with one of the courthouse clerks." He opened the folder he'd brought with him and ran his finger down the middle. "He and a Margaret Swinson disappear a couple minutes after Langley Mulligan is taken into a holding cell by one of the guards. Do you know Margaret Swinson, Ms. Justice?"

"Yes. I work with her occasionally." I glanced at Ashton, who pursed his lips.

He, no doubt, knew I wanted to blab about Maggie's proximity to the crime scene.

"In fact, I spoke with her earlier today. I didn't see her enter the courtroom after Langley was detained—I guess I'd already stepped outside—but she did mention this morning she went back into the courtroom mid-recess to speak with Mr. Harriston."

"I assume you've had time to interview them," Ashton asked, "did either one of them give any indication of their whereabouts?"

Detective Daniels tightened his mouth, and I thought he wasn't going to answer. "They both claim to have stepped into the jury room together to discuss employment."

"Hold on." I held up my hand. "I don't follow. Why do you accept that they went into the jury room as opposed to somewhere else?"

"All the public areas, including the courtrooms, have eyes in the sky—"

"Excuse me for a second." Ashton stood, clutching his cell phone, and scurried out of the room.

I hadn't heard his phone ring or buzz, so I assumed he'd chosen to make his escape.

Daniels shot an irritated glance at Ashton's back. "We've accepted that response for now because Jury Room Four is the only possible point of departure for the pair. The keycard log doesn't show Ms. Swinson swiping into any of the personnel offices at that time. She has a full access card, so any movement would have raised a flag."

"What about the judges' hallway?" My voice grew anxious. I needed to keep him talking, for Ashton's sake, but also for my own curiosity. He seemed receptive enough, but how far could I push him? "I've seen cameras in there. Did you get that footage?"

"We have video coverage of the judges' hallway."

"Well, what about Ms. Freddie? Did you see…"

My throat tightened, and the sting of tears clouded

my vision. The emotion I'd faked earlier had grown real. If someone had ambushed her in that narrow corridor, no one would hear her scream.

"Ms. Justice, calm down. I can assure there was nothing unusual from the footage in the judges' hallway. Wannamaker simply uses that route to escort Phyllis Dodd into the kitchen." The detective flipped through his paperwork and skimmed a passage. "The two linger in there for a few minutes then step out together into the personnel hallway between the kitchen and the Protho-notary's Office." He looked at me. "Did you happen to see Phyllis Dodd moving around the personnel areas of the courthouse during the recess?"

"No, but I remember she left the courtroom as soon as the trial broke. She wanted to speak with the judge in private—something about needing to leave for an-other trial. The bailiff took her back to chambers." My voice cracked at the realization that almost everyone I'd encountered that day could have murdered Ms. Fred-die. "I didn't see Phyllis again until I went outside. She was in the parking lot arguing with Mr. Stevenson and Corporal North. I also ran into her leaving the lab this morning. She mentioned Ms. Freddie invited her for tea…although she claimed to have only stayed a few minutes because she was in a hurry."

"Ms. Dodd volunteered that information? Did she mention them having a quarrel or a disagreement?"

"Between Ms. Freddie and Phyllis?" I shrugged, but I'd learned from Ashton that Daniels wouldn't have asked if he didn't think it was possible. "Not exactly. Phyllis simply said she wasn't fond of Ms. Freddie. But shouldn't we be more concerned about Mr. Stevenson?

Is there any truth to what the reporters are saying? I already know he was in the kitchen. He told me as much."

Daniels closed his file and nodded. "The footage shows Judge Wannamaker return to the kitchen after Ms. Dodd's departure. Minutes pass and Stevenson follows her inside. We checked the video feed at the back entrance to the kitchen—the one off the judges' hallway. She doesn't leave and no one else enters at that time."

"When Stevenson goes in there, she's alone?"

"Yes. But the courthouse doesn't have cameras in the kitchen or the bathroom, where the murder occurred, so we can't confirm anything. We can't even confirm what went on in chambers prior to the crime." He scratched his mustache as if lost in thought. "If we had a few more angles, we might be able to figure out how Stevenson's tie got into the bathroom. He claims he wasn't wearing it or carrying it, but we lose track of it on the video after Harriston picks it up."

The detective stiffened and leaned across the conference table until I couldn't look anywhere but deep into his droopy brown eyes. "Are you *sure* you didn't see that tie with anyone else?"

"I didn't see it with anyone else." I drew out each syllable to avoid the question on the tip of my tongue—but my words crashed out. "Why not arrest both attorneys and see if one of them breaks?"

Stupid question, of course. Law enforcement preferred a certain amount of direct evidence to make an arrest, but maybe his response would give me some insight into who was at the top of his suspect list.

"Ms. Justice," he sighed at my ignorance, "two more people enter the kitchen after Stevenson and neither one of those people was Harriston. Phyllis Dodd doubles back after a few minutes, and Corporal North joins her. Nearly five minutes pass before they leave the kitchen with Stevenson and another ten before you arrive and discover the judge. That leaves a lot of information open to interpretation."

"Well, what are you doing to narrow down the suspects?"

He raised a bushy eyebrow at me. Had I pressed him too far?

"I can assure you everything is under control," he said. "We're taking this case seriously, and we don't want to make mistakes. The governor has expressed his concern about the safety of our state officials, and everyone is looking a lot harder at security measures for all of the government facilities. For now, we'll remain focused on interviewing people, mainly employees, but also everyone and anyone who—"

"What about the crime scene, Detective?" We both looked up to find Ashton leaning against the doorjamb. Despite a little sweat along his hairline, the corporal seemed as relaxed and as charming as ever. "Any fingerprints?"

"No usable fingerprints at the scene." Daniels grunted. "Our techs think the bathroom got wiped. We did, however, find some traces of powder, so maybe the perp was wearing latex gloves that contained talc."

"So you don't have anything concrete on Stevenson?" said Ashton.

"What we have on him is circumstantial," Daniels twitched his mustache, "which is why this office hasn't made an official statement to the press."

"Well," Ashton said, "if the information didn't come from *this* office—"

I faked a phlegm-filled cough.

Between the conversation with Stevenson and the morning's confrontation with Maggie, I bet my busty blonde coworker not only blabbed to the press about me finding the murder scene, but also dished about Stevenson being in the personnel area—a convenient way to take focus away from her own suspicious behavior.

"With the speed information travels these days," Daniels rose from his seat and stepped toward Ashton, who still occupied the doorway, "the leak could be anyone's handiwork. Word to the wise, North, forget the gossip and start dealing with your own mess so you can get back on track for that promotion."

Ashton agreed and thanked Detective Daniels for his time while I followed them out of the conference room. Once we'd left the detective and stepped outside, I whispered to Ashton.

"I don't know if I feel better or worse after hearing all that."

"I take it Stevenson is guilty?"

"I don't know. I guess it sounds like it, but with Maggie and Harriston unaccounted for, who knows?" I scanned the crowded parking lot for Ashton's wannabe monster truck and trudged toward it. "I felt for Stevenson back at his office, but now…" I shook my head. "How did you do?"

"I got everything I needed and then some," Ashton opened my door and held my arm as I climbed up. "The sergeant's evidence log confirms what I seized at arrest. As long as that information comes to light during the state audit, I should be golden."

"Cool." I sat back and let my mind drift while he walked to his side of the truck.

"Where to next? Harriston's?"

I nodded, but his questions were simply background noise. My thoughts alighted on Spencer Stevenson and his necktie. Why bother to kick up all that dust about the missing drugs if he was just going to kill the judge in retaliation? And why was Harriston the only person—the last person—seen with that stupid tie?

Something was missing.

FOURTEEN

"You've got to be kidding me," I muttered as we walked toward Harriston's colonial storefront.

The old attorney stood on the sidewalk fielding questions from a handful of news reporters and camera operators. Curious, I pushed our way through the group of onlookers who'd gathered behind the press in the parking spaces in front of the doorway where Harriston reigned.

"Oh, yes, indeed," he said, "I believe the missing evidence in the Mulligan case may point to a large-scale drug conspiracy. However, I also believe my client was innocent from the get-go. No drugs were ever in her possession," he turned and gave the WSYS news camera to his left a megawatt smile, "and what happened in court is further indication of that innocence. Justice was served yesterday, and it pains me to think the media would attempt to invalidate a young lady's innocence simply because one state facility shows signs of corruption."

A discontented growl exploded from Ashton's throat, and I moaned softly along with him, barely suppressing an urge to scream. *Langley innocent?* Those words didn't belong in the same sentence. Someone stacked the deck in her favor—most likely Harriston himself—and the fact the old attorney seemed content to stand in the middle of The Quad and crow about such duplicity made me wonder why Detective Daniels didn't consider Harriston a suspect.

"Large-scale drug conspiracy, Mr. Harriston, or an error exploited for profit?" asked a tall dark-skinned man I recognized as Mike Slocum from *The Bugle*. "I mean, I can't help but question how this drug lab issue affects your business when I see a 'For Lease by DelaCorp' sign in your window. Yesterday's trial makes you relevant again, wouldn't you agree? No matter how this story is spun—corrupt lab, botched chain of custody, evidence tampering, or innocent client—you profit, correct?"

"Can I help it if an unsympathetic organization has acquired this building and raised my rent beyond what is sustainable? I am a victim of DelaCorp's greed. That's what you need to report. To imply anything else is slander." Harriston shook his jowls and stepped away from the crowd.

"Please, sir, one more question," said a Latin woman with teased hair and too much lipstick. "What do you think of the assertion the Magistrate Murderer is a courthouse employee or may even be someone present for your trial?"

Finally, a question Harriston wouldn't be able to dodge or manipulate for his own gain. I reached over, clutched Ashton's arm for support, and found his muscles as tense as my own.

"I'd hesitate to follow that line of thinking." Harriston dismissed the question with a flick of his hand. "The whole idea of guilt by association or location or approximation fails to take into consideration our government officials and law enforcement officers are *always* at risk since they sit atop the food chain. The police would be foolish to rule out the possibility of other suspects."

"Are you implying the police are following false leads and their murder investigation is misguided?" yelled a bearded reporter in a navy-blue trench coat.

Harriston ignored the jab and shut things down. "If you'll excuse me, I have a business to run. Please direct further questions to my administrative assistant, Ms. Margaret Swinson,"

Harriston inclined his balding head toward Maggie then escaped through the doorway to his practice. A chorus of shouts followed his back while Maggie slid into his place. What was she up to?

"Ladies and gentlemen, I can assure you Mr. Harriston loves our law enforcement community and works tirelessly to aid them in their quest for peace in Bickerton. Please, if you would kindly clear the door to the premises, we can get back to business as usual. We don't want to intimidate our incoming clients." She began passing out business cards. "You can direct additional inquiries to us by telephone, where we would be happy to make an appointment for a one-on-one interview. Thank you."

When she spun around to go inside, I dodged through the dispersing crowd to grab her.

"Maggie, what are you doing?"

"Helping." She snatched her wrist free.

"Grace said you were assisting Harriston because he lost his secretary, but when did you start working here? What about your job at the courthouse?"

"Why, Corporal North." She slinked over to Ashton and held out the back of her hand like he was supposed to kiss it. "I barely recognized you out of uniform. Will we be seeing you at Cooper's for karaoke tomorrow night?"

"I believe Victoria asked you a question," Ashton replied.

"Excuse me," said the female reporter with the teased hair. Up close, I recognized her as Ana Ortega, the anchor from the nightly WSYS broadcast. She'd been on the edge of our threesome having her mic removed by a cameraman. "Are you Victoria as in Victoria *Justice*? We'd love to get a statement from you about the Magistrate Murderer."

"No comment." Ashton placed his hand on the small of my back and pushed me past the reporter and through the doorway to Harriston's storefront. Maggie must have barreled in behind us because I heard the twang of her lazy accent overpower the clamor that took place outdoors.

"Haven't you caused enough trouble for one week?" Maggie pressed her shoulder into the door and locked the dead bolt against the encroaching horde. "You shouldn't be here. Mr. Harriston is expecting—"

"Seriously, Maggs." I detached myself from Ashton and confronted her, fueled by anger from the reprimand she'd given me earlier in the day. "Give me a straight answer. When did you start working for Harriston?"

She busied herself, removing the "For Lease by Dela-Corp" placard from the window by the reception desk.

"What do you care?" She ripped the sign in half, tossed the pieces aside, and plopped down on one of the three ivory couches arranged in a semicircle near a gas fireplace. "I'll only be in your hair for two more weeks."

"You didn't mention that this morning," I replied.

"Well, you didn't give me half a chance, did you? You were too busy pitching a boogie to let me tell my side of the story."

"Maggie," Harriston bellowed from the recesses of his office, "do you have my next appointment out there?"

"No, it's just Victoria Justice—"

"And I have your transcript from the Mulligan trial," I hollered over Maggie. "I'd love to collect payment on that if you don't mind."

"Why, yes, yes. Come on back," Harriston said in a refined but commanding downhome accent that reminded me of Foghorn Leghorn.

I flashed Maggie a smug grin, beckoned Ashton, and headed toward the sound of the lawyer's voice. We crossed through a set of open French doors, just beyond the waiting area, to find Harriston sitting in the middle of a room resplendent in golds, tans, and mahoganies.

"Excuse us for barging in without a courtesy call, but I was surprised to find Maggie working for you so I—"

"Oh, my, yes. I offered her a job after the trial yesterday. Figured business would pick up once word spread about the evidence mishap," Harriston chuckled, "and I was surely right."

My mouth fell open, and Ashton stiffened at my side. What about Ms. Freddie? Didn't this man have any sympathy or respect for her passing?

"Intuition and opportunity, my friends, not deceit and duplicity as those journalists would have you believe." Harriston gestured us toward the set of club chairs that faced the daunting fortress of his leather-topped executive desk. "I figured some of my old clients, and a few future ones, would consider the doubt cast upon the lab's credibility a prime opportunity to seek a miracle in the form of sentence modifications, post-conviction relief, and the like. Couldn't have come at a better time, if you ask me." He leaned back. "Of course, my intention wasn't to throw Ms. Swinson directly into the thick of things. She stopped by for a word during lunch and, before you know it, the press arrived. Hope you two didn't get caught up in that."

"A little. Nothing Ashton—Corporal North couldn't handle."

"Ah, yes, excuse me, Corporal North, to what do I owe this unexpected pleasure?"

"Routine visit. I offered to escort Ms. Justice around town for her safety."

"I hope it's not because of that assault nonsense with Ms. Mulligan." Harriston fixed his stare on me. "I can assure you that you're perfectly safe."

"Langley Mulligan attacked you?" Ashton half rose from his seat. "When?"

"After you left the courtroom yesterday." I wasn't sure I wanted to rehash the situation in front of Harriston.

"What happened?" He returned to his seat and placed a palm on my knee. "Were you hurt?"

Harriston raised a hand to discourage Ashton's alarm. "Ms. Mulligan meant no harm, and she feels horrible about yesterday. As a matter of fact, we were hoping Ms. Justice would consider a written apology and damages—for her outfit—in lieu of pursuing prosecution." He opened his hands wide in a pleading gesture and addressed me. "She's already spent a night in jail over this. And, with the ink barely dry on her plea deal, she doesn't need this new set of charges ruining her probation."

Ashton snorted, and I joined him. The idea of going easy on Langley was unfathomable.

"Absolutely not. I merely came here to make good on my promise." I pulled out the final transcript of the day and tossed the hefty packet of paper onto his desk. "I would ask you do the same. You can make your payment out to Victoria C. Justice."

Harriston gripped the arms of his leather club chair. He examined me for several seconds before reaching into the top drawer of his desk and pulling out a checkbook. He slipped on a pair of bifocals and filled out the lines as he spoke. "Ms. Justice, I know you're a businesswoman, so I don't blame you for rejecting my first offer. Nevertheless, let's get real here and negotiate. We can arrange a time to meet with a DAG about the case or if you prefer—"

Bam. Bam. Bam. Bam.

A cacophony of sound floated in from the reception area. Maggie's loud drawl followed the sound of a brusque New York accent, then the heavy thunk and click of the deadbolt unlatching. Seconds later, the French doors to Harriston's office crashed open.

A man with an intense tan and an unkempt goatee barged into the room. Despite the frigid temperature outside, he wore nothing but a white V-neck thermal and white corduroy pants. A silver wallet chain and I.D. card hung from his waist, while a white knit cap held back his stringy, shoulder-length hair.

"Why do I bother paying you, Harriston?" The stranger thrust a vascular forearm in the attorney's direction. "You're supposed to keep my wife out of jail. And yet, I get another call last night about bailing her out. If I'd known that cop's B.S. was going to cause this much trouble, I'd have taken care of him myself."

"Is that a threat?" Ashton shot out of his chair.

"What the—are you following me again?" The intruder's face, already pinched from frustration, hardened into stone at the sight of the officer. "You best believe that's a threat. I should sue your Barney Fife-looking mug for harassment."

Harriston, his round nose and saggy cheeks twitching, recovered and intervened. "Please, my apologies, Mr. Mulligan. I thought our appointment was at four." He rose and buttoned his suit jacket. "We were just finishing up." The attorney ripped out the top check from its book and reached across the desk to hand it to me.

"I don't care who you have in here." The man stared at me as I folded the check and slid the tiny rectangle into my bag.

Pinpricks ran across my skin. This was Langley's grislier half.

The man continued, "As much dough as I'm laying out, I should be able to talk to you twenty-four/seven."

"Funny," Ashton stepped into the stranger's personal space, "I didn't think innocent people kept defense lawyers on retainer."

"Don't test me, Pig."

I jumped up and tugged at Ashton's arm before he could respond. I didn't know what was going on, but I wanted out. No need to draw attention to myself or my connection to Mr. Mulligan's wife.

Harriston clearly shared my concern because, as I struggled to drag Ashton toward the door, the attorney dismissed us. "Have a seat, Chance. I'm sure Corporal North and his guest will close the door on their way out."

FIFTEEN

"WHAT IS GOING ON? Have you lost your mind?" I asked when we were standing outside of Harriston's storefront. Luckily the sidewalk, though sprinkled with people from the nearby polling center, was free of reporters.

Ashton clenched his teeth and stared at the trees in the middle of The Quad. A vein at the center of his forehead pulsated in rhythm with the clenching of his jaw.

After a long silence, he said, "Why didn't you tell me Langley Mulligan attacked you?"

"You're stalling." I was tired of running in circles. I was tired of being the last one to know everything. I was tired of being the studious little court reporter who was on a need-to-know basis. For once, I wanted the truth, the whole truth, and nothing but the truth. "What's with the screaming match between you and Langley's husband?"

Ashton tore his gaze away from the town center and glared at me. His shoulders sagged. "I don't know how familiar you are with Langley Mulligan, but her husband is a known drug dealer. I've been trailing him for several years."

"So, this is about some drawn out police investigation?"

"I wish." Ashton took my elbow and shepherded me across the street toward the evergreen hedgerows that enclosed the town's four-tiered fountain and meditation garden. "I was covering some shiftwork for a coworker down by the beach three years ago when I first arrested Chance. He was driving a stolen car, and he had a few packets of oxy on him. I suspected he was dealing and arrested him, but he managed to get the charges dropped."

"How?"

"The owner of the car came forward to recant her report, and Chance miraculously produced a prescription for the drugs. Suspicious, but worthless to pursue. Not every arrest leads to conviction." We settled onto one of the garden's wooden benches, a few yards from the dreaded water feature. "None of that would have mattered if it weren't for the events that happened a few days later in the shooting death of Master Corporal Natalie Knowles."

"I don't understand what that has to do with—" My hands flew up to my mouth as details of the Knowles case came flooding back to me.

Ms. Freddie had recently discussed the matter over dinner with Ma. As Bickerton's only cop killing, the tragedy was never far from people's lips—especially since the case had been our county's last capital murder investigation before Delaware repealed the death penalty.

I refocused on Ashton. "Isn't that the case where only two men were tried because the judge suppressed the theory of a third gunman?"

"Exactly. I believe that third suspect is Chance Mulligan." Ashton grabbed my hands and forced me to meet his gaze. He took a deep breath. "I was there as backup. I arrived after the suspect vehicle had crashed and opened fire on the officers in pursuit. I was *sure* I recognized Chance fleeing the scene, but our search produced nothing. When detectives followed up, Mulligan's wife gave him an alibi. Supposedly, he'd accompanied her to the dentist's office. He even got the receptionist to confirm it. I didn't buy it, but no one could prove otherwise, so the information was deemed inadmissible."

I wasn't super familiar with the case, having only worked the arduous jury selection, but I remembered Ms. Freddie had gotten a ton of flak from the press for granting defense's motion to sever—doing so gave the two defendants separate trials. What most people didn't know was Ms. Freddie came to that decision based on the scenario Ashton had just described: Since both defendants faced the death penalty for Corporal Knowles's murder, those who knew about the suppressed evidence thought it was suspicious neither defendant chose to rat out the existence of a third culprit.

Ashton released my hands. "Natalie was my partner during my probationary training period with the troop. She championed me when people thought I wouldn't cut it. When I finally made rank and started earning my marks, she encouraged me to apply to the Drug Task Force. She was even going to sponsor my first bid for detective, but…"

His voiced cracked, and the words crumbled into nothingness. He stood up and seemed to replay some event in his mind. "She lived with honor and helped me become the man I am today. She didn't deserve death at the hands of a coward. I may not have been there in time to stop it, but I *will* find a way to make Chance pay."

"Ashton, I'm so sorry." My words came out ragged. I recognized Ashton's pain. I hadn't been there in time for Ms. Freddie either, and the guilt gnawed at me. "But you're acting like this Chance guy is some mastermind who can get out of any crime. He's human. He's fallible.

You'll get him. Just like you got Langley. He couldn't work his magic for her, right?"

"Didn't he, though?" Ashton's voice grew heated. "Think about it. Langley got out of her felony charges on a technicality. Do you think that's coincidence? I know this sounds crazy, but maybe the two of them figured out a way to switch the drugs and discredit me at the same time. I don't know how much you were watching Langley during trial, but she never looked surprised about the missing evidence. Neither did Harriston."

As much as I hated Langley and wanted to hate her husband by association, I couldn't wrap my head around the prospect. Chance would need to have access to the drug lab, the troop, and/or the courthouse for Ashton's theory to fly. The last option was one I didn't want to consider, especially since that implied Chance Mulligan could have accessed the courthouse prior to my mentor's murder.

Ashton must have sensed the skepticism behind my eyes. "Maybe I'm overthinking things, but the point is Chance is dirty."

He left my side and paced along the fountain's basin, which acted as a reflection pool and wishing well. Watching him walk so close to the water caused a stinging sensation to surface in my chest, so I squeezed my eyes shut and concentrated on my breathing for a moment.

"I've been keeping an eye on him," Ashton explained when I opened my eyes. "He hangs out around the high school and mingles with the beach tourists. Money changes hands, but I haven't been able to catch him holding or distributing. The few times I've gathered enough probable cause to put him under official surveillance or petition for a warrant, he comes off clean. He doesn't seem to have any suppliers or accomplices. I think he's either getting the drugs legitimately or stealing them."

"Or maybe Langley was the dealer all along, and you were too busy watching him to notice her." I hated to play devil's advocate, but I needed to say something. The man sounded obsessed.

"It's not that simple." He collapsed onto the lip of the marble fountain, his back bowed in defeat.

We sat like that for eons, me on the bench and Ashton by the fountain. He stewed silently, while the distant sound of construction floated over from the south side of The Quad. I couldn't see the municipal workers for all the trees surrounding the meditation garden, but I could hear shouts of frustration as they struggled to erect the bandstand for the next day's Post-Election Festival. The light drone of their hammers and drills mingled with the steady gurgle and splash of the fountain just enough to keep the dull burning in my chest from becoming a four-alarm panic attack.

"When were you going to tell me about Langley Mulligan and the assault?" Ashton asked as if we'd never paused the conversation.

"I wasn't." I rose, to test the idea of leaving. As long as my breath stayed steady, I could take care of myself. "She thought she could bully me, like in high school. She was wrong."

"Look." He extended his hand, but I stepped out of reach. "I didn't mean to upset you. I haven't given you much reason to trust my judgment. But, believe me when I say Chance and Langley are dangerous. You should be careful." He held up his cell phone and tossed it to me. "Call your number so I have yours in my phone and you have mine. Ring me if either one of them approaches you."

SIXTEEN

I WAS ONLY a few steps away from the meditation garden when my cell rang. I dug it out of my bag, and turned to look across the street for Ashton.

"Seriously?" I said into the phone. "I think I can walk the half a block to my car without you checking up on me."

"Of course you can, Angel, but it's my job to worry about you," said a voice from the speaker.

"Ma?"

I searched the greenery around the fountain only to find Ashton had vanished. I'd insisted upon walking alone to my car because I wanted to clear my head. Now that he was gone, my heart sank a little. He'd trusted me with his fears and failures, and I'd managed to push him away. I should have acknowledged we shared the same demons, even if I didn't subscribe to his theory.

"Victoria, are you still there? Is everything okay?"

"I'm fine. Everything is fine. Work was quiet. But, you were right. Today was a wash. Even Candi suggested I go home."

"As she should. Under the circumstances, I can't understand why you'd want to be there."

"It's my job, Ma." I twisted the phone away from my mouth so she wouldn't hear me groan. I wasn't in the mood to rehash our mini-argument from last night. "Relax. You'll have me all to yourself for the rest of the week. I'm walking to the car now. I should be home in ten minutes."

"Don't bother. Just come over to Cooper's as soon as you can. We're going to start the results party early. The numbers are already pointing to a landslide victory." She half-squealed, half-giggled. "I just want to thank my team and wrap this thing up quick. I don't feel comfortable celebrating with everything that's going on with Freddie."

After running around town all day, I'd forgotten about the culminating moment of my mother's new career as a politician. The mayoral race was between her and another newcomer to politics, but Ma's illustrious career as an educator put her name at the top of everyone's list. At this point, the election was a formality.

"Of course," I said. "I'm practically around the corner. See you in a bit."

"Wonderful. Love you, Angel."

"Love you too." I hung up the phone and had barely put the device away before it rang again. This time I took a second to check the caller ID before I tapped the screen.

The words "Grace Tisdale" greeted me in bold letters. "Hey, look who's finally learned to answer her phone. I went looking for you at lunch. They said you'd gone home, but nobody answered at your house. You okay? I texted you three times. Where'd you go?"

"Not far. I'm actually in the courthouse parking lot, but I'm about to swing by Cooper's for Ma's party." I unlocked the Mustang and slipped inside. "Sorry. I wasn't trying to ignore you. I should have stuck my head in to see you before I left work, but things got—weird."

"Why am I not surprised? Did those reporters start calling your office?"

"No. They were too busy rallying around Harriston and his new secretary, Maggie Swinson." I took a deep breath, hoping to dampen the temper that bubbled underneath the words that came tumbling out of my mouth. "But that was only after Maggie practically accused me of murder, even though she's the one running off into dark corners with Harriston planning goodness knows what." I got in my car, put Grace on speaker, set the phone in the passenger seat, and started the engine. "Has she even told anyone she's quitting yet?"

"Hold on. One thing at a time." The sound of rustling came over the phone, which made me think Grace was trying to press her ear closer to the receiver. "Maggie accused you of murder? Who's going to believe that? That woman has some nerve. She's just jealous of your relationship with Wannamaker—and because you make, like, three times more money than her. She's done nothing but gripe about her paycheck since she lost her job in chambers. Those clerks don't even get paid half as much as the secretaries."

"Wait. Wait. Wait. What?" I put the car in gear and eased onto the roundabout that serviced The Quad. "Are we talking about the same thing here? I meant Maggie got a job working for Harriston, not the judges."

"Yeah, I heard you. I'm just saying Maggie's been a beast since Judge Wannamaker reassigned her to the clerk's office. That was before your time, but I can remember when losing her secretary gig was all Maggie could talk about. I'm not surprised she's jumped ship to go to Old Beau Harriston's, but I *am* surprised she's stupid enough to try to ruin your rep on her way out the door."

"Well, now I'm the one who feels stupid." I turned down Bickerton Boulevard and sped toward Route 1. "I always figured she hated me because I sided with Jillian during that fiasco with Shaun."

"Don't try to figure out anything Maggie does. You'll just give yourself a migraine." Grace chuckled. "And if it makes you feel any better, she got herself demoted. I mean, does Maggie strike you as the type of person you'd trust to maintain your schedule, let alone the secrets of the realm?" The mockery in her voice was so thick that her words rose an octave and cracked when the question hit home. "She was shooting off at the mouth about everything that went on in chambers, misplacing files, and buzzing complete strangers into their front office. She should be grateful Wannamaker didn't put her in jail. Old Beau is going to have a handful."

That behavior sounded like classic Maggs, and the thought of it tugged at the corners of my mind. "Do you think Maggie has a grudge against Judge Wannamaker? Enough to hurt her or let someone into the courthouse who—"

"Don't go there, Victoria. Let the police handle all that. Detective Daniels has the surveillance footage. He'll come to the right conclusion."

"Sure, in another decade or two." I picked up the phone with one hand and merged onto Route 1 with the other. "I was just at the troop talking to Daniels. He didn't seem to be in a hurry to make an arrest."

"No?" She paused. "Well, I'm surprised to hear that since I dragged North, Stevenson, and Ms. Dodd out of the kitchen not too long before everything went to hell. Gotta be one of them."

"Or Maggie or Harriston." I tucked the phone between my cheek and shoulder so I'd have both hands free to navigate onto the pot-hole ridden tire buster better known as the vast parking lot spread out in front of Cooper's. "Just hear me out. Indulge me. Today's been brutal."

"Fine. Shoot."

"Daniels says Harriston and Maggie disappear off the surveillance feed around the time of the murder. He also said Harriston was the last person seen holding the murder weapon. Add that to Maggie's bad attitude about Wannamaker and the odd timing of her new job offer, and it all starts to sound a little suspicious, don't you think?"

Grace made a clucking noise with her tongue.

"Maybe we should compare notes," I said. "Do you think you can make your way over to Cooper's?"

"Yeah, I think I have a change of clothes somewhere in my office. Let me get out of this uniform, and I'll meet you there in twenty."

When she hung up, I lifted my chin and let the phone slip down my chest and into my lap while I backed into a cramped space between two SUVs. Even though it was barely 4:00, the lot overflowed with dozens of vehicles cocked at funny angles to avoid the child-sized craters in the dirt parking area.

To the untrained eye, Cooper's looked like a 1950s Howard Johnson's restaurant gone to seed. Yet, it was the best dive bar in the state. The joint was open Wednesday through Sunday for karaoke, and known for serving a mean fish sandwich, a meaner crab cake,

and every brand of alcohol known to man. Regulars—
or those allergic to seafood—might manage to convince
the kitchen to put together a BLT or a grilled cheese,
but don't dare ask for a salad or ketchup for your fries.
Do so and earn an ejection from the bar courtesy of
the owner himself. According to Ian Cooper, salt, vin-
egar, and potatoes were all any person required in the
way of vegetables.

While Cooper's wasn't exactly the most elegant place
for a mayoral kick-off celebration, the venue was avail-
able for private party rentals on Tuesdays, had plenty of
open floor space around the bar, and boasted a raised
stage with a sound system, all of which combined to
give Ma a serviceable site for her event.

I stepped out of the car and traversed the length of the
crowded lot to find Russell Wannamaker, Ms. Freddie's
husband, sitting on the steps outside the entrance. He
hunched over the concrete and concentrated on packing his pipe, a sandblasted Peterson P-lip. I watched and
waited while he carefully pinched and tamped tobacco
from the gold tin of Dunhill 965. When he finally noticed me, his bloodshot eyes lit up in recognition. I tried
for an upbeat expression, but my emotions must have
betrayed me, because he abandoned the usual pleas-
antries.

"Don't be like the rest of them. Fix your face. I'm
a grown man. I'll survive." He stood with the unlit
pipe between his lips and gave me a long hug. He was
still quite sturdy for a man of seventy, and his embrace bound me tight. His toasty body warmed me even
though he wasn't wearing a coat, just a loose-fitting
navy-blue suit. A matching herringbone fedora covered

his graying Afro. I patted his back, in lieu of offering the condolences he obviously didn't want to hear.

When we separated, he gestured for me to join him on the step as he started the ritual of lighting his pipe. A cloud formed around us. I resisted the urge to fan away the pungent smell of roasted leather and burnt brown sugar.

"I'm surprised to see you here, Mr. Russell."

"I wouldn't miss an opportunity to support your mother. Neither would Freddie." He looked at the reddening sky. "I imagine she's here in spirit."

Content to listen, I closed my eyes for a moment and took solace in the idea.

"But I just couldn't spend another minute in there." He jerked a thumb over his shoulder toward Cooper's glass doors, which had become lost behind a wall of fumes. "Too much noise, too many questions. You can only listen to people say they're sorry for so long before you snap." He took a lengthy draw from his pipe. "They're all tiptoeing around the subject of murder as if facing the truth will break me."

Smoke curled out of the corners of his mouth as he studied the cars zipping past on the highway. Traces of frustration and distress tinged his voice. "Here's the truth: Freddie was tough. She lived for justice. We were married forty-two years, and I can tell you the only thing she loved more than me was the law. She sacrificed everything for that job—health, happiness, kids, our relationship. The day she took her oath as judge was the best day of her life. I hate that someone took that away from her."

"Me too." Those were the only words that seemed fitting since he didn't want my sympathy. I pulled the collar of my coat tight around my neck, trusting the warmth of the added fabric would bring me a little comfort. Death wasn't something I'd contended with before, and I was a little disappointed he'd closed the door on commiseration. "She deserved better. We'll just have to hope for a speedy arrest."

Mr. Russell let out a heavy grunt that soured into a cryptic chuckle. "You sound like that one-trick pony Detective Connor Daniels. He talks a big game, says he has a suspect in mind, but I don't believe a word of it. Whoever did this wanted to punish Freddie. This was personal. That stupid courthouse employee theory doesn't fly with me. They need to look more closely at her peers, starting with old Beauregard Monroe—"

"Harriston? Why?" I had my suspicions, but I had no idea anyone else shared them.

"You've always been so mature. Sometimes I forget I have almost half a century on you." He wrenched his eyes away from the road and gave me a melancholy smile. "You couldn't have been more than three when Freddie was in line for her first appointment to the bench. Back then, Old Beau was on the short list too."

He let out a long exhale from his pipe until a screen of milky white smoke separated us. I held my breath as I waited for him to continue.

"Everyone assumed the governor would choose Old Beau. Turns out, he picked Freddie. And since you can't fight the man in charge, Old Beau blamed Freddie for his failure. Don't get me wrong. His surface demeanor has always been respectful, but he's turned her courtroom into a circus over the years and made quite a name for himself while doing it."

"She never mentioned—" I stopped myself.

Why *would* she have mentioned something like that to me? I wasn't in a position to help her. Knowing something like that would have colored my opinion of Harriston, and Ms. Freddie was too professional to let her personal woes interfere with productivity. Though I wish she had confided in me, particularly since this information fell in line with Grace's description of Harriston's cutthroat trial tactics.

Mr. Russell chewed on the end of his pipe. "But if I was ever in doubt of Old Beau's intentions, he made his position obvious today. I was driving around The Quad, trying to make my way over here, when I spotted him playing politician outside his practice. I should have stopped to see what he was up to, but I was sickened by the thought of him trying to capitalize on her death."

"I was there—on The Quad—for part of his statement." I looked over to see if the admission upset him, but his face was inscrutable. "I didn't hear him say anything about Ms. Freddie, but one of the reporters accused him of benefiting from the drug lab investigation set off by the case she presided over yesterday. Harriston denied it at first and tried to spin the question to put the focus on some business called 'DelaCorp.'"

"He would manage to do that. Just another dig at my wife's expense. DelaCorp is a subsidiary of Axelrod Financials."

I nodded as he spoke. I hadn't been as close to Mr. Russell as I had to Ms. Freddie, but I knew he was one of Axelrod's chief financial officers.

"I'd heard rumblings about them acquiring Old Beau's building, but I didn't think to mention the deal to Freddie because I don't have ties to the commercial real estate division." Mr. Russell pulled the pipe from his lips. "We normally discuss investments that may become a conflict of interest so she can recuse herself. I guess Old Beau made the connection and tried to shine a light on the situation. Should have known he'd take advantage of this tragedy and avoid his responsibilities when it comes to the real issue."

"The *real* issue?" Jealousy or murder? Did Mr. Russell even realize what he was implying, or was he merely waiting for me to catch up? "Do you think Harriston had a hand in her death—would Ms. Freddie's passing open up the opportunity for him to make another bid for a judgeship?"

Mr. Russell inclined his head and spoke with purpose, as if measuring each word for accuracy. "He's substantially older than most appointees, and they could always pull a replacement judge from another county or stick with the ones they've got, but I suppose the door is open. Though, the process isn't exactly simple. First, he'd need to get back on the list of attorneys the judicial nominating commission sends to the governor—"

Just as I was trying to make sense of the conversation, the husky growl of Grace's Shadow Phantom filled the parking lot. Her motorcycle commanded attention as she glided around potholes to make her way toward us. She'd changed out of her uniform into black jeans and a leather riding jacket that matched the matte black paint of her bike and helmet.

As she parked the machine against the building's façade, Mr. Russell tamped out his pipe and leaped to his feet as if embarrassed about the indulgent pastime. I joined him at the bottom step because I figured it was my job to facilitate an introduction.

"Mr. Russell, I don't know if you've met Grace Tisdale. She's the chief bailiff and head of security over at the courthouse."

"Yes, we've met a few times in passing." He removed his hat and extended his hand. "Russell Wannamaker. You are lovelier than I remember."

"Is that so?" Grace grinned. Then she added, in a low voice, "I'm terribly sorry for your loss. If you don't already have plans, I insist you join us."

"Thank you, but I must decline." His left eyelid twitched and the corners of his mouth turned down. "I don't think I'd make great company, and Victoria has reminded me of a few issues that require my attention."

"Understood. But if you change your mind, we'll be in one of the back booths." Grace gave a playful wave of her fingers as she moved toward the bar's entrance.

"Another time perhaps." He mirrored the hand gesture while he watched her disappear.

I lingered on the steps, eager to finish our conversation about Harriston, but Mr. Russell seemed to have his own agenda.

"Thanks for indulging on old man, Victoria. Don't keep your mother waiting—or your friend, for that matter." He reached into his pants pocket and pulled out a fifty, which he thrust into my hand. "Enjoy yourself, have a glass of bourbon on me."

Without pausing for a reply, he donned his hat and strolled toward the center of the lot, where his Silverado towered over a handful of subcompacts. I stood there dumbfounded. Mr. Russell hadn't handed me money since I was in grade school and, even then, he wasn't the gregarious type who did such things on a regular basis. He usually pulled out money when he wanted me to get lost and keep my nose out of adult business. I imagined today's gesture was no different—a way to keep my mind occupied while he made his escape. Apparently, the Harriston conversation was a festering wound too painful to readdress or maybe there were parts of the story he wasn't willing to share.

Either way, I didn't have time to analyze the odd behavior because, as soon as I crossed Cooper's threshold, my mother descended.

"Where have you been?" she shouted over the barroom chatter and flapped her arms in exasperation. Election updates blared from the flat screens mounted above the bar behind her. "You missed my victory speech."

She was still wearing the fitted white Ashley Stewart suit I'd seen her in that morning, but she'd replaced her usual American flag pin with a huge *Corinne Justice for Mayor* button emblazoned with her picture. The effect was unintentionally comical since the button sported the big haired, bright teeth commercialized version of my mother. Yet, the person standing in front of me had a creased brow, compressed lips, and a no-nonsense topknot. I could tell she was attempting to rein in her emotions by tightening her exterior.

"Already? Oh, Ma, I'm sorry. I left as soon as I hung up the phone, but I ran into Mr. Russell outside and—"

"Say no more." She held up a perfectly manicured hand. "I'm glad you took the time to talk with him. That man stood around here for an hour looking miserable. Bless him for coming. I spent a good portion of the afternoon trying to help him make funeral arrangements. Of course, we didn't get very far—he had complaints about every little thing—but we at least secured Wesdale United Methodist for Saturday morning. Freddie loved that church."

She tugged at the neckline of my sweater until it accentuated my nonexistent cleavage and pushed a few frizzy strands of hair away from my eyes.

"Seriously, Ma?" I swatted at her hands. "People are watching."

"Now that you're here, please try to mingle a bit. I caught Grace uprooting a couple of volunteers from one of the tables. Don't hide back there with her all night."

"I won't. I'll make the rounds. I'm here to support you."

"You'd better. This is just the start. Don't forget we have the big festival tomorrow. The whole town will be there. I want you at that speech." She kissed my cheek and left me alone in a sea of bodies.

Ever the hostess, Ma shook hands and patted backs as she threaded her way toward a group of her Kappa Mu sorority sisters. The gaggle of women stood by the stage, wineglasses raised in her direction. Based on their animated whoops, Ma would soon have on rosé goggles so thick my presence would scarcely matter.

I turned in the opposite direction and made a beeline for the back of the joint, where I found Grace holed up in a booth by the restrooms. Whenever I came to Cooper's—which wasn't very often since alcohol wasn't my thing—I liked to luxuriate at one of the eight tables left over from its diner days. The owner had retrofitted the relics so each had plush velvet seating and a tabletop jukebox. By the sound of things, Grace had already put on a classic Journey song from her era. The opening bars of the iconic piano chord progression drifted over the partitions of the booth as I approached.

"Heard you kicked a couple innocents to the curb to get this table." I slid into the seat across from her.

Grace sighed and lifted her face skyward. "Tell your mom to relax. They were cool with it. All they had on the table were shooters. Everybody knows Coop's motto, 'diners get dibs.'" She held up her hands and cracked her knuckles. "All-you-can-eat shrimp demands a will to succeed and plenty of elbow room." She frowned at me when I didn't reply. "We're ordering food, right? You didn't just ask me here to talk."

"Food…and drinks." I tossed the fifty on the table. "Courtesy of Russell Wannamaker."

"I'll be damned. He's one hell of a guy to maintain that kind of chivalry." She fingered the bill. "I don't know if I'd be thinking about anyone else if I was in his situation."

"I think you may be giving him too much credit. I got the impression he was using the money as a diversion. We were having a pretty intense conversation about Harriston when you drove up."

"Oh really?" She leaned forward over the table. "You told him everything you told me about Maggie and Old Beau disappearing during the time of the murder?"

"Actually, no. He brought up the subject of Harriston on his own. He suspects the attorney is holding a twenty-year-old grudge." I pulled off my coat and leaned back. "I'm not sure if Mr. Russell knows about the surveillance video or the murder weapon, but he mentioned meeting with Detective Daniels and being unimpressed by the investigation."

"Okay." Grace drew out the word. "I'm not sure what you want me to say. I don't know any more about Old Beau than you do, and I still haven't had a chance to look at the video. My only real conversation with Daniels was yesterday after the crime scene investigators arrived. At that point, his focus was squarely on Dodd, North, and Stevenson being in the wrong place at the wrong time."

"I get that, but hear me out. Remember, during trial, right after we broke for recess, you said Harriston has a reputation for causing chaos in the courtroom to win cases. Well, just now, totally unsolicited, Mr. Russell basically said the same thing."

"Yeah. So? That's the definition of a bad reputation."

"Seriously, Grace? Work with me." I slapped my hands on the table, causing our mini jukebox to skip. "You've been around long enough to understand how Harriston operates. Don't you think it's possible the missing drug evidence could be a distraction for something bigger…like murder? Couldn't Harriston have been working with someone inside the courthouse? You said yourself he has been in and out of the clerk's office for weeks getting help from Maggie who, not only works for him now, but—news flash—has an all-access keycard and a grudge against Wannamaker."

"Holy sh–"

"Easy there, Tisdale," said a ragged voice. "Nothing looks worse on a broad than a potty mouth."

Ian Cooper, clad in deer hunter camo, strutted up to our table with a dishrag. We both clamped our mouths shut as he bent over the laminate surface to give it a cursory swab. Coop, whose faded good looks echoed those of Clint Eastwood, was a crotchety old gossip with a mouthful of brutally honest insults. Most locals let his comments slide because he'd been a driver on the NASCAR circuit in the late eighties. In Delaware, that was as good as being able to turn straw into gold.

"What can I get for you girls?" Cooper shook out the rag and squinted at us.

Grace pointed at me, and I mimed tossing her the ball.

"I'll have the all-you-can-eat shrimp special," said Grace, "and a Red Stag on the rocks."

"I used to think more highly of you, Tisdale." Coop snapped his rag at her. "Didn't I tell you last week when you were in here with—"

"I know. I know." Grace waved her arms in front of her face to halt the conversation then pushed Mr. Russell's fifty toward Coop.

"How could you know? You keep interrupting me while I'm talking. Let me finish." He plucked up the fifty. "Flavored bourbons are for chumps and people with no class. But, I'll allow it since you're paying up front. And what'll it be for the lovely lady who lives with our new mayor?"

"A BLT with fries and some lemonade."

"Dangit, girl. Why do you start this every time you come in? You see all these people in here?"

My gaze followed his hands as he gestured at the crowd, and I caught Grace riding low in her seat. She covered her mouth to hold in the what-were-you-thinking laughter.

"Do you honestly believe I have any bacon left? Here's what I'm going to do for you, since it's your mama's special night." He tucked the rag in his waistband and started miming his plan with his hands. "You're gonna get the shrimp special like Tisdale here, but I'll get the bartender to send you over some booze-free

Blood Mary mix along with a stalk of celery and some olives. There's your BLT. Shrimp, celery, olives, and tomato."

I wrinkled my nose about to protest.

"You're welcome." He walked away.

As soon as Coop faded into the background, Grace hooted. "Why does he even bother taking orders from people? He might as well have just come out here with some shrimp."

"You think?" I said with all the sarcasm I could muster. "Thanks for having my back."

"You're welcome." Grace mimicked the gruff finality of Coop and succumbed to another fit of laughter. She didn't sober up until moments later when a waitress whizzed by and sloshed our drinks onto the table. After a swig of bourbon, she got serious. "Okay. Who told you Maggie has an all-access card?"

"Daniels."

"Detective Daniels?"

"Not intentionally." My celery came wilted and soggy. I tossed it and munched on the olives. "I think it was just a slip in his thought process. I don't think he considered it out of the ordinary when he said it. But after you told me Maggie used to work for Wannamaker, everything made sense. The woman uses the card every day to buzz into my office. She shouldn't be able to do that. I should have known."

"No. I should have known." Grace cursed under her breath. "I didn't even look at the keycard report. I could catch hell for not correcting that glitch, but how was I to know? Maggie changed jobs nearly a decade ago. I wasn't running the show back then. I couldn't even carry a firearm yet. Zeke should have reprogrammed her card before he retired."

She took a long draw from her glass, but the action didn't appear to erase her paranoia. She hunkered down and lowered her voice to a whisper. "Hopefully, the new protocol will clear all of that up. The governor already has a task force in place to analyze security. They're dreaming up a completely new set of standards for all the state buildings. We'll be doing a full keycard recall on Monday. Additional cameras, new metal detectors: the works."

"Sure, but that doesn't solve our current problem. What about the murderer? Whoever it is probably had a keycard or access to one. What did Daniels say to you about that?"

"Nothing. When we met this morning, I just handed over the surveillance footage and keycard logs, so there wasn't anything to say."

"What about your interview with him on the night of the murder? Tell me everything."

"*Everything*?" She shook her head in exasperation when I stared at her and didn't blink.

"Everything. Start with the trial."

"Okay. The trial. Fine. When you guys went to sidebar, the judge sent me out to wrangle the jury. I got them settled in the jury room, told them to stay put, and returned to the courtroom. Everybody was still up on the bench when I came back in. Stevenson was swinging his arms around. He looked like he was having a fit."

"He was. Harriston was trying to get Langley's felony charges dismissed. Go on."

"I took the secondary post over by the defense table so I could watch the defendant. Not long after that, things got loud, so I looked at the bench and saw Stevenson whip off his tie like he was laying down an ultimatum. Then Wannamaker did that iron glare she's so good at."

"Did you see Harriston pick up the tie?"

"I don't think so. Situations like that are always a little uncomfortable, so I turned back to the defendant. I didn't really look around again until Phyllis stepped down and made a break for the gallery. Stevenson wandered off to his table. I assumed you guys were finished, so I was about to walk up to the bench to ask Wannamaker what she wanted to do about the jury, but I noticed you'd stuck around to talk to her."

"What about Harriston? Did you get a good look at what he was doing?"

"Not really. He caught me off guard. I was still staring over at you trying to gauge how long you'd talk with Wannamaker when he rammed into me. Told me to get out of the way so he could consult with his client in private. But just as I was about to walk away, he handed me his business card. Said I should tell you he wants a trial transcript and to contact him directly about payment."

"Then?"

"Then I got out of the man's way. Moved over to the Corrections post."

"Translate. I don't speak bailiff."

"Position three, where the Department of Corrections guards usually stand when we have a defendant they've transported over from the prison. I positioned myself between the door to the courtroom's holding cell and the door that leads to the judge's chambers. I could watch the defense table, you, and the jury room door from there. Then I waited for my turn to talk to the judge."

Grace paused when a harried high schooler shuffled up to our table with two steaming baskets of shrimp and fries. Once he dropped the food in front of us, the conversation resumed.

"Turns out," she said, "the judge called for a thirty-minute recess, so I didn't go up to talk with her because that was a clear sign we were in a holding pattern. Instead, I stepped up to the bench to see you."

"What are you saying? You never saw Stevenson's tie after he took it off?"

"Nope. I'm looking at the courtroom to assess potential threats. Most of my focus is on the judge and the defendant—who was an absolute a-hole by the way. She bossed Old Beau around like she ran the show. And when she wasn't doing that, she threw shady looks at you."

"Figures."

"Don't tell me you two have a history."

"I won't right now. Maybe later. Eat your food."

We both took a second to grab a couple shrimp tails and dip them deep into the flimsy paper containers holding our cocktail sauce. The savory crunch of the golden fried panko breadcrumbs was a welcome relief. I hadn't eaten since the lemon cake at Jillian's, so the shrimp melted like butter on my tongue.

I stuffed three more bites into my mouth. "Tell me what happened after Phyllis Dodd came up to the bench and interrupted us. You offered to take her back to chambers. Daniels implied she'd gotten into an argument with Wannamaker. Anything unusual go down?"

"Meh. Seemed routine to me. We went into reception, asked Wannamaker's secretary if we could go back, and got the greenlight. I escorted Dodd into the judge's office, and they seemed chummy enough. What actually surprised me was Wannamaker said I could discharge the jury. So, I hightailed it back to the courtroom and supervised their departure. By the time I got back to chambers to escort Phyllis out, they were both gone."

"Right. Daniels said they took the judges' hallway to get to the kitchen. Did you see anything else?"

"Uh-uh. Nothing." She looked at the ceiling like the answers were written large above her. "I talked to the secretaries in chambers for a few minutes longer than I should have, then thought about going back to the courtroom. Actually, I was excusing myself to head that way when radio chatter from Corrections threw me off course. They were asking permission to put the defendant in one of the holding cells while they waited for Bickerton P.D."

I pointed at myself. "That's the upshot of the history between Langley Mulligan and me, but, like I said, I'll fill you in later. Keep going."

"Hmm." She sucked her teeth. "Normally, I would have given the affirmative over the radio, but since all I had to do was walk through chambers and the courtroom to get to holding, I had them standby. I wanted to prepare the cell and act as backup. But, I didn't get that far because a second radio call came in from the Prothonotary's Office about a disturbance in the kitchen. That's when I went ahead and gave the affirmative over the radio. Figured I'd let Corrections do what they do best while I hightailed it down the judges' hallway toward the kitchen."

"Is that when you nabbed Stevenson, Dodd, and North?"

"Yeah. They were in there barking at each other about the missing drug evidence. I threw them all out the employees' entrance and went back to the courtroom. I suppose I should have known something was up when I didn't see Wannamaker in the kitchen, but I really had no reason to think she'd be anywhere but chambers." Grace emptied her basket of food and set the container aside to signal for more. "Point being, none of it seemed out of place until I got a third call about you screaming."

"Screaming?" I voiced the word as a question, but the statement was the articulation of my thought process as snapshots of Ms. Freddie's lifeless body ticked through my mind like an old film reel. Bile welled in my throat.

"Well, I should say a call about *someone* screaming. I didn't know it was you at first. I'd just walked into the courtroom to do a sweep. I got the call, doubled back to the personnel area, and followed the noise. I found you passed out in the alcove between the kitchen and the lavatory."

"Right. I remember coming to with you crouched over me."

"You started babbling about the judge being murdered, so I called it in."

"*You* called it in?"

"Yup."

"Nobody should have seen the body but us?"

"Nobody but us and the killer."

SEVENTEEN

"THOSE FAMILIAR WITH Trident County know our little corner of the world is unique," said the chipper teenage tour guide in colonial military garb. "Often referred to as 'Delaware's Dixie,' life is slower and more genteel in Bickerton because our rural ties to the land and sea reflect a grassroots approach to community pride."

He walked backward and faced our group as we lumbered down Bickerton Boulevard toward the south side of the crowded quad. Part of me wanted to tell the kid to give it a rest. Everyone knew the Post-Election Festival's history. He'd have been better off showing us where they put the pit beef booth this year. However, I didn't want to embarrass Ma, who stood beside me looking surprisingly alert, despite the wine consumed at Cooper's the night before. Instead, I politely suppressed a chuckle of satisfaction when the discordant thrum of bagpipes from a nearby street musician forced the guide to yell his next statement.

"That's not to imply we don't share the same valiant history as the rest of the counties in 'The First State.' On the contrary, our customs go even deeper because this festival is a tradition borne of necessity."

"Seriously, Ma," I hooked her arm and squeezed my petite frame against her fur-covered curves, "a historic walking tour? Couldn't we have gone to the *indoor* craft show?"

The sun hung high in the noonday sky, but the air was arctic. Even though fall temperatures fluctuated in our area, a twenty-three-degree day was unusual for Bickerton. The weather should have given the town an innocuous excuse to cancel the festival following the judge's death. However, the municipality chose to move forward with the biennial event because the festivities doubled as a state holiday, celebrated by not only Trident County residents but also history buffs and politicians throughout the region.

I leaned closer to Ma's ear and relished the plushness of her faux mink coat, while internally cursing my stiff wool one. "Could we please cut out of here and head to Cake & Kettle? I'm sure Jillian could set us up with some tea."

"These are the trials a leader must endure," Ma whispered.

Joy danced across the lines of her sienna skin when she alluded to her new job. Mother's mayoral victory put her at the heart of all planned activities, and she'd insisted on having me by her side every step of the way.

"This is what they have for us on the schedule. Just five more minutes. Let the boy finish his speech. Think of the tradition."

We stopped in front of the worn stone façade of the original Trident County Courthouse, and the guide raised an arm toward the relic as he continued his presentation.

A sharp breeze cut across our cluster, causing the teen to clamp his other hand onto his tri-cornered hat. "This event dates back to the Revolutionary War. All the residents of Trident County cast their votes right here in the county seat to protect against the combative protests of Loyalists content on keeping British rule. The tallying of votes required staunch safeguards to prevent interference. Therefore, the following day, citizens gathered on The Quad to hear the results and to ensure the succession of the newly elected officials. The tradition of announcing the results in this fashion continues today with a ceremonial truce between the political parties, a parade—"

"Can't we just hurry up and get this first photo-op out of the way?" One of the four newly elected town council members, a burly man with no neck, interrupted the pink-faced tour guide. "I want to head over to the candidates' luncheon and get a good seat. I can only imagine the length of the receiving line for the governor."

The burly interrupter cupped his hands over his mouth and blew a billowy stream of vapor onto the fingers of his knit gloves. Apparently, I wasn't the only person who saw the futility of a walking tour in freezing weather.

"But we're supposed to—" The tour guide's voice cracked, and his nose beaded with the sweat of uncertainty. "Oh, I guess it's all right."

The boy waved a reluctant surrender to the photographer, who'd been lingering at the back of our group. The cameraman elbowed his way to the center and arranged the councilpersons in front of the Old Courthouse. I let go of Ma's arm and watched from the side, along with the other family members, as she posed with her new coworkers. Her tawny pageboy was perfectly coiffed, except for a series of strands near her ear that she often tugged out of nervousness or excitement.

While we waited, I kept my head on a swivel, looking for people I knew so I could slip away from my mother and escape the cold for a few moments. That was when I saw Russell Wannamaker. Actually, I noticed the hat before I noticed the man.

Across the street, the navy-blue herringbone fedora was unmistakable in a sea of baseball caps and toboggans. I lost the fedora for a second as it mixed in with a group of Shriners. But when the fez brigade moved toward The Quad, the fedora reappeared and an opening in the crowd exposed its owner. Mr. Russell stood with his back to me, talking to someone. His body blocked the face of the shorter and slightly wider person. I took a step off the sidewalk, hoping to cross the street and join the duo, but stopped suddenly.

Maggie was his companion.

She was too busy watching Mr. Russell to spot my vantage point. Her eyes were demurely downcast, her hands pressed against her chest, and her lips puckered into a pointed smile.

I could tell the two were having an amiable conversation. His body and shoulders displayed an easy confidence. One hand slipped into his pocket while the other offered the scarf she must have dropped. The pair stood on the sidewalk that ran in front of the county administration building and led up to the bandstand, where Cooper had secured a seafood sandwich booth near the stage. Mr. Russell appeared to have caught her getting in line for a meal and stopped to have a word. Since I wasn't aware the two of them knew each other, I found myself transfixed by the interaction.

"What are you looking at, Angel?" Ma had approached from behind, apparently free of her publicity duties for the moment, so I tore my eyes away from the couple.

"Mr. Russell. I'm surprised to see him out again today. Yesterday, he seemed…"

Reclusive. However, the thought quickly vanished. He had every right to behave in any manner he felt appropriate. Besides, the fact he was dealing with a tragedy didn't mean he had to isolate himself from the world.

I tilted my head toward the scene across the street. "Feels a little odd seeing the two of them together. Kind of like my professional and private worlds are colliding."

"Ah, yes, I know what you mean." She looked over at the twosome. "They used to be quite chummy before Freddie dropped her from the secretarial pool."

"Huh. Well, she's officially leaving the courthouse for good in a couple of weeks. She got a job working with Beau Harriston."

"Beau?" Ma snapped her head back to look over at me. "Talk about water seeking its own level. Good riddance. Freddie always gave people too much credit. First, Harriston runs amuck in her professional life. Then that hussy comes along and upsets her personal one."

My mouth hit the floor. "What are you saying?"

Ma froze for a moment then seemed to catch herself. She surreptitiously steered me away from our tour group, who hadn't yet departed for the candidate's luncheon at the community's fire hall.

"You didn't hear that." Her words were sharp and cut as viciously as the frosty air. "And don't you dare repeat it. Freddie shared that information with me in confidence, and she never confronted Russell about the affair. She loved her job too much to cause a scandal. She simply removed the unwanted element and moved on. Every marriage has its…challenges. I just—I…" Her mouth disappeared as she pressed her lips together. "I don't want you thinking less of Russell. He's a good man."

"I know, Ma. He's always been phenomenal to me, and he still seems devoted to Ms. Freddie despite…everything." Besides, I was quite familiar with Maggie's skill set. This wouldn't be the first time I'd had to compartmentalize my shock, betrayal, and anger over her behavior. She'd already destroyed Jillian and Shaun's marriage, so I had no desire to let her think she'd spoiled another. "I won't say anything."

"Good, because we've been spotted." She tugged at her favorite strand of hair. "Smile."

I straightened my posture and turned to put on a congenial mask. I expected to see Maggie, but I found someone worse.

"I just want to extend my congratulations." Beau Harriston slipped in on us through the mingling crowd. "I have every confidence you will bring this town continued prosperity."

"That's surprisingly kind of you, Mr. Harriston," Ma said. "Now, if you'll excuse me, we were on our way to the candidates' luncheon."

"Why, yes, yes, of course. Do you need an escort? I know you're new to politics. I could introduce you to some of the more distinguished members of our community. You know, my father, grandfather, and great-grandfather were once senators of this fine state, and I went to college with former Vice President Joe Biden."

"Yes, you've been telling all of us that for decades, but I think I can see fit to do my own networking. After all, the luncheon is for candidates—"

"And their honored guests," he added.

"Yes. But in this instance, the honor is all mine." Her voice took on an aggressive growl I didn't recognize.

"And anyway, she has an escort." Mr. Russell stepped into the vacant space between them. I looked for Maggie, but she was nowhere in sight. "I always enjoyed attending that luncheon with my wife. She loved meeting the candidates and showing her civic pride."

"So true." Ma shuddered a bit, but capitalized on Mr. Russell's improvisation. "The occasion contains such history and prestige. Would be a shame not to feel her distinguished presence through the proper representative."

"All righty." Harriston's heavy jowls drooped as his sycophantic request fell flat. "I suppose you all have things well in hand. I'll just continue to enjoy the festivities. Good day." He gave a feeble half-bow and receded into the crowd.

The three of us walked west across the lawn and passed behind the historic courthouse toward the firehouse hall.

"Thank you, Russell." Ma beamed. "Your timing couldn't have been better. Do you actually plan on attending the luncheon?"

"No. Things were getting lonely at the house today, so I decided to take a stroll along the parade route." He sniffed as a gust of wind slammed icy air into our faces. "I suppose I could use Freddie's invitation, but I don't know how long I'll feel sociable. The emotions come and go. Speaking of which, I apologize for leaving your party without saying goodbye."

"Stop it." She swatted his arm. "No apologies necessary. In fact, you should come with us. Talk as much or as little as you want. Step out any time. We won't take offense. You're family."

He looked back and forth between us. "That's mighty kind of—"

"Congratulations, Mama Justice. Or should I say Madame Mayor?" Grace came striding toward us in a state-issued black rayon jacket that complemented the bailiff uniform.

"Madame Mayor sounds wonderful, but I can't answer to that until I'm officially sworn in." Ma grabbed Mr. Russell's arm and urged him forward. "Grace, surely you've met Russell Wannamaker."

"Good to see you again, Ms. Tisdale." He removed his hat and placed it in the crook of his arm.

She extended her hand, which he cupped in both of his.

"Likewise. Thanks for picking up our tab last night. That was very generous of you."

"Least I could do after infringing upon your get-together with Victoria." He patted Grace's hand several times before resuming his place by my mother, who checked her watch.

"Still, please, consider me grateful," Grace said. "Sorry to interrupt. I just came over to give all of you my best. I have to work. With so many elected officials here, the governor's security team wants to do a sweep of each state-run facility, so I need to be on hand when Capitol Police accompanies them through Superior. They're already over at the Family and Chancery courthouses now."

Sensing an opportunity to make my escape, I invited myself on Grace's journey. "Ma, I should go with Grace. I think I may have left a few items in my desk at work."

"Go, go. No need to lie. You've been complaining all morning. All I ask is that you meet me at the foot of the stage after the parade. I want you on the dais when I give my speech."

"Absolutely." I meant it. I hadn't been thrilled about being tied to her hip all day, but I did want to support her when it counted.

"Ms. Tisdale." Mr. Russell tipped his hat then followed my mother to her destination.

"I appreciate the save," I said after Ma had left with Mr. Russell.

"Don't start thanking me just yet." Grace twisted her way through the crowd to get to the east side of The Quad, where the Superior Courthouse stood. "I'd love to have you tag along, but we need the building clear. You understand."

"No worries. I get it." I could see Cake & Kettle's gray and gold striped awning in the distance. "I actually planned to head over to Jillian's place anyway. You want me to grab you some coffee or something?"

"Nope. I'm good. I'll text you when I'm off duty."

"All right. See ya."

Grace headed off to the right toward the courthouse while I crossed to the left toward the teashop.

When I stepped through the Cake & Kettle entrance, I found chaos. The place was packed. Every wingback chair, sofa, and ottoman contained festival revelers and their cold weather gear. Jillian scurried toward me with a massive tray containing a full tea service, a tower of finger sandwiches, and several ramekins of shepherd's pie.

"Thank heavens you're here." She streaked past.

I could barely hear her above the din of conversation and the clank of china teacups. She set the tray on a coffee table in front of a quartet of octogenarians then went rushing to fetch silverware and linens. After a few seconds, she came back to the entryway where I stood.

"With Shaun gone," she panted, "I've lost a set of hands. I hate to ask you, but I could use your help."

The statement was a warning rather than a question. Instead of waiting for a response, she dragged me toward the bookshelves that marked her makeshift ordering area and shoved me onto the stool behind the register.

"Mind the cash and take orders while I serve and keep a proper eye on the boys in the kitchen. Just 'til things die down. All right? Thanks, love." Jillian gave me an air kiss and dashed away.

I barely had time to shrug out of my wool coat and adjust my cardigan before I sensed the approach of a customer.

"Oh, great," muttered a husky male voice. "Isn't this the perfect cherry on an increasingly crappy week?"

I looked up to find Spencer Stevenson waiting for service. He examined me with a loathsome expression that made my skin flush.

"Excuse me?" I was unsure if he was talking to me or someone else.

"Forget it. Just give me a Jug O' Java and a dozen Chelsea buns to go." He put extra emphasis on the last two words. Then he slipped off his leather gloves, unbuttoned his dress coat, and pulled a wallet from the inside pocket of his three-piece suit.

"No problem. Sorry for the wait." I wanted to challenge his snarky demeanor, but I had to be respectful of Jillian and her business. No need to cause a scene. "That will be…"

I groped around for a menu to note what prices to punch into the register. Stevenson beat me to my goal.

He grabbed one from the end of the counter and tossed the laminated square in my direction. "Cut the clueless act. If you're looking for an excuse that'll keep me around long enough to answer more of your stupid questions, don't bother. I know you went straight to Detective Daniels after you left my office yesterday."

"To drop off a transcript."

I made an unsuccessful attempt at keeping my voice even. I didn't have to be a genius to know he was implying I went to the police to snitch about our conversation. While I certainly went to Troop 11 hoping to determine whether Stevenson's status as prime suspect was legit, I didn't share anything with Daniels that the detective didn't already know.

"And for the record, Counselor, what I do in my spare time is none of your business."

"You made it my business when you took your accusations to the police." He made a quick appraisal of the room and lowered his voice. "I didn't kill Judge Wanna-maker, but any chance I had of proving that disappeared when you went rogue and tainted public opinion."

"Went rogue?" I hoped the repetition would diffuse my desire to say something rude.

Stevenson leaned across the counter and invaded my space—a cross-examination intimidation tactic I'd seen him use several times in the courtroom. I took offense he had the audacity to use it on me, so I avoided eye contact and concentrated my gaze on the crown of his head. He must have shaved recently because the over-head light glinted off the smooth peach surface.

"Come off it," he growled. "*The Bugle* printed a story this morning about surveillance video of the prime mur-der suspect, an attorney—a DAG *lurking*—their word not mine—near the scene of the crime. Now, how would they have gotten that information if you hadn't been running around town shooting off at the mouth?"

"You can't blame *me* for something written in *The Bugle*." I hadn't seen the article, but I was positive I wasn't the cause. "They had that information long before I crossed paths with you."

"Information they wouldn't have printed if you hadn't validated things by taking my story to the police."

"What you're saying doesn't even make sense." I pivoted toward the register and sped through the task of tallying up his order. When I finished, I pointed to the total on the matchbox-sized screen that faced outward for customers. "If you have a problem, you need to talk to Detective Daniels or, better yet, Mike Slocum at *The Bugle*. He was the first person to mention video footage of you near the scene of the crime."

"Get real. You're smarter than that." He opened up his wallet and dropped a glittery American Express Platinum card in front of me, as if to offer the caveat I wasn't smarter than Spencer J. Stevenson. "*The Bugle* was discreet enough not to mention the attorney's name. If I run over to the paper to complain or visit Detective Daniels for another chat, I'd just be adding more fuel to the journalistic fire, wouldn't I?" He scowled at me and exhaled so menacingly that his nostrils flared. "But then again, why bother doing anything when the AG and his executive staff have already come to their own conclusions about me and turned their festival trip into a witch hunt."

"Sounds like a personal problem." I scooped up the platinum card, swiped the overrated piece of plastic, and ripped off the receipt that bubbled up from the spool. I slid the flimsy piece of paper and his card toward him, without offering a pen.

He produced his own. A sterling silver one, by the looks of it. Pretentious prick.

"My advice," I snatched up the signed receipt, "if you don't have the balls to deal with it, don't complain about it."

Suck on that, mister. I stood up from the stool and moved away from him toward the pastry display, where I boxed up his Chelsea buns.

"Go ahead. Laugh it up." His words were a hoarse whisper but sounded surprisingly close.

I looked up, startled to find he'd followed me over to the glass casing.

"Easy for you to talk tough. Your life isn't on the line. Look around. I'm not the enemy. I'm the victim. I'll admit it. I didn't like Wannamaker or her sanctimonious nature, but she was right about the need to investigate the drug lab. So, I made the effort and started every investigation she asked for and then some. Now somebody is framing me for my efforts."

"No. You started an investigation to save your own butt, hoping to throw the blame on Phyllis Dodd or some other hapless state employee." My mind went straight to the argument turned browbeating session he'd started with Phyllis Dodd in the parking lot of the courthouse the day of the murder. "Don't try to paint yourself as a saint."

"Saint or sinner. If it weren't for you, I'd be out there enjoying my state-mandated holiday. Or better yet, spearheading the investigation into the controlled substance lab rather than getting coffee and sweeties," he tugged at his tie when he referred to the currant buns, as if he had one stuck in his throat, "for the man who holds my career in the palm of his hand. In the future, do us both a favor and keep your mouth shut unless you know exactly what you're talking about."

"Victoria, are you okay?" The sound of Candi's sweet voice hovered over Stevenson's shoulder. "I thought you were taking some time off. What are you doing in here?"

Candi and James had gotten in line behind Stevenson. Relieved to have the interference, I scampered from behind the dessert case and dodged around the ordering area to greet my coworkers. I trusted that doing so would give Stevenson time to cool down.

"Great to see you." I hugged them both. "I'm just helping Jillian for a while. She's slammed. What can I get for you guys?"

"A round of cider." James chivalrously handed me cash to pay for Candi's drink as well.

"Make that to go." Candi surveyed the crowded room and exchanged a disappointed glance with James.

"Coming up. Give me a minute to finish up with Mr. Stevenson."

I hustled back around to the ordering area and used the insulated plastic carafes to fill the Jug O' Java and my coworker's to-go cups of cider. Then I taped closed the folded flap on the box of buns and handed Stevenson his full order. "Have a nice day," I said without a trace of pleasantness behind the phrase.

"This is not over." He stalked off.

With the attorney gone, my coworkers were able to step forward and grab their beverages.

"We're going to get spots for the parade across the street in front of the courthouse, if you want to join us later." James was experiencing his first Post-Election Festival, having moved to Bickerton from Virginia just shy of a year ago. "I heard each candidate gets to ride around The Quad in a horse and buggy."

The newbie twinkle in his eyes righted the mood Stevenson had attempted to destroy. I laughed to relieve the anxiety in my chest and bid them farewell.

Jillian rushed up soon after. "While we have an empty queue, could you run back to the kitchen and check the bins? I need to keep my hands clean for table service, and I don't want the boys abandoning their stations when we're backed up on orders."

"Sure."

I threw on my coat and pushed through the swinging door that led to the kitchen. I expected to spend a few minutes gathering trash, but someone had already done the work for me. I waved my thanks to the Thompson triplets, a skinny set of teal-haired twenty-somethings, who barely looked up from the countertop where savory pots steamed, knives sliced, and fryers crackled. I grabbed one of the four industrial-sized garbage bags and lugged my load through the back door into the alley.

Once outside in the nippy autumn air, I realized I wasn't the best person for the job. The task required me to haul the ginormous sack of dense trash into a dumpster whose lip reached well above the height of my shoulders. I leaned the bag against the receptacle and analyzed the logistics. All I needed was an empty milk crate to give me a boost. I stepped away to search the alley for such an item, when the heat of another person pressed against my back.

Panic flooded my chest. Fingers gripped my shoulder. I screamed.

EIGHTEEN

"YOU SHOULDN'T BE out here alone." A voice boomed overhead in satiny bass tones.

"Ashton?" I spun around.

My terror morphed into surprise as I recognized the man standing in front of me. A day's worth of copper-colored stubble had formed along his jawline, and the jeans/North Face jacket combo that had become his new uniform looked rumpled. His rough appearance, however, held no menace. He stepped past me to grab the bag of trash and tossed it into the dumpster with ease. I let my shoulders relax.

"I didn't mean to scare you. Is everything all right? What did Stevenson say to you just now? Did he threaten you?"

"Stevenson? No. He accused me of—wait. What? You saw that?" I stepped back and found that the Dumpster blocked my retreat. My throat tightened. "I didn't see you inside…have you been following me?"

"No—well, yes, but—"

"*Yes*? Why? What do you want?"

I glanced at the service door to my left. Could—should—I dash back inside before he made another move?

"It's not what you're thinking." Ashton held up his hands. "I can explain."

"Really?" I took a step toward the door.

"I was keeping an eye on you—for your safety."

"Well, couldn't you have come up to me like a normal person?"

He shook his head and mumbled, "I suppose, but I wanted to make up for yesterday—for the way I went off the deep end with those stories about Chance. I shouldn't have bothered you with that stuff, especially since you have your own problems. I pushed it on you. I was wrong for that." His skin went pink, and he shuffled his feet. "This was a way to keep my promise to look out for you, while still giving you a little space." Ashton hesitated.

I waited. "And..."

"And," he cleared his throat, "I saw Chance and Langley on The Quad. They headed in this direction. I thought they might come after you or something. I had to warn you."

Part of me wanted to laugh at his concern. Ma was the only other person who'd ever displayed such an absurd level of protectiveness. Another part of me, however, wished he'd respect my decision to put Langley behind me. While I absolutely considered her a threat, I refused to harbor contempt for her in the same way Ashton did for Chance. I would never let Langley consume me. She didn't deserve that power.

"Be honest," I sighed. "This isn't about me. You think they're up to something, and you want my help." I crossed my arms and popped my hip. "Well, I don't have time to run around town swapping conspiracy theories. Not today. I have too much going on. I promised Jillian I'd help her out. After that, I'm going to support my mother—"

"Whoa. Whoa. Whoa. I'm not asking you to do anything. If they're not here, that's a good sign, but my gut tells me there's more to this. The festival is the perfect camouflage for mischief." He swept his head left then right as if to scan the open ends of the alley. "Just stay alert. They loitered for nearly an hour on the corner of York Road and Merchant Street near the Controlled Substance Lab. I think they were casing the building."

His final sentiment seemed to linger between us. We were just two blocks north of the lab, and I got the feeling he'd been watching them for much longer than he let on.

"Ashton." I softened my response, but the truth of the matter was I didn't know how much I could trust him, and the whole spying and skulking in the alley scenario wasn't helping matters. "Don't you think, maybe, just maybe, they were trying to enjoy the festival? Not everything is about drugs and violence."

He clenched his jaw and glared at me. "I thought you of all people would understand how dangerous Chance and Langley are."

His eyes glistened with tears that refused to fall, and I remembered our conversation about his former partner, Natalie Knowles.

"I do, but—" I didn't know how to answer him.

Part of me didn't understand why Ashton wanted to put his career and life on the line for a low-level hunch about the Mulligans. If he really wanted vengeance for his fallen friend, he should play it cool and do it with a badge. Hadn't he told me yesterday he'd gotten everything he needed to clear his name? Why bother making waves when he could have his job back in a matter of days?

We were still for a long time, and the crisp fall air that swirled around us seemed more ominous than ever.

"Look, I don't know what you want me to say. The lab is closed and padlocked for the investigation, remember? Phyllis told us as much yesterday before she bit our heads off. Even she doesn't have access. And with all the cops on the street, only an idiot would try—"

"To break into a state-run facility. I know." He ran a massive hand through his shaggy crew cut. "I guess—I just wanted to share the idea with someone who might take it seriously for a second."

The laugh lines of his handsome face hardened and took on the stoic formation of a person used to betrayal. Then he turned and lumbered down the alley toward York Road.

His words resonated with me as I watched him go. *State-run facility.*

That phrase seemed oddly familiar. Hadn't Grace said something like that earlier today? I sifted through my conversation with her until I stumbled upon the key ingredient.

"Ashton. Wait. You might be on to something."

I had to sprint to catch up with him. He'd made his way onto York Road and moved swiftly through the festivalgoers. When I reached him, he didn't stop. Maybe I deserved that.

I jogged alongside and did my best to appease him. "Ashton. I'm sorry. You were right. They weren't loitering because they were trying break into the lab—they were loitering because they didn't have to."

Ashton still wouldn't look at me, but he reduced his

stride to a length that was manageable for my short legs. I took it as a positive sign.

"A friend of mine from work said the governor's security team is doing a sweep of all the state buildings. That means the drug lab is probably going to be unlocked for a few moments. All Chance and Langley have to do is be in the right place at the right time. A little misdirection might get them in and out unnoticed."

"Hiding in plain sight." He inclined his head. "It's a long shot. But, at this stage, any theory is worth checking out." Ashton picked up his pace and continued down York Road. I ran after him, but he blocked my progress with a muscular forearm. "Stay here, Victoria. Go back inside. Make sure you're always in public view. I don't want you getting hurt."

"No way. You came to me for help, and now you're trying to get rid of me?"

"Exactly. We don't know what we have here yet, and things could get dangerous. I don't have the resources or the authority to protect us both. If you want to help and you feel like you have the time," he finally cut his gaze toward me, and I could see they were still full of hurt, "call Troop Eleven or flag down a city patrol officer. Just stay out of the way. Things will go smoother if you're not involved."

"I'm already involved." I pointed at the intersection of Merchant Street and York Road.

We couldn't have been more than fifty yards from the Controlled Substance Lab, which occupied the southeast corner of the roadway. The two-story red-brick building had large industrial-sized windows with black shutters. A façade of faux Grecian columns outlined the glass entryway into the facility.

Chance and Langley were nowhere in sight. The foot traffic in front of the lab was moderate and everyone moved with purpose toward the festival at the center of town. No one stopped outside the facility. No security officers patrolled the area. Everything seemed… normal.

With our enemies at bay, Ashton relented and allowed me to follow him to the front of the building. The first thing I noticed was someone had attached a safety hasp to the doors for a padlock. The effect was overkill since the deadbolt was still securely in place.

"No overt signs of forced entry," Ashton noted.

I used a hand to hood my eyes and pressed my face against the glass door to get a look inside. The interior was deserted. No signs of life at the receptionist's desk. However, I noticed the security procedures for entering the building were surprisingly similar to the courthouse's. Once a person walked through the main doors and past reception, a keycard was required to enter a plexiglass pass-through that had an antechamber containing a metal detector and another keycard door on the opposite side. I stepped back and found Ashton busy inspecting the padlock.

"Either someone hasn't figured out how to use a key," he showed me the scrape marks around the keyhole for the padlock, "or that same someone has been picking at this lock with tools. Not a very sophisticated technique, if they succeeded." He examined the dead bolt, which appeared untouched. "That's weird…maybe they gave up."

"Or maybe they had a key. We know the padlock is a new addition. The deadbolt, not so much. Any employee could have a key."

"That's a fair assessment. How familiar are you with this facility?"

"Not at all…except for what Phyllis told us yesterday." I mulled over our prickly encounter with the chemist. "She mentioned getting fired over the lack of video surveillance equipment, so that definitely leaves this place vulnerable."

"Speaking of which," Ashton straightened, "they have a place in the back where officers ring for a lab tech to come down and do intake on a drop off. That area is secluded and may lend itself to a breach. C'mon."

Ashton led me along the York Road edge of the building for a hundred paces where the festival foot traffic thinned until we found ourselves alone on the street. We came to a parking lot surrounded by a ten-foot security fence with barbed wire at the top, and another padlock. This lock was much larger than the one on the front doors and held the fence together with a rusty link of chain.

Ashton inspected the setup. "They usually have the gates open. Otherwise, I don't see anything new as far as security. No scrape marks on the lock. If someone tried to get into the lab earlier, it doesn't look like they considered this entry point a viable option."

I leaned against the fence and squinted at the back of the facility. A standard-sized steel door sat in the middle of the building's brick back. Embedded in the wall beside the entrance was a keycard fob panel and an intercom.

"Where does that entrance lead?" I asked.

"I don't know. I've never been inside, but I know it doesn't go directly into the lab. The lab and the drug vault are on the second floor. The first floor are administrative offices."

"It looks like anyone trying to get inside is going to need an electronic keycard, keys for the deadbolt—"

"Possibly a code for a building alarm," said Ashton.

"Right. Plus, they'll need to know their way around to get to the second floor—"

"And don't forget lock picking tools." He looked up and down the street then refocused on the rear of the lab. "Sounds like sneaking in during a security sweep may be the easier bet. Let's do a final perimeter check then I'll walk you back to Cake & Kettle. I can always—"

Ding! Ding!

The double chime from my phone caused Ashton to stop and raise his eyebrows, as if curious to see who'd sent me a message. But his manners must have kicked back in because when I pulled the device out of my coat pocket, he sauntered toward the front of the building. The message was a text from Jillian.

We call the café Cake & Kettle, not Cut & Run. You leave my kitchen full of rubbish and then pop off?!? Where'd you go? I need you! No more sanitation duties. I promise. Free scones for life if you come back.

Free scones. I lived to consume those flaky domes of floury goodness. Jillian knew how to make me feel guilty and loved at the same time. I didn't mean to blow off my promise to help her but, but the revelation about the lab had been too peculiar to leave unexamined. I sent a quick reply.

Sorry. Took a break to walk with Ashton—that guy from
yesterday. On my way back now.

I glanced up from the phone, when I reached the
front of the lab, and found Ashton using his cell to take
pictures of the padlock.

"Hey," I yelled. "I'm heading back."

He held up a finger, but I waded through the growing
crowd of pedestrians without him. I'd promised Jillian
I'd make a speedy return.

Ding! Ding!

Her response filled the screen.

I had a feeling about you two. He's a cutie. Glad to
know my scones can compete with those hot cross
buns. Bring him with you. And ask if he has a brother!

I stuck my tongue out at her comments.

Nobody's looking at his buns but you. I've got eyes
on your storefront. Fresh scones better be waiting for
me at the register.

The idea of warm baked goods appealed to me so
much that when I reached for the door of Cake & Kettle, I was blind to the fact Chance blocked my path. He
wore the same outfit as the day before, but in shades of
black—a V-neck thermal, a knit cap, a douchey wallet chain, and a self-satisfied sneer. Without missing a
beat, Chance knocked the phone out of my hand, where
it crashed to the ground, cracked, and died under the
heel of his biker boot.

"I know you," he said in a New York accent so thick

the words congealed into one big blob. "You're North's girl. I seen you with him in Harriston's office. Where is that Sherlock wannabe anyway?" The question curled out of his mouth as violently as a rattlesnake's hiss.

Before I could respond, he grabbed me by the scruff of my collar and steered me through the crowd toward the alley behind the café. I tried to scream, but he squeezed the nape of my neck so tight the sound came out as a feeble yelp. I wriggled against his grip, tried to pull forward and away into the crowd of festival patrons, but he was heavier, taller, and stronger. As we drew deep into the alley and away from civilization, his arm snaked around my neck until the pit of his elbow locked under my chin and the coarse cotton fibers of his shirt bit into my flesh.

"Consider this payback for getting my girl thrown in lockup," Chance said, "and tell your boy to stop following me and mine, or next time I won't be so generous with your life. His neither. He's not the only one who knows how to work a frame-up."

I clawed at my throat. I needed air, but I couldn't pry myself free. My hands were too numb, my body too weak. My vision dimmed. The alleyway narrowed into a sliver of light.

Chance's thick accent drifted overhead. "Stop whining and get your lanky butt over here. Grab her legs. Grab her legs, dammit."

Was someone else there?

I fought to understand what was happening, but the vise on my throat made it difficult to concentrate. A blurred version of a woman's face appeared in front of me. My vision faltered. A floating sensation took over. I felt myself rise then hover.

I closed my eyes. A bitter autumn breeze stung my face. The grip on my neck lightened. Air returned to my lungs. My body began to sink—so hard and fast that the air flew right back out of me.

I opened my eyes. Everything seemed miles away. Chance's face materialized above me. His levitating head chortled. The woman's head was there too. Her head wasn't laughing. Her freckled face and prim mouth held a doleful expression. She was crying.

Phyllis?

I attempted to speak, but the effort left me lightheaded.

Everything went black.

NINETEEN

THE SMELL OF sulfur was the first thing I recognized—
that stench of rotten eggs mixed with the underlying
musk of decaying produce. The combination stung my
nostrils and caused a sour mucus to form at the back
of my throat.

I coughed.

The sound reverberated around me, but I could also
hear the voices of a female and a male arguing above
me.

"You've got to get her out of there. Is she all right?
Should I call an ambulance?"

"Hold on. She's breathing. Thank goodness—I
shouldn't have let her out of my sight."

"How were you to know? How was I to know? She
just sent me a—wait. You'll drop her."

"Do you want me to do this or not? We can't just
leave her in the dumpster."

The sound of their voices detonated in my skull.

Blinding flashes of white-hot pain shot through my
neck and back. I longed for my vision to clear, but no
further input arrived other than sharp tingling sensa-
tions from my hands and feet. Even still, I was grateful
for the pain. Pain was the one thing I recognized. Pain
let me know I was alive. I laid there for a couple more
inhalations. My back rested against something lumpy
and unfamiliar.

The male voice spoke again. "I'm going to lift you out of here with a fireman's carry, but I need you to tell me if I'm hurting you. Okay?"

I blinked rapidly and hoped the male voice understood I was listening. Blinking was the only thing that didn't take maximum effort.

Seconds later, the comforting warmth filled me of another body bending over me, followed by the giddy sensation one experiences when rising in an elevator. My aches were still there, but they seemed to matter less once I began floating and the smells changed from sour to sweet.

"Which way?"

"Through there to my office. Steady. You can put her down on the sofa. I'll fetch some tea."

The female had an accent I recognized as Jillian's. I had trouble placing the first voice, the male voice, so I decided to test my eyes again once I'd stop floating. Cushions cradled my back and a hand the size of a catcher's mitt engulfed mine.

My eyes swam into focus.

"Are you in pain?" Ashton sat on the opposite arm of the overstuffed couch looking down on me. "We should get you some medical attention."

"No," I croaked. "I'm fine. Freezing, but fine."

I swallowed hard. My throat was scratchy. The throbbing in my neck and back continued, but being inside helped everything else. "Chance sent you a warning… and I think I saw Phyllis."

"Chance did this?" Ashton took off his jacket, revealing the hoodie he wore underneath. "And he's with Phyllis? Dodd? The *chemist*?"

I nodded and propped myself up against the arm

of the sofa so Ashton could wrap the jacket backward across my chest like a Snuggie.

I tried my voice again. "How'd you find me?"

"I saw you come out from behind the lab, but you kept walking. I figured you wanted to be alone to finish your texts, so I hung back." He stood and went to lean against the edge of Jillian's desk. "When I got to Cake & Kettle, I found your smashed phone in front of the entrance. Your friend Jillian said you hadn't come back. After a few minutes passed, I assumed the worst, and we went looking for you in the alley. We could hear you moaning."

I started to thank him, but his face grew grave.

"Look, Victoria, this is the second time you've been attacked in two days." He opened and closed his mouth several times before speaking, as if sensing the need to tread lightly. "You've got to tell me what's going on so I can help. You could still be in danger."

"I told you. Chance did this so you'll stop following him. He's probably using Phyllis—"

"We'll get to Phyllis. That's not what I meant." He waved his hand. "I meant what's going on between you and the Mulligans. First Langley. Now Chance. Why would they both want to hurt you?"

"Aren't you listening? Chance attacked me because of *you*." Raising my voice caused my head to throb, but I preferred it over having some macho cop play armchair psychologist to my pain. "He knows you've been following him. Leave it alone. Your obsession with him is out of control. You don't see me chasing Langley all over town, and she almost succeeded in—" I covered my mouth with both hands.

"She almost succeeded in what?" he asked.

I thought back to the Bickerton High swimming pool, the mascot costume, the near drowning—that was a lot of baggage to throw at someone new. Someone whose only knowledge of me was through a series of troublesome situations. Someone whose intentions I considered murky at best.

"Forget it. It's a long story."

"I've got nothing but time, remember?" He tugged at the front of his hoodie. "Listen, I'm sorry. Really. I know this is my fault, but I told you my history with Chance. The least you could do is tell me about yours with Langley."

He inspected me in a way that made his thirty-something face age a decade, and creases of concern appeared along his forehead, eyes, and mouth. "I know you've lost all reason to trust me, but we share the same enemies now, so help me understand."

He crossed his arms and waited.

I considered his words. I certainly had nothing to lose. I took a deep breath. "Langley used to bully me in high school. We were on the Pep Squad together."

I closed my eyes for a moment, taking the physical pain I was feeling and balling it into a mass of anger and courage to tell the tale. I refused to let Langley defeat me. If Ashton wanted to sign on for this crap, he deserved to know what he was up against.

"I joined the squad to make friends, not really thinking I'd get tasked with much. I assumed since I was smaller and lighter than most kids, I'd get put on the top of the pyramid or used for those basket toss stunt thingies."

I grabbed my left wrist with my right hand, threw

my arms in the air to demonstrate, and immediately regretted the ambitious exertion.

Slightly dizzy, I closed my eyes again. "Remember those?"

"Yeah. For sure. Best thing about the pep rally at my school."

"Well, that's not what they had in mind for me." I reduced my gestures to the wag of a finger to conserve energy. "I was stuck being the mascot. Scrappy the Seabird. Which is as good as saying I was stuck being the school's punching bag. Actually, things weren't that bad at first. Most kids treated me okay as a freshman. I was two years younger than everyone else, but we were all in the same boat—a bunch of young kids in a new environment. But as everyone got older and started hitting milestones—dating, learner's permits, driver's licenses—I was the baby holding everyone back."

"Let me guess. Langley took advantage of that."

"Yup. Turned me into the scapegoat for everything that went wrong. But, things didn't hit bottom until the first football game of our senior year. Langley's clique decided to hang out on the football field and get drunk after a game. Somebody ratted them out—probably an underclassman—but, of course, the blame fell on me. Langley convinced everyone I was jealous because I was too young to join in. Half the squad got arrested, revoked licenses, fines, community service, suspensions, the whole nine."

"I recall seeing that on her record, along with a more recent DUI. Only a matter of time before she got caught one way or the other." He'd stumbled into cop mode but acknowledged his misstep and dismissed it with a sober nod. "I take it her revenge was swift."

"Not so much swift as calculated. She let me think my only punishment was social suicide, that is, until Homecoming. That's when she pushed me into the school pool. Full mascot costume. Left me to drown. I could swim, but the suit dug into my shoulders and weighed me down. What I remember most is the moment I ran out of air and the instinct to breathe took over—"

My voice caught, because that was the moment I died. I couldn't bring myself to say those words, especially since the realization made me all too aware of the fire in my throat where Chance had recently gripped my neck—the sensation erased the distance between past and present. I shuddered and concentrated on Ashton's sympathetic eyes. I had to finish the tale. I couldn't let her win.

"They say a security guard spotted the costume bobbing below the surface. EMTs from the game pulled me out."

"I take it from your expression…she wasn't charged." Ashton came over and crouched next to me so we were on the same level.

"Charged? According to her friends, she was nowhere near the pool."

"And that doesn't bother you?"

"I try not to think of it. You could drive yourself mad thinking like that. I keep to myself and stick with people I can trust. That's how I survive."

We locked gazes. I could sense he wanted to say something, although I wasn't sure what it was, so I rambled through the awkwardness.

"Well, you know, swimming is never going to be my thing. I get a bit phobic about water situations I can't control. And yes, Langley tried to exploit that. After the trial on Monday, she assaulted me with a pitcher of water, but I handled it because I can't afford to live in fear."

Ashton didn't seem convinced. "You were just attacked by someone whose wife recently assaulted you and tried to kill you in the past. We need to report this to the authorities. The law is on your side."

"The law might be on my side, but nobody saw Chance attack."

"I'll say I saw him."

I stared at Ashton, not sure what to think. On one hand, the offer was valiant. He'd come to my rescue, and this was an opportunity to take Chance down for good—maybe Langley too. On the other hand, how much of this was about me, and how much of this was about busting the Mulligans to clear his name and get a promotion?

"But you didn't see the attack. Why take that risk?"

"Because you deserve retribution." He paced around the miniscule office. "And Chance deserves a life behind bars."

"What if the whole thing backfires?" I sat up and swung my legs over the edge of the couch, but my head swam so I laid down again. "You said Chance is a master of deception, and she's—Langley knows my soft spots. Believe me, I want to see him punished, but it's our word against theirs."

"Yeah, well, that doesn't change the fact they both deserve what's coming to them. Langley assaulted you earlier this week, right? Not to mention how she lied to cover up Chance's involvement in the murder of a state trooper that forced Judge Wannamaker to suppress my testimony." Anger crept into his voice with every syllable. "This week the judge tosses out Langley's felony charges on a drug case you're now telling me Chance might have a connection to, in some cryptic way, because you saw him with Phyllis—the woman who used to run the lab where the drugs went missing." He slammed his fist against Jillian's wooden desk. "C'mon, Victoria. Langley and her husband deserve what they have coming. I just pulled you out of a dumpster, for goodness sake."

The door creaked, and we both turned in the direction of the sound. Jillian stuck her head through the opening and entered the office with one of the huge ceramic mugs she usually reserved for coffee.

"Thank goodness you're all right." Jillian sat on the couch beside me and handed over the tea.

Ashton drifted toward the doorway, giving us room to talk. I took a sip of the beverage and relished the rich smell of ginger. Jillian placed an apologetic hand on my knee. "I—I thought… I blame myself really. I didn't—I had no idea you were in danger. If I hadn't sent you outside—"

"This is not your fault. I'm just as surprised as you are. Ashton tried to warn me. I should have taken him seriously."

I looked over at Ashton and lifted my chin in tacit acceptance of his earlier apology. After all, he'd practically saved my life.

Ashton met my gaze and nodded.

Jillian gave the corporal a little side-eye. She must have overheard our argument. "I can sit with you if you'd prefer."

"That's okay. You have a business to run. I'm fine. Ashton and I just need to figure out what to do."

Jillian raised her eyebrows disapprovingly, but she eventually added a smile and reached out to squeeze my free hand.

"Really," I said. "I'll be okay. I'm just a little achy."

"Don't worry. I've got her." Ashton stepped forward from the office doorway.

Jillian's eyes turned to slits. Perhaps out of skepticism, perhaps out of a need to challenge Ashton's sudden possessiveness. Either way, she breathed a sigh of resignation, gave my hand a second squeeze, and tiptoed out of the tiny closet of an office, gently closing the door behind her.

"Tell me how you want to handle this," Ashton commanded.

Just then, the faint sound of several drum rolls, cymbal crashes, and horns, belting out "Louie, Louie," seeped through the four rectangular windows that lined the alley-side of the office ceiling. Cheers and applause followed.

"What time is it?" I motioned for Ashton to relieve me of his coat and hold the mug. With some effort, I pushed myself to a full sitting position. "Is that the parade? No, no, no. Don't tell me it's one already. I can't afford to miss my mother's speech. I bailed on her last night. She'll kill me if I do it again. I need to get to the bandstand before the parade ends."

"Who's your mother?" Ashton asked.

"Corinne Justice. She just won the mayoral seat."

"I think she'll understand once she hears what happened."

I rubbed my palms over my eyes, hoping to circumvent the frustration building into a massive headache. I didn't want Ma hearing about this. She'd only go off the deep end with worry. Besides, my main concern was Chance's timing. The whole event was eerily similar to how Langley had distracted me from getting to Wannamaker on time. Sure, I was jumping to conclusions, but the correlation terrified me.

The last time I was distracted from reaching my destination, someone wound up dead.

"Okay," I relented. "If you're willing to help make the charges stick, I'll report everything I saw today. But first, I have to get to The Quad before the candidates reach the bandstand. I need to know my mother is safe. I'll contact the police after her speech."

"I'm not letting you go running out there by yourself."

"Fine. Of course. Whatever." I rose slowly. My head didn't swim, so I stepped toward the door.

"Hang on." He handed me some tissues from Jillian's desk and his cell phone camera to act as a mirror. "If you're going to go, freshen up a bit."

I pulled bits of dirt and paper out of my tight curls and wiped my face until I looked presentable. Ashton was too much of a gentleman to tell me if I smelled, so I chucked my scarf, which looked stained and seemed like the most likely offender. Then I dusted off my coat and checked for smudges.

When I finished, Ashton held a gun in his left hand. He removed the clip, reinserted it, and tucked the firearm into a holster under his hoodie.

"Relax. Even as a private citizen, I can carry concealed in Trident County as long as I have a permit, which I do." He patted his jeans to indicate his wallet. "Where are we headed?"

"Bandstand." My neck and back still ached, but I couldn't let that stop me. I bolted out of the office and didn't wait to see if Ashton followed. Four big strides got me through the kitchen. Ten more got me through the dining area, where I blew a kiss goodbye to Jillian and sailed out the door.

Wading through the festival crowd, however, was like trying to walk through quicksand as people formed roadblocks and stood steadfast to maintain their positions on the parade route. We trudged behind clueless individuals who inched along in front of us and were too busy staring at the marching band majorettes and shiny, black convertibles to care about walking with purpose. But the worst were the people who clung to me to give well wishes and those who tried to keep pace in order to force a friendly chat.

When we finally reached the south side of The Quad, where the bandstand stood, we watched the candidates from each race sit together in horse-drawn carriages and ride around the center of town.

After a quick wave to Ma and her former opponent, I led Ashton toward the heavily bundled female state trooper who guarded the stage-left side of the bandstand's perimeter. She stood in front of a wooden sawhorse that was about ten feet out from the roped area that led backstage. As we approached, she held out her arm to warn us.

I looked up at Ashton and whispered, "Do you know her?"

"Yeah. She's one of our rookies. Let me handle this." When we reached the officer, he said, "Trooper Mc-

Intyre, good to see you. My friend Victoria and I need to get through. Her mother is the Mayor-Elect."

"I need to see some I.D., please." Trooper McIntyre's mouth was a fine line. The shadow from her campaign hat masked shrewd eyes. "Only parties pre-approved by the festival committee beyond this point."

"You know who I am, right?" Ashton threw his shoulders back.

"I.D., please, Corporal North. Protocol."

I handed the trooper my identification. Ashton did the same. The officer compared them to her clipboard and looked up.

"Thank you, Miss Justice." She returned my license and slid a portion of the sawhorse aside so I could walk through. "You're not on the list, Corporal." Her voice fell flat as she returned his identification.

I waited by the barrier.

"I realize that, McIntyre, but you know my credentials." He flexed his jaw, clearly impatient. "We work at the same troop. Pencil me in. I need to escort this young lady for her safety."

"I'm sorry, Corporal." She became remarkably still and stared into the space between Ashton and me. "The lady is free to go, but I cannot accommodate your request."

"You do understand I outrank you." He pointed to her uniform's navy-blue dress coat to highlight the fact it held no stripes.

"I understand, Corporal, but I have specific orders. You have to either be on the list or be a uniformed officer with preapproved credentials. We cannot afford to take chances with the governor, attorney general, and congresspersons here."

Ashton stuck out his chest so he reached the full extent of his already intimidating height. He was about to speak when his cell rang. The young officer took advantage of the distraction and waved forward the group of men behind him. The act of which pushed me past the barrier and separated me from Ashton, who was blocked by the sturdy frame of the determined female trooper.

McIntyre slid the sawhorse back into place and began checking the next set of I.D.s.

Ashton and I locked eyes through the crowd. His features warped inward as if the betrayal was personal. Guilt sent a flash of heat across my skin. He'd fought for me today. I should have done the same for him—I suddenly wanted to do the same, but I couldn't keep my mother waiting. So, I did the only thing I could do. I mouthed the words "I'm so sorry."

TWENTY

"I AM HUMBLED and honored by the great trust you've placed in me to serve as your next mayor. The campaign was long and arduous, but now we get to focus on our communities. This Post-Election Festival is the prime time and place for that process to begin." Ma's angelic voice reverberated through the bandstand's sound system.

I stood behind her while she commanded the podium that overlooked the sea of Delawareans gathered for the event.

"Due to the tragedy in our judiciary, we need to put aside our differences and do everything in our power to uplift our neighbors and protect one another. The First State is a small wonder, where we all seem to know each other and our lives overlap in more ways than we can imagine. May I suggest that we never allow our ideological differences to tear us apart. We need that for Bickerton. We need that for Trident County. We need that for the mighty State of Delaware."

The crowd roared as she hit her stride, and she soaked in their applause.

I was proud of her and content in the decision—be it naive, dangerous, or misguided—to attend her speech before filing a complaint with the police about Chance Mulligan. Ma had been overjoyed I kept my promise, and I was actually having a wonderful time meeting all of the candidates. The mood of the festival was jovial and serene, and even though Ma was the last of six politicians to give a short speech, the post-election ceremonies moved quickly.

"Let's work together to make decisions that will uphold our traditions, establish long-standing new ones, and bring us closer together. Many thanks to everyone in attendance today. May God bless our communities and keep them safe."

Ma raised both arms in victory and waved to the applauding crowd. I followed suit, and we stepped away from the podium.

"Let's give another warm round of applause to Mayor-Elect Corinne Justice," said Ana Ortega, the nighttime news anchor for WSYS, who acted as master of ceremonies for the event.

"That was fantastic, Ma." I wrapped an arm around her waist as we moved to the wings and waited for the final portion of the ceremony.

"You don't think it was in poor taste to refer to Freddie without saying her by name?" She tugged at a strand of hair. "I don't want people to think I'm using a tragedy to fulfill a campaign agenda."

"Enjoy your moment. You were tasteful. Your speech was a rallying cry."

She squeezed my arm, and we huddled together against the chilly air.

"The time has come for the hatchet ceremony." Ana Ortega held the foot-long axe above her head. The crowd cheered in response. "If I could have all the candidates from each race come up together and hold the ceremonial hatchet as a symbol of solidarity between the parties now that election season has ended."

The Bickerton High School Marching Band played a rousing rendition of "Proud to Be an American" as each group of politicians took turns holding the hatchet overhead together and waving their thanks to the crowd.

The mass of media photographers who lined the front of the stage snapped pictures of each group of participants and demanded the candidates in the more hard-fought races hug or shake hands. Once everyone had cycled through, Ana Ortega returned to the podium.

"Now, I'd like to invite the Democratic, Republican, Libertarian, and Green party chairs up to bury the hatchet in the Trident County war chest." She turned and gestured with a flourish toward the red curtain that concealed the chest and the back of the stage from the audience. "The ceremonial chest was hand carved in nineteen forty-two, when the festival was briefly suspended for the Second World War."

As the four chairs stepped forward, Ana handed them the axe. "As is tradition, the sand provided for this burial comes from the shores of Trident County." Ana stepped toward the curtain and pronounced with a trill, "Let the burial begin."

The curtain opened sluggishly to reveal, not a war chest, not a bucket of sand—just a bald but dashing young attorney in a three-piece suit, hanging by his neck from a rope attached to the lighting scaffold of the bandstand.

TWENTY-ONE

GASPS. SILENCE. SNIPPETS of confused laughter.

If I had to guess, I'd say everyone thought the moment was some kind of perverse joke.

But as we took a collective breath and surveyed the scene, as we recognized the figure dangling overhead, as we accepted that Spencer Stevenson was dead, panic ripped through us.

Screams erupted from the crowd as some pressed forward to get a better look, pulling out cell phones. Others covered the eyes of their children or pushed an upstream path through the crowd in an attempt to run for safety.

The governor, who'd maintained a place of honor on the bandstand to the left of the speaker's podium, was tackled by his personal security detail and swept away from the scene.

Flashbulbs popped from the media. Several reporters rushed the stage and yelled questions at the stunned faces of the congresspersons in an attempt to capture candid reactions to the event in real time.

The party chairs, all of whom were closer to the body than anyone else, ran over to Stevenson to block his corpse from public view and attempted to free the attorney from his hang by hacking at the rope with the ceremonial hatchet. This brought protests from the half dozen police officers who'd reacted too late to secure the stage.

As a result, their professional efforts contributed to the chaos. Most of them collided with the press and hollered at people to move away from the victim, while a couple other officers recognized the deputy attorney general and, in turn, helped to liberate his body.

Poor Ana Ortega, whose proclamation had revealed the tragedy, stood motionless in the midst of the pandemonium. Her arm was still outstretched toward the curtain and the missing war chest. Her ruby red mouth was frozen in the shape of a perpetual "oh".

My mother was the only person who reacted rationally. She broke from my side, stormed toward the podium, and shouted into the microphone for everyone to remain calm. She commanded the State Police and Bickerton P.D. to evacuate The Quad in an orderly fashion and told her constituents they had nothing to fear. Her voice urged everyone to go home and to trust that what was happening would be investigated with the utmost swiftness, thoroughness, and dignity. Her words praised the fallen attorney for his service and asked that we all respect his privacy and the privacy of his family.

Those who didn't know her might have thought she'd seized the moment to show her strength as a leader. The truth was she did it out of love. She would have wanted someone to step up and keep her death from becoming a circus. Something she didn't have the chance to do for Ms. Freddie.

My mind ran wild as I struggled to make sense of what I was seeing. Stevenson had spoken to me less than an hour ago. Alive. Angry. Feisty even. Ready to fight me. Ready to fight for his job. Ready to tear the world a new one. Now he was lifeless. Motionless. Purposeless.

As if in a trance, I pushed a path through the confused collection of police and politicians who raged against the bloodthirsty press. I needed to see Stevenson's body. He wasn't my favorite person in the world, but this wasn't a proper end, even for him.

When I reached the back of the stage, I was torn from my reverie by the grisly roar of the burly councilman who'd torpedoed the latter half of our walking tour. He'd been one of the handful of people who'd helped to free the attorney's snapped neck from the noose. He bent over Stevenson's corpse, yelling at the top of his lungs. We were in the middle of bedlam. Nobody was listening to him but me. I hunkered beside him.

"I found something. Do you see it? There's something pinned under his jacket." The councilman used a gloved hand to pull back the front flap of Stevenson's three-piece suit and revealed a sheet of paper fastened to the attorney's vest with a safety pin. The paper was a handwritten letter, Stevenson's suicide letter.

My burly companion opened his hand to snag the paper for a closer look, but I blocked his efforts. "Leave it. Don't touch anything else. We need to preserve the scene. Grab an officer. Who knows what other evidence moving the body may have disrupted."

The councilman nodded and concentrated his efforts on finding an authority figure who wasn't preoccupied by the chaos. I did my best to preserve a space around the body, warding away errant photographers and panicked onlookers, but I expended most of my efforts attempting to elude the glassy void of Stevenson's eyes.

His placid expression seemed both distant and present at the same time. I couldn't bear to witness what was behind that unblinking stare, but, as the seconds ticked by like hours, I couldn't stop myself from wondering what had gone wrong. My focus drifted to the letter that contained Stevenson's final thoughts, I could just about make it out without touching it.

Citizens of Trident County:
The act of taking one's own life is a serious endeavor. One does not do so without a purpose and mine is to save myself from death at the hands of the system. Judge Wannamaker blamed me for mishandling evidence, and I killed her for it. I didn't expect to get caught. No one who commits a crime does, but they always do. I, of all people, should know that.

A nervous impulse to glance over my shoulder or obscure the page rushed to the surface. The frigid afternoon air—or maybe apprehension—stung my cheeks. From afar, I heard the approach of determined voices. Yet, in the space Stevenson and I occupied, there was no sound except a pounding in my chest. I settled deeper into the prose, soaked up every syllable, and shivered at the pomposity hidden behind Stevenson's words.

And now that *The Bugle* has exposed me, I am left with no choice. Rather than face prosecution, I am exercising the most fundamental right our civilized society has to offer: free speech. Making a statement, going out on my own terms. Peacefully demonstrating my defiance of a system that would have me at its mercy. Thus, in keeping with my oath as an attorney to serve the people and avoid all malice, I will do to myself what our laws would do.

This is what you've made of me, Bickerton.
I hope it makes you happy.
Spencer O. Stevenson

As the weight of what I'd just read sunk into my consciousness, the world around me came into focus. A firm hand pressed into my shoulder, and the gravelly bark I'd come to associate with Detective Daniels said, "I think you need to come with me."

TWENTY-TWO

"HERE WE ARE AGAIN."

Under the circumstances, I didn't know why Detective Daniels bothered with idle chitchat. Everyone who had been on stage, as well as those people near the perimeter of the bandstand at the time Stevenson's body was unveiled, found themselves herded into the community fire hall for questioning. Daniels and his investigative team had nearly fifty people to interview, so time should have been on his mind.

We'd all been waiting for hours while officers combed the scene. I thought of my mother, who was now sitting alone vacillating between outrage the entire community witnessed such a ghoulish display, and dread she couldn't do enough to help the town face another tragedy. I wanted to be there to console her, but they'd broken us into four groups: civilians, politicians, press, and security.

I was unlucky enough to go first in the civilian group, due to my proximity to Stevenson's body and my request to file a complaint against Chance.

Daniels was unlucky enough to have the cramped fire hall kitchen as his interview room. We sat on stools at a wooden island cluttered with a butcher block of utensils, a Crock-Pot, and an enormous bowl of browning bananas. A trio of gnats circled the fruit as Daniels pushed the kitchen items to one side and set out the tools of his trade—coffee, digital recorder, legal pad, and pen.

He wasted more time gulping down his drink, wiping his mouth with his hand, and clicking open his pen. "Bickerton P.D. will follow up on your statement against Chance Mulligan. In the meantime, tell me what you saw on the bandstand."

"I saw exactly what everyone else did, but I don't believe it."

"What don't you believe?"

"I don't believe Stevenson killed himself."

"What makes you say that?"

"The suicide letter."

"Are you saying you knew about the letter ahead of time?"

"No, no. Of course not. I meant this whole thing doesn't sound like something Mr. Stevenson would do. He didn't seem like a man on the verge of killing himself. When I saw him earlier, he was more arrogant and obnoxious than ever."

"With all due respect, I'm not asking for a judgment call. All I need to know is if you saw anything out of the ordinary." He ran the tip of his pen down the center of the legal pad then worked the lines of his leathery skin into a friendly facade. "According to my viewpoint from the crowd, you were standing off near the wings stage right with the Mayor-Elect when the incident occurred. Why move toward the body?"

"The idea that Mr. Stevenson could be dead was unreal. I wanted to help."

"You wanted to help?" Daniels scratched his mustache and bore into me with his hound dog eyes. His voice was gruff but quiet. "Why do anything? You're a court reporter, not a police officer or a medic."

"Yes, but I know the rules of evidence." I squirmed on my stool and let a tuft of hair fall across my eyes. If I was honest with myself, I had no good reason for moving toward the body other than morbid curiosity.

With my face hidden, I tried to make logic of my choice. "Pulling down the body probably caused more harm than good. I didn't want anyone to do anything else that could damage the scene. In fact, when I got over there, the big man—I think my mother said his name is Mr. Iverson—was about to rip the letter off the body. Nobody else was paying attention, so I stepped in and demanded we keep everything intact." I brushed aside my wiry strands of hair and looked up.

"Okay. Let's put your involvement on the back burner." He didn't appear to have bought my reasoning, and his taut mouth let me know he had bigger issues on his mind.

"We're hoping that you and this Mr. Iverson are the only civilians who know about that suicide note, and I'd like to keep it that way—at least until we finish the investigation—for the sake of the potential publicity. Understood?"

I nodded.

Daniels drew a bullet point on his legal pad. "For now, tell me about your conversation with Stevenson. You said you talked to him earlier. Was that today?"

"Yes. I talked to him right before the parade...around twelve thirty, or thereabouts. He didn't seem suicidal. He seemed determined, like he wanted to clear his name."

I recalled the last words the attorney spoke to me—"This is not over"—and shivered.

"Your assessment of his mood aside," he said, "what was the nature of your conversation?"

"We argued. He was mad at me because he believed I motivated the article that was in the morning paper. I haven't seen it, but he said it made him look guilty. I told him what I told you yesterday, that the press already had that information, but he persisted. He claimed someone was framing him for murder, and he warned me to stop spreading lies."

"Did you believe him—about him being framed?"

"Not at the time, but I do now."

Daniels's head jerked backward in disbelief, but his voice remained neutral. "What's changed?"

"I read the suicide note."

"You read it?" He gripped the edge of the kitchen island with an intensity that turned his knuckles white and gnawed at the inside of his jaw. Eventually, he asked, "Why'd you read it?"

"I couldn't help it. I didn't touch it or anything. I just—I mean—I'd *just* talked to him. I did what anyone would have done."

He challenged me with his hound dog eyes. This time I didn't back down.

"What about the note changed your mind?" he asked.

"It seems too pat, too presentational, too rehearsed. Like it was trying to tell us something without telling us anything. A vapid political statement on the day when our politicians are supposed to be their most sincere. No real emotion, not like Stevenson at all. He's a raw nerve. But more to the point, who signs a suicide letter with their full name? The idea of that alone was odd. Nothing in that letter makes sense."

"You're saying the letter doesn't make sense because Stevenson was his normal self when you saw him?"

"No. In the letter, Mr. Stevenson said he killed Ms. Freddie because she blamed him for mishandling evidence. That's the exact opposite of what he told me in Cake & Kettle. He said the judge made the right call and he'd done everything she suggested regarding the drug investigation. He made a point of telling me, without solicitation on my part, that he didn't kill her—not just that he didn't do it but that he was being framed *because* he was working so hard to nail the drug lab."

Daniels shifted on his stool. "Okay. You lost me. Are you claiming Stevenson didn't kill the judge or Stevenson didn't kill himself...or both?"

"I don't know." My eyes began to water as confusion took over. "Maybe...both."

"Look," the word came out in a huff that highlighted his apparent frustration, "I know this must be difficult for you since this is the second death you've been a party to in less than three days, but I need you to stay on track. We need to talk in facts, not speculation." He patted the table to keep me from crying. "If you want to go down this road, I'm willing to listen. But why would Stevenson commit suicide if it wasn't for the reasons stated in the letter?"

"That's just the point. I don't think he did kill himself. Or if he did, it wasn't because he killed Ms. Freddie." I wiped my eyes with the back of my hands. "Last time we talked, you said Harriston was the last person seen holding the murder weapon, not Stevenson. Doesn't that leave open the possibility that the judge's murderer could have been someone else?"

I might have been round holing everything into one

big square peg of troubles, but the more I spoke, the more things began to make sense. Harriston, Maggie, and even Phyllis Dodd had more to gain from killing Ms. Freddie than Stevenson did, especially since Phyllis seemed entangled in some kind of forced relationship with Chance. I wondered how I could work all of that information into the conversation when I noticed Daniels holding up his hand in a stopping motion.

"Isn't it also possible Stevenson killed himself because the media account was accurate?" Exasperation seeped into the detective's voice, and he let his pen clatter onto the wooden surface of the kitchen island as if resigned to abandon his notes. "Surveillance shows Stevenson following Judge Wannamaker moments before the estimated time of death and several courthouse employees confirm his attitude toward her was hostile. Until we can prove otherwise, we're talking about Spencer's murder confession and *suicide*." Daniels exaggerated his lip movements to make sure I understood.

"Now, for the last time, is there anything you can tell me about your conversation with Stevenson, what you saw or heard before his death, or what you read in the suicide note that proves—"

"Letter. It was much more of a letter to Bickerton—" I blinked. Considered. And blinked again.

That made sense. The idea drifted to life and grew until the real issue with the suicide note came into focus.

"Stevenson didn't write that letter." I clasped my hands, determined to make him believe. "Or, if he wrote it, he wrote it under duress. The signature on that letter read Spencer O. Stevenson. I've seen his signature before. Today at Cake & Kettle. I am 100 percent sure his middle initial is 'J' for James. I should have known as many times as I've looked up his full name to put on the coversheet of trial transcripts. Whoever wrote that letter didn't know his middle name—or maybe Stevenson was trying to send us a message that he was in trouble, that his death wasn't a suicide. S.O.S!"

Daniels shut off the voice recorder and leaned forward. His face showed patience, but his body language conveyed the opposite.

"Ms. Justice, I understand your desire to play detective. You work in a courthouse. You know the law. These victims are your friends." He held up his hand, anticipating my urge to speak. "But, I can't do anything with theories. Stevenson left a suicide note and claims to have committed murder. I have to take that seriously until *real* evidence proves otherwise. Real evidence—that's fingerprints, eyewitness accounts, the condition of the body, and, in this case, notes found on the scene. Not speculation, hunches, or minor discrepancies—who's to say Stevenson's cursive 'J' isn't your cursive 'O' and vice versa? Handwriting is subjective—"

"What about confessions?" I snapped. I wasn't going to let him condescend to me like a child. My theory had merit. "Are confessions reliable facts? Because, the last time I checked, those aren't one hundred percent accurate either. At least do some kind of handwriting analysis before you run with this letter. False confessions made under coercion are the leading cause of wrongful convictions in homicide—"

"Enough. You're talking in circles and mixing metaphors. This wasn't an interrogation. No one put pressure on Stevenson to confess. As far as we know, he did so of his own accord."

Daniels went to the kitchen sink, where he filled a

plastic cup with water and plunked it in front of me, his attempt to pacify me. A fruit fly from the nearby bananas landed on the surface of the liquid. I pushed the cup away and rolled my eyes at him.

"I understand you're frustrated. I am too. The whole town witnessed Stevenson's death. We all want answers, but there's no need to make them more complicated than they need to be." He sat back down and let his finger hover over the start button on the recording device. "The State Police are committed to working this case to its logical conclusion, so let's just avoid the Agatha Christie amateur hour and show our governor we're making a serious effort to reestablish the safety and integrity of our State facilities…"

The moment Detective Daniels started towing the party line, I tuned out and shut down. He, of all people, should know crime and the law are not like science. The simplest answer is rarely the correct one.

TWENTY-THREE

THE FIRST THING I did once Detective Daniels released me from his kitchen-office was borrow Ma's cell phone to call Jillian. I wanted to see if Cake & Kettle was still open so I could get a look at Stevenson's receipt and compare the signature with what I remembered about the suicide letter.

The café normally closed well before 6:00 p.m. because traffic on The Quad slowed by that hour and most of the offices in the vicinity shut down mid-afternoon. Jillian, however, must have made an exception for the festival because she picked up my call on the second ring, saying I could come by whenever I was ready.

Ma wasn't keen on the idea of me walking over to Cake & Kettle by myself in the aftermath of Stevenson's death, but she relented once they called her name for the police interview. We agreed she would drive over to the café to pick me up as soon as she finished.

I grabbed my coat, made the quick jaunt across The Quad, and found Jillian drinking tea and talking with Grace. The place was empty, and, by the looks of the sweet feast set before them—finger sandwiches, macarons, scones with clotted cream and jam, mince pies, and trifle—the two women had been waiting for my call.

"You guys know me too well." I wiggled out of my coat and took an armchair beside Jillian.

She poured me a cup of what smelled like peppermint tea from a kettle shaped like the Tower of London.

"I wanted to get in touch with you earlier," Grace was still in her uniform and stretched out on a sofa, "but I was hanging out at the back of the crowd and got roped into helping evacuate The Quad."

"Don't worry about it." I reached for the teacup to take a sip. "My phone died an untimely death at the hands of Chance Mulligan."

"Who?" asked Grace. "Why does that name sound familiar?"

"We had…" Jillian cleared her throat and glanced at me, which caused Grace to furrow her brow in confusion, "…a bit of a situation this afternoon."

"Chance is Langley Mulligan's husband." I set down my teacup and began the formidable task of loading up a scone with butter, strawberry jam, and cream. "Forget that for now. We'll talk later. Ma could be coming to pick me up any minute."

Frankly, I was too on edge about Stevenson's suicide letter to rehash my run-in with the male Mulligan, especially after spending the afternoon reliving the event for the Bickerton police detective who took my statement before the interview with Daniels. Both officers acted as if there wasn't much they could do until they located Chance, and I didn't want to admit that fact to my friends or my overprotective mother.

"Well, at least tell us what happened on stage." Grace sat up in her chair.

"I don't know for sure, but I have my suspicions."

Against the advice of Detective Daniels, I told them about the suicide letter, my conversation with Stevenson, and my doubts about the attorney's signature. This prompted Jillian to dig through the register to find the receipt.

"Stevenson tells you he suspects he's being framed for murder," Jillian handed me the paper slip, "then dies of what his letter claims to be suicide, and you think that means his death is related to Judge Wanna-maker's murder?"

I bobbed my head in agreement and stuffed half of the loaded scone into my mouth, wishing I had more time to savor the unctuous concoction. "If Stevenson was honest about being framed, he probably didn't kill himself and that could mean two things—he may have been murdered for getting out of line, and he probably didn't kill Ms. Freddie. Whoever killed Stevenson must have meant for his death to take the steam out of Ms. Freddie's murder investigation." I unfurled the receipt and spread it out on the coffee table among the desserts. "See this. The 'J' Stevenson wrote on this receipt is a perfect cursive 'J.' The 'O' on the suicide letter is in standard print—almost like it was meant to stand out."

"Yeah, that's all fine and good," said Grace. "But if Stevenson was really in trouble—feeling threatened and in fear for his life—why mess around with some-thing the cops could never notice. Why not put some clues in the letter?"

"Maybe he couldn't," I said. "Maybe he was being told what to write. If he had no choice about what the letter was supposed to say, his signature would be the only way—the sneakiest way—to ask for help."

Grace clucked her tongue at me and closed her eyes, while she dismissively sipped her tea. Jillian curled up in her wingback chair and pulled a bottle of Bushmills whiskey from the cushion.

I cursed under my breath at both of them. Why wouldn't anyone take this seriously? "Look, I know there's something to this. What about what Stevenson said to me earlier today? He didn't mention feeling sad or going home. In fact, he talked about having to fight for his job with the Attorney General—"

"He was riled up," Grace said. "So what? Stevenson was always charging at the wind and getting into fights. If someone killed Stevenson—"

"—or forced Stevenson to kill himself," I added.

"Or forced Stevenson to kill himself," Grace repeated with a breathy note of sarcasm, "to cover up for the murder of Judge Wannamaker, who do you suspect is the real murderer?"

"Who does she suspect killed Stevenson?" asked Jillian. "Or who does she suspect killed Judge Wannamaker?"

"Both?" Grace's gaze slid back and forth between us.

Jillian turned to me. "How do you figure they were killed by the same person?"

"That's the part I need to work out, but they were both strangulations of a sort…and there are plenty of other people who had more motive for killing the judge than Stevenson—take Maggie for instance." I wrinkled my nose at my mistake. "Sorry, Jillian. She-Whose-Name-Means-Shame."

"That bloated slag?" scoffed Jillian. "You're joking, right? She's a homewrecker for sure, but I don't see her being a murderess."

"Yeah. She's too lazy," Grace said, "and she's far too smug to keep such a huge secret. And anyway, she wasn't near the kitchen at the time of Wannamaker's murder. Stevenson was, though. Screaming and yelling at Corporal North and Phyllis Dodd. He was making so much noise I had to throw them all out into the parking lot. And, if I remember correctly, Stevenson had nothing but nasty things to say about the judge."

"Most of that's true," I said, "but I forgot to tell you how Stevenson got back there in the first place."

Grace leaned in, finally showing eagerness for the tale, and I mirrored her, hoping to draw her in further.

"I dropped off a trial transcript with Stevenson yesterday, and he told me Maggie—I mean, *she*—took him back to her desk. She made coffee for the two of them in the kitchen not long before everything went haywire. Put that together with what we already know about her sudden allegiance to Harriston and what I learned today about her having another affair, and you have proximity as well as motive."

"Bloody hell." Jillian set down her teacup and saucer with a clank. "That gal gets around, doesn't she?"

"Stop right there. Even if Magg—" Grace peeked over at Jillian, who snarled and rolled her eyes. "Even if *she* was in the right place at the right time to hurt Wannamaker, we're still left with a ton of loose ends when it comes to Stevenson's death. How the heck did she get clearance to go backstage during the festival or get him to write the suicide letter or force that bullheaded Stevenson to do anything she said?"

"That's the tricky part." I bit into the other half of my scone and spoke with a full mouth. "Maybe she threatened him—"

"Face it, Victoria. This whole thing is based on wishful thinking," said Grace. "I know you're still hurting and you're trying to do what's best for Judge Wannamaker, but maybe you should see Stevenson's death for what it is…a gift. The killer confessed."

"Or maybe that harlot seduced him." Jillian held up the whiskey bottle and tipped a second helping into her tea. She tested her enhanced beverage and mumbled, "Honestly, I wouldn't put it past that woman to have a gun."

Her words floated through the air like a grenade and left me stunned. But, the possibility stirred my brain—coercing Stevenson would be easy if Maggie lured him into position with her usual charms and pulled out a gun. Of course, Maggie would still need clearance to get to the stage. I'd experienced that roadblock first-hand when it came to the standoff between Ashton and Trooper McIntyre, so I'd need to figure out how she'd accomplished that.

"That's definitely an avenue worth exploring." I loaded up another scone. "Now we just need to find proof."

"*We*? Not me." Grace leaned away from the coffee table. "I think you're getting ahead of yourself. What are your other options?"

"Harriston. He never went back to the kitchen with Wannamaker, but he could have had help with that in the form of Maggie—or Phyllis."

Was it possible Phyllis's new association with Chance meant she was working with Harriston and Langley? They were all spotted on The Quad at one point or another during the day and could have conspired to pull off Stevenson's death, as well as Wannamaker's murder.

"Did either of you see Mr. Harriston on The Quad today, or Phyllis, or Langley?" I looked at Jillian. "Langley has tacky orange hair."

"Orange hair?" Jillian giggled and touched her own

bleached-blonde pixie cut. "Gosh, no. No on Phyllis, too. But Harriston came in this morning for his usual round of coffee and blood sausage."

"Figured that'd be the go-to meal for a vampire like him." Grace cringed and unbuttoned the thick cuffs on the sleeves of her polyester uniform before reaching to scoop a spoonful of trifle. "The only time I saw Harriston is when I met up with you and your mom earlier today. He was standing a few feet away from you, watching your mother and Mr. Russell. Nothing other than that."

Our conversation came to a halt when the bell over the door rang to announce the presence of a patron. We all looked up to find my mother walking through the door.

"Jillian. Grace. Nice to see you. I'm sorry we can't stay." She clipped her words, and I could tell the festival's unexpected finale had drained her of her graciousness and patience. "Angel, I need to go home."

"Gotta go, ladies." I grabbed a linen napkin to wipe my hands. "Call me at the house if you come across anything interesting."

I widened my eyes as I spoke so they'd know that, even though I was telling them to call me at home, this wasn't something I wanted to share with Ma.

"Jillian, email me a copy of that receipt when you get a chance." I pointed to the slip of paper I'd left on the table then followed my mother, who had already turned and pushed her way back through the door.

Ma moaned when I stepped onto the street beside her. "I thought I'd seen everything, but today was just—" Her gaze moved toward The Quad, and I followed her line of sight.

We couldn't see the bandstand from where we were standing, but the roundabout that serviced the town center had several sawhorses and orange barrels wrapped in bright yellow police tape blocking the route. Officers in riot gear replaced the mass of festivalgoers, food vendors, and musicians who'd lined the streets earlier. They patrolled the town's square and directed the occasional trickle of cars toward the convoluted detour of side streets.

Ma's Buick sat at the curb in front of Cake & Kettle. She handed me the keys.

"How can our town move forward from this?" She pulled at the handle of the passenger door before I could unlock the vehicle and expressed her frustrations by yanking the lever back and forth. "People are going to remember this day for the rest of their lives. Why would someone create such an ugly display for public consumption?"

"I don't know, Ma. I don't think we were meant to understand."

We collapsed into our seats and stared out the windshield. The evening had taken on a blueish-gray haze from where the rising moon gave the darkened surroundings an ethereal glow. I cranked the ignition and turned on the heat, letting the engine warm up before I put the car in gear.

"Someone dropped the ball," Ma said. "How does a young man die of a hanging in the middle of a festival designed to promote bipartisanship and goodwill mere days after Freddie is killed inside the courthouse?" She snapped her seat belt into place then looked to me for an answer.

I guessed my mother didn't have an opportunity to talk with Mr. Iverson or Detective Daniels about the suicide note. I debated sharing the contents of the letter with her—doing so would give her the peace of knowing who killed Ms. Freddie and why. On the other hand, she'd have a completely new reason to feel guilty about the events of the day and a fresh set of frustrations regarding the unjust nature of her best friend's death.

Since I didn't believe the letter or the simple solutions it suggested, I followed Detective Daniels's advice and kept my mouth shut. I didn't want to get Mom's hopes up if the confession turned out to be false.

"Someone is clearly trying to send a message that our town has something sinister raging at its core." Buildings flew by her window as we traveled the short distance to our home. "We have Freddie's funeral in two days. What if there's another tragedy? I don't think I can take anymore. What I did out there today—what I said. People are going to expect me to be strong. I don't think I can do it."

"Yes, you can." I reached over the center console and squeezed her hand. "Remember what Ms. Freddie wrote to me in her letter. When life gets difficult, we must 'rise above and forge your own path.' Those words were meant for you too." I pulled onto our street and slowed the car to a crawl so I could look her in the eyes. "The town believes in you. They wouldn't have elected you for the job if they didn't think you could rise above tragedy and transform it into triumph."

She cut me with the kind of sharp look of sardonic reprimand perfected by mothers everywhere.

"Seriously, Ma. I have faith in you. Ms. Freddie had faith in you. Everyone does. Nobody has worked harder in this community teaching kids right from wrong, upholding ethics, and living with integrity." I pulled the Buick into the drive, put the vehicle in park, and gave her a hug. When I released her from my embrace, she seemed to sit a little taller.

"I guess I could suggest an emergency meeting of the outgoing and incoming city council members so we can all work together with the police to form some kind of special investigative committee or coalition." She tugged at a strand of her tawny pageboy, and her voice became deeper, more official. "I know this isn't the time to point fingers, but someone made a mistake that left everyone vulnerable. The stage should have been more secure. How did Mr. Stevenson's body get up there? The Quad was crawling with police officers, reporters, and news cameras recording our every move—if we're not properly protected under a circumstance like that, how are any of us supposed to feel safe?"

Again, I had no words. But as I shifted the car into drive and eased into the garage, my thoughts drifted to the courthouse. We had those protections for keeping people safe—bailiffs to keep the peace, court stenographers to capture the verbatim record, and video surveillance to document misdoings—and Ms. Freddie had still been killed.

If I wanted to prove Stevenson didn't kill himself over Ms. Freddie's murder, I'd have to start by proving the real killer was still out there. The best way to do that would be to use all of the resources at my disposal, starting with my transcript and the AudioSync recordings of the Mulligan trial then Grace and her access to the video feed at the courthouse.

After all, the people with the most to gain from Ms. Freddie's death were all in the courtroom with her at one point or another, and maybe someone said or did something incriminating on tape.

TWENTY-FOUR

THE HARSH LIGHT of my laptop screen bathed my little bedroom in a dull shade of blue. Apropos since, between the evening news coverage of the tragedy at the day's festival and Ma's anxiety-ridden dinner conversation, I almost felt too depressed to undertake the task of sifting through Langley Mulligan's trial transcript. Normally, I'd work in the luxurious office space my mother had created in the room across the hall, but I didn't want to arouse her curiosity or attract her company. She'd shared so many concerns throughout the night, I feared she'd want to sit at my shoulder and help once she discovered my true intentions.

"Good night, Angel. I'm going to bed." Ma's voice drifted in from the next room. The closing credits music of the 11:00 news disappeared as she turned off the television and slipped onto her creaky mattress.

"Good night," I called back through my open bedroom door, which I quickly jumped up and closed before returning to my perch. I sat stock still on the edge of my bed and listened until the sounds from her room ceased.

Sequestered and alone, I settled cross-legged in the middle of my queen-sized bed hunched over the laptop screen. I had no idea what I was looking for, but I had to find some snippet of testimony that would link Ms. Freddie's murder to Mr. Stevenson's death.

If the attorney really killed her, the connection

should show itself. If not, that meant the murderer was still out there, and someone else might turn up dead. That thought sent prickles across my skin. With no one taking me seriously, I'd have to rely on innovation and ingenuity to find the truth.

The Mulligan transcript was still stored in the computer software that translated my machine shorthand into English. I slid my hand across the laptop's touch pad and the cursor soared across the blocks of text. I debated where to begin.

The microphone on my laptop was set so it recorded from the moment I made the first keystroke on my steno machine until the second I closed the program. This meant I had sound for almost every conversation that happened near my computer during and after the trial.

But what made the court reporting software special was the AudioSync feature, a component that synchronized the audio recording with my verbatim capture of the proceeding. Therefore, I could click on any section of the text and go straight to the same spot in the audio.

Some court reporters cursed this little gem because the presence of built-in recording software suggested we're unable to do our jobs, but its true value as a review tool for garbled testimony and sotto voce conversations would become my saving grace tonight.

"Let's start where things fall apart," I muttered to myself as I placed the cursor near the start of Ashton's trial testimony about Langley's drug bust. Plugging my earbuds into the headphone jack, I leaned forward, clicked the microphone icon on the menu bar, and listened.

THE WITNESS: I slowed when I saw a vehicle parked on the shoulder of Route 1 about a quarter mile north of Cooper's. Naturally, I was a little suspicious with the motorist being so close to an establishment known for its alcohol. When I approached the vehicle, I found a woman sitting behind the wheel. She told me she thought she had a flat tire and had stopped to check.

MR. STEVENSON: Is the individual you approached in this courtroom?

My stomach clenched. Hearing Stevenson's disembodied voice, after seeing him hanging lifeless mere hours ago made me realize how difficult this endeavor was going to be. I tapped the space bar to stop the recording. Would I be able to handle it when Ms. Freddie's voice surfaced? I scanned the page for her name. Finding nothing, my stomach slowly unknotted.

Steeling myself, I used the touch pad to move the cursor ahead a few beats to get to the heart of Ashton's testimony. Then I took a deep breath and plunged back into the audio.

THE WITNESS: I was going to offer my assistance, but I noticed her eyes were glassy and her words a bit slurred. I also detected the faint smell of alcohol.

MR. STEVENSON: What did you do next?

THE WITNESS: I asked her to step out of the vehicle and that's when I observed what looked like a large quantity of pills on her front passenger seat.

I held my breath as the magic AudioSync cursor skipped through the words on my screen and hovered over the period when Ashton's voice lingered between sentences. This was the portion of the case where he gave his probable cause for searching Langley's car. I remembered this testimony from trial, but two things bugged me about it now.

First, Cooper's wasn't open during the daytime hours when this arrest took place, so why imply concern about a bar being in the vicinity? Was it all lip service to justify his search of her car? Second, how was Ashton able to stumble upon Langley so easily when Chance had eluded him for years? Langley was self-absorbed and had a history of drinking, but I imagined no amount of alcohol would cause her to forget to hide her drugs with a cop approaching.

With both of those issues plaguing me, my mind flashed to Ashton's offer to act as witness to my run-in with Chance. At the time, the gesture seemed valiant, but now I wondered. If Ashton was so preoccupied with the Mulligans that he was willing to lie for me, what else was he willing to lie about?

I hit the spacebar to stop the audio.

Ashton had been nothing but helpful and sympathetic to my plight, so I had stopped considering him a suspect for Ms. Freddie's death. But the truth of the matter was he was at the scene of the crime during the time of the murder and had no other legitimate reason for being there.

Now that I knew more about Ashton's obsession, I could see he might have a motive.

Was it possible he harbored animosity toward Ms. Freddie for refusing to admit evidence of a third suspect in the Natalie Knowles case, thus allowing Chance to get away with murder? Could Ms. Freddie's decision to drop the felony charges against Langley have been the act that pushed Ashton over the edge enough to kill her?

I flinched. If there was the slightest grain of truth to either consideration, I'd essentially spent the last two days laying the investigation at the feet of a potential killer.

Still, the real litmus test was Stevenson's death. Could Ashton have killed the attorney as a cover-up for his crimes against the judge?

Well, he had escorted me to the bandstand around the time of Stevenson's death, and he had his—I flinched again. Tension gripped my shoulders the moment I remembered—Ashton had a permit to carry a concealed weapon. He also wasn't fond of Stevenson. He could have easily used the gun to bully the attorney into slipping on a noose and making a false confession.

Although Ashton didn't strike me as a murderer, all the pieces were there. I stared into the flat void of the computer screen unsure of what to do next when the sound of a woman's voice jerked me back to reality.

"Stay away from the internet."

Huh? I looked up.

My mother stood in the doorway of my room, wearing a paisley headscarf and a fuzzy green robe.

"I didn't hear you knock." I tugged the buds from my ears by their cord.

"I knew you'd be up late. I just wanted to warn you to stay off the internet. I scrolled through on my cell out of curiosity and…." She pressed one hand to her heart while she squinted at the screen on her mobile device. "They're making the worst speculations about the festival with headlines like 'Magistrate Murderer Strikes Again?,' 'Post-Election Execution: Mishap or Murder?,' and 'Bickerton's Ballot Day Disaster: Backlash Against Bipartisanism?'"

"Don't worry, Ma. I'm not on the internet. I'm doing something for work." The last statement wasn't wholly untrue.

"Well, good." She blew me a kiss. "Don't stay up too late—even if you don't plan on going to work tomorrow. Sweet dreams, Angel." She closed the door, leaving me with my thoughts.

Despite Ma's warning, part of me was curious to see what information the print press had gathered and how their spin differed from the WSYS evening news, whose coverage focused on the inconvenience of the public display rather than the details of the death.

Another part of me considered what would happen if I took my curiosity and my theories directly to Mike Slocum at *The Bugle*. Perhaps I could convince him to publish my theory about Stevenson's suicide note in an attempt to flush out the killer. I wasn't sure how feasible this was, but I filed the idea away as a possible activity for the next day.

Determined not to let Ma's distraction slow me down, I slipped the earbuds back in and returned my attention to the trial transcript.

Even though the speculation against Ashton weighed heavily on my thoughts, I'd started this endeavor convinced Harriston and Maggie carried the heaviest blame, so I tabbed down to the area of the transcript where the judge had called for a recess to accommodate plea negotiations. Maybe my computer mic caught some of that off-the-record conversation.

As for Maggie, she typically didn't say much on the record while trial was in session. If I hoped to find anything with her voice, this break in trial was my best shot.

I started the AudioSync and was surprised to hear Grace.

THE BAILIFF: Oh, dear. Please excuse me, Mr. Harriston. I can be so clumsy sometimes.

MR. HARRISTON: Quite all right.

Their voices were faint due to the distance of the defense table from my computer. I pumped up the volume and pushed the earbuds a little deeper into my ears.

MR. HARRISTON: Oh, wait a second, madam— Ms. Tisdale. Terribly sorry to impose. Could you please tell the court reporter I'd like a copy of the trial transcript? Here's my card. Tell her to contact me directly when the document is ready. I'll have my office send payment.

My mind started working so fast I barely heard Grace's reply. When I last spoke to Grace about this scenario, she told me Harriston had rammed into *her* and made a rude comment as he stepped down from the sidebar with the judge. This exchange didn't reflect that. Not only was Harriston polite, but the exchange sounded as if she'd bumped into *him*. Why would Grace exaggerate the situation? The conversation was innocent, if not insignificant.

But I didn't have time to dwell on an answer. I'd left the audio rolling, and it wasn't long before Stevenson's militant bark filled my ears. His voice was distant, but the echo in the courtroom made his words distinct enough to cut through the ambient sound of people moving around the space.

MR. STEVENSON: What the hell are you looking at?

MR. HARRISTON: I thought I was the only one who could get on that woman's bad side.

MR. STEVENSON: What do you care?

MR. HARRISTON: Care? You're not looking at the big picture, Son. I've hated that woman for decades, but you don't see me behaving in ways that undermine my professionalism.

MR. STEVENSON: I'm not in the mood for another lecture, Harriston. Back off.

MR. HARRISTON: Take it easy. We might be enemies today—and, yes, I came out on top—but men of our caliber have to stick together. This is just a court case. You haven't been truly hurt until one of them steals your job. Don't worry about that old spade. Focus on keeping your nose clean. Her time will come to an end. And when I get my chance to run things, I'll be sure to remember who's on my side. Now, about my client—

I paused the audio so as not to lose my place. *When I get my chance to run things?*

What did Harriston mean by that? Was he aware the judge was about to lose her life? Harriston had basically won his case at that point, so what did he have to gain from Ms. Freddie's death?

My mouth fell open, a new notion punching me in the gut. Maybe what Ms. Freddie's husband had suggested was true. Granted, I hadn't spent a lot of time talking to Russell Wannamaker, but he had mentioned Harriston might attempt to court the governor for the judgeship for which he'd been passed over in favor of Ms. Freddie.

That made a lot of sense when juxtaposed with Harriston trying to convince my mother to let him escort her to the candidates' luncheon during the festival—where the governor was in attendance. Luckily, she'd refused. But if she hadn't, Harriston would have been able to unabashedly schmooze the governor face-to-face.

Although, for all I know, he still could have made his way into the event and succeeded in making his pitch. Maybe Ma saw him at the luncheon. If not, maybe I could whip up an excuse to visit Harriston's office again. Probe him about the governor and Stevenson's tie.

Ping!

An email notification drew my attention back to the screen. The message was from Jillian. She'd scanned Stevenson's credit card receipt and sent me the picture.

I reached beside the bed for my purse and rummaged around for Detective Daniels's business card so I could forward him Jillian's PDF. Not that it mattered since he'd treated me like an idiot and didn't believe me anyway. Still, if I expected to make sense of this mess, he was my only hope until I figured out some alternatives.

When I finished the email, I clicked the screen to

resume the audio and found myself submerged in Maggie's heavy southern Delaware drawl. Her voice overpowered the conversation between the two attorneys, and I assumed she must have been closer to my computer and its microphone.

Curses. I needed to hear more of Harriston and Stevenson's conversation in case they mentioned the murder weapon, Stevenson's purple tie. Instead, I'd stumbled upon the moment when Maggie walked up to my desk to flirt with Ashton.

I paused the audio once more as an idea formed. If I could see what the two men were doing physically and their positions in the courtroom when this conversation took place, maybe I could ascertain what happened to the murder weapon.

I slapped my laptop closed and reached for the cordless phone on my nightstand. I dialed Grace's number and crossed my fingers she'd answer at such a late hour. Four rings later, I had a cranky, husky-voiced Grace on the line.

I plunged into my request without preamble. "Do you think you could get me a copy of the surveillance footage you gave Detective Daniels?"

"Well, good evening to you too." She yawned. "Thanks for waking me to make sure my phone works. I'm going to hang up now."

"Grace, I'm serious. If I can just get a look at that footage, I might be able to wrap my head around Ms. Freddie's death."

"Fine," she huffed. "For Freddie. Friday. After work. My office. Tell no one. Me sleep now."

Friday? That was two whole days away. Much later than I'd hoped, but I accepted her terms, offered an apology for disturbing what she referred to as "the best sleep of her life," and filled her in on my transcript discoveries before hanging up the phone and returning to the task of examining the trial audio.

WHEN THE RECORDING RESUMED, Maggie's voice oozed through my earbuds.

MS. SWINSON: What are you doing sitting here all by your lonesome?

CORPORAL NORTH: Making sure Langley gets what's coming to her. I didn't put my career on the line to let some lush make a fool out of me.

MS. SWINSON: I'm sure a fine-looking man like you has never let a woman make a fool out of him. Is there anything I can do to help?

CORPORAL NORTH: Not unless you can turn back time.

A lot of scratching and rustling interrupted the audio. This led me to believe I'd reached the point in their conversation where Maggie placed her ample bottom on my teeny-tiny desk.

CORPORAL NORTH: Are you sure the courthouse evidence closet is secure?

MS. SWINSON: I'd bet my life on it.

CORPORAL NORTH: Well, you may have to because I know what I put in those evidence envelopes. Those drugs were specifically picked out for her.

MS. SWINSON: I believe you, darlin, but the trial is over. Why don't you let me help take your mind off things?

Scratch. Rustle. Rustle. Scratch.

MS. SWINSON: You married?

CORPORAL NORTH: Uh, no.

MS. SWINSON: Good. I've learned my lesson about married men.

CORPORAL NORTH: But I am—uh—dating—someone—uh, surely a gal like you has someone special in her life.

MS. SWINSON: Nope. Decent single men are hard to come by.

The sound of rustling returned. When the audio settled, Maggie's drawl was low and husky.

MS. SWINSON: You know, most of us clerks hang out at Cooper's on Wednesday night for karaoke...

I quickly lowered the volume. My own voice would be next from where I shooed Maggie away from my desk. I had no desire to hear the contorted sound of my nasal tones on digital audio.

While my words played faintly in the background, I closed my eyes. What did Ashton mean when he said, "Those drugs were specifically *picked out* for her?" Such a strange choice of words.

My heart fluttered. Something deeper was at play. Was I jumping to conclusions because of my epiphany regarding Ashton's potential involvement in Ms. Freddie's murder, *or* had he actually implied the possibility of knowing more about the drugs in Langley's car than he claimed under oath?

If the latter was true, Ashton couldn't be trusted… to be telling the truth…about anything.

That idea robbed me of breath. Why hadn't I realized this earlier? Ashton had already hinted at his willingness to lie when he offered to act as a witness to Chance's attack. My heart had wanted to believe he'd done so for *me*, but the bastard had probably lied about that too.

I bit my lip to pull my focus back to the audio since Maggie's responses weren't to be ignored either. She'd implied she was single but failed to fully acknowledge her affair with Mr. Russell. Though, I suppose, why would she? His wife had just left the courtroom, and an adulterer wouldn't confess her sins to a complete stranger. Or maybe the tryst ended years ago.

But *if* Maggie was no longer seeing Mr. Russell, what was her motivation for possibly killing the judge? Demotion? Grace had mentioned how angry Maggie became after her reassignment to the clerk's office. Maybe the rift between the two women had become a matter worth murder.

I set the computer aside and stretched out my legs while the audio droned through my conversation with Ashton and the catty encounter with Langley. I wished I could have avoided replaying her bullying attempt, but the mechanics of the AudioSync made that impossible. Since our interaction fell into the spaces of the transcript where I wasn't writing on my steno machine, I had no way of rewinding or fast forwarding the material without having to restart at the beginning or zipping straight to the end.

Anger rose and subsided as I relived Langley's bitter venom and my sweet victory. At the end of our fight, I raised the volume to see if the mic caught any residual conversation.

What I got was the sound of Langley's snarky attitude reduced to a blubbering mess.

THE DEFENDANT: Harriston, you bastard, do something. You know I'm innocent. I shouldn't even be here. Things weren't supposed to happen this way—

An unidentifiable male voice interrupted Langley. I could only conclude from context that it was a guard. This must have been right after she assaulted me with the pitcher of water, during the moments they dragged her away to a holding cell. I was on the verge of a panic attack at the time and could only remember groping for the nearest exit to escape the scene.

THE GUARD: Let's walk and talk, lady. You can hash things out with your lawyer in holding.

THE DEFENDANT: Call Chance. This is all his fault. If he'd just stop toying with that stupid cop, none of this would've happened.

THE GUARD: I said, move it.

The guard yelled so loud I had to pull out one of my earbuds to recover from the abrupt increase in volume.
Snap. Crackle.
A walkie-talkie popped with static, punctuating the brutal sharpness of the guard's voice. I couldn't make out the words coming over the radio. Based on the banging and slamming that followed, it must have been a call from his backup team in holding.
I was about to shut off the recording when I heard Mr. Harriston's voice break through the din.

MR. HARRISTON: Don't worry, Ms. Mulligan. I will do everything in my power—

Thump. Thud. Bam!
More hollers, curses, and the sound of a door slamming.
A new woman's voice joined the cacophony. After a couple of beats, everything became clear again.

MR. HARRISTON: Ms. Swinson, please...

Maggie? What was she doing back in there?
Then I remembered she'd confessed to going back into the courtroom after she took Mr. Stevenson to view the courthouse's evidence closet. I heard the volume of her voice crescendo as she approached the front of the

courtroom, where my computer captured the rest of their conversation.

MR. HARRISTON: I told you I'd speak with you after the trial.

MS. SWINSON: What does it matter?

MR. HARRISTON: It matters to me. My reputation and how people view me while I'm in this building matters to me.

MS. SWINSON: Relax. Nobody knows anything yet.

MR. HARRISTON: Good. I don't want any trouble.

MS. SWINSON: We shouldn't talk out here.

Their voices seemed to move away from the microphone toward what I presumed to be the jury room. Detective Daniels mentioned they'd disappeared into one during the recess.

Sure enough, the faint clunk of a door closing led to an audio feed that hummed with the dull buzz of an empty room.

I removed the earbuds with trembling hands. Those final moments left a lot open to interpretation.

For one thing, Langley declared her innocence of the drug charges. If she had no expectation that anyone was listening, except Harriston, why bother…unless there was some truth to it?

I also had Maggie and Harriston colluding over

something. Perhaps murder, or perhaps Maggie switched the trial evidence to help Harriston win his case. After all, she had access to the drugs prior to trial during the brief time they were stored in the courthouse evidence closet.

The alleged switch led to several gains for Harriston: an easy trial victory, a high-profile disruption in Ms. Freddie's courtroom, a monetary business boost…and the perfect alibi for murder.

The real question, however, was what did Maggie gain from taking such a huge risk for another person? The only advantage I could see was a new job, but Maggie wasn't the type to be content with such a small piece of the pie.

My brain was full to bursting with questions, yet the answers remained elusive.

Nothing on the audio pointed to a definitive culprit for the deaths that haunted our town. In fact, when I added everything I'd just heard to the loose-end issue of me spotting the state chemist with Chance, an alleged drug dealer, I was stuck with more suspects and suspicions than ever.

And yet, all those unanswered questions meant there was much more to this than Detective Daniels cared to believe. The dull ache in my stomach made that much crystal clear.

As the laptop powered down, I blinked against the fading glare of the screen and debated just how much of my mother's fear, anger, and paranoia from earlier in the evening had seeped into my own thinking. I couldn't let those emotions cripple me. My mother, with her proposed city council meetings, might have been content to let the slow hand of justice swipe blindly at moral turpitude. But for me, justice meant catching the killer.

Sifting through theories wasn't enough. I needed to take action.

To accomplish that end, I'd have to confront Ashton, Harriston, Maggie, and Phyllis. Tomorrow, I'd forge my own path to the truth.

TWENTY-FIVE

"IF YOU HAVE something to ask me, Ms. Justice, make it quick. I'm due in court in a half hour." Beau Harriston slammed shut the top drawer of his filing cabinet and shoved the folders he'd extracted into a large box strapped to a luggage cart.

I fiddled with the belt on my wool coat and shifted in the leather club chair in front of Harriston's massive desk. In the light of a new day, the idea of confronting Ms. Freddie's murder suspects seemed like a foolhardy endeavor—one I had undertaken with no preparation.

I bowed my head to summon some courage, but all I managed to discover was my feet didn't touch the floor due to the enormity of the chair. Harriston and I were all alone, and I had no recourse if he chose to use our size difference to his advantage. This revelation made me wish I hadn't arrived at his office the minute it opened at 9:00 a.m. I should have waited until I had someone like Ashton to come with me. But since now I couldn't trust the corporal any more than I could trust Harriston, I was stuck.

I stifled a groan and forged ahead. "What was your relationship with Ms. Freddie?"

"We had no relationship of which to speak. She was a judge, after all, and I'm merely a private criminal defense attorney doing my best to keep my business afloat." He rattled the box that was now brimming with paperwork.

Oh, boy. He was going to play dumb, but I was ready.

"Let me rephrase the question. What was your relationship to the weapon that killed Ms. Freddie?"

"What on earth are you—"

"I saw you pick up the tie Mr. Stevenson left on the judge's desk when you all stepped down from the bench for plea negotiations. The police are saying that's the murder weapon. I know you never gave the tie back to Stevenson. He told me so before he died. What did you do with it?"

The red-faced tirade he almost flew into melted into a twisted look of innocence, complete with wide eyes and sagging lips. He must have realized I was on a fishing expedition and he'd almost fallen for the bait. He abandoned the files, came around to the front of his desk, and rested his rear on the edge so we were only a couple of feet apart. He peered down his nose at me.

I refused to squirm.

"You are speaking out of turn. If you are trying to accuse me of something, you have severely underestimated with whom you are dealing."

I dealt him my first ace. "Did you give the tie to someone? Maybe Maggie? I know you met with her in the jury room during recess."

Harriston swallowed a couple times and blinked rapidly. His wrinkled features formed a tight mass, but I wasn't sure if it was because he was hiding something or because he was pissed I didn't back down. "Now you're just firing blanks into the dark. Maggie and I were discussing her new job here at my practice."

Yeah, right. "And as for the tie?"

"I don't know what happened to the tie. I had it in my hand one moment, and it was gone the next. I probably left it sitting on one of the counsels' tables when I reached in my pocket to pull out business cards. Once we started our plea negotiations, anyone could have grabbed it. I only bothered to pick up the tie as a courtesy."

"Then why not hand it right back to Mr. Stevenson?"

"Good gracious, child. I don't have time for this." He stepped behind his desk, grabbed his coat, and gripped the handle of the cart. "If I'd known you were coming in here to implicate my involvement in something I obviously played no part in, I never would have let you—"

"I heard what you said to Stevenson during the recess. You made it sound like you knew the judge's life was in jeopardy."

"Jeopardy? Please. Judge Wannamaker and I have a history that you can never—or will never—understand. Anything I might have said about that woman was surely routine."

He wheeled his cart out of the office toward the deserted reception room and motioned for me to follow. I stood, but I couldn't leave until I'd obtained at least one straight answer. I loitered in the archway between the two spaces.

I had to push him. "Earlier, you said you and Judge Wannamaker didn't have a relationship. Now you're saying the two of you have a history. I'm confused. Maybe I should have a talk with Russell Wannamaker. He could clear this up. I swear I heard him mention you and his wife were once up for the same judgeship."

Harriston stopped mid-stride. His back curved like a cat splashed with water. He released the handle of his cart and slowly turned to face me. The quiver of his jowls let me know he wasn't pleased about being on the wrong side of a Q&A, but he made the vocal effort to remain calm.

His words were soft but deliberate. "Did he bother to tell you I attended Cornell Law School? Did he tell you my ancestors have lived in this county for centuries and my family holds three generations of senators? No way on God's green Earth that woman should have beaten me out. Downright Machiavellian of the governor to put us in that position. Everyone knew she'd just joined my practice as a partner. That alone raised her profile when most people wouldn't have known who she was. She didn't have half my win record. That appointment should have been mine. So, when I said Judge Wannamaker and I didn't have a relationship, I meant it."

We stood, staring at each other from across the vacant reception area. No way was I leaving now.

"Sounds like you're still holding a grudge." I crossed my arms and tilted my head. "Russell Wannamaker says you've spent years trying to undermine his wife."

"Are those supposed to be questions? Are you trying to intimidate me by suggesting I had motive to do her harm?" He laughed and slipped on his coat, pulling out a pair of keys in the process. "Let me tell you something, little girl. If anyone here is guilty of threats, it's Russell Wannamaker. He's come in here over the years throwing his weight around—trying to intimidate me by using that DelaCorp sham to threaten my business and buy out the building. Of course he'd lead you to believe I had something to do with her murder. He'd love to see me take the blame."

"DelaCorp?" I repeated. "Mr. Russell said he didn't

have anything to do with the commercial real estate dealings—"

"*Mr. Russell said, Mr. Russell said.*" He mocked my words in discordant nasal tones, the act of which rattled my confidence and slowed my attack. "You sound ridiculous, Victoria. Think for yourself. Don't let that man fool you. He was behind the sale of my building to DelaCorp. Took me a while to figure out why the management company was so quick to put this place up for sale. Russell Wannamaker has an agenda, and I have the paper trail to prove it."

"But that still doesn't—"

Harriston didn't stick around to let me finish. He ripped open the door and stepped outside onto The Quad. I debated the idea of staying put when I heard him bellow.

"I've got to get to court. Come out, or I'll have you arrested for trespassing and disturbing the peace. I've had enough games for one day."

With my head held high, I stepped into the cold and onto the busy sidewalk. Harriston locked the door without acknowledging my presence and rounded The Quad toward the courthouse. As I watched his back moving through the crowd, a fire welled in my stomach. He couldn't get away with ignoring the issue. I raced after him.

"I know you're up to something, Harriston," I panted when I'd reached his side. "I don't believe the Wannamakers would harass you if you weren't harassing them first. Whatever you're into needs to stop. Innocent people are getting hurt. Did you know Chance—another one of your unsavory clients—attacked me yesterday? He and Phyllis Dodd threw me into a dumpster. Don't you think it's a little odd that his wife weasels her way out of a drug conviction and now he's running around with the state chemist who was supposed to testify in her case?"

At that point, Harriston stopped and turned on me so quickly the trio of parking enforcement officers walking behind him had to stop short. One of them even muttered a few curses at Harriston's expense. The old attorney, constantly aware of his public image, smiled at the women and inclined his head in polite regret. Once they'd passed, he glared at me and cut a hand through the air in a sharp hacking motion that signaled for me to shut up and get lost.

I ignored him. Emboldened by the safety of having witnesses to any possible malice, my words bubbled over.

"If you or your clients had something to do with that drug switch or the judge's murder, I am going to find out about it. Corporal North already told me Chance has been dealing drugs for years. And despite that pious sob story you're pedaling, I know you think you have a chance to replace Ms. Freddie now that she's gone. Just don't be surprised if whatever you and your clients are hiding blows up in your face."

"Listen to me, young lady." He pointed a fat finger at my nose. "I understand you've now had—shall we say—challenging encounters with two of my clients, and I sympathize with your predicament. However, I rebuke your attempts to put them on trial through innuendo and conjecture. Your allegations about drug tampering and distribution are scurrilous. Have you ever seen Chance or Langley sell drugs? Talk about drugs? Do drugs? You'd do best to check your sources."

He took a step to depart but stopped and leaned down to whisper a cryptic message in my ear. "Everyone is innocent until proven guilty, including me. Don't be so quick to suggest I'm part of some grand conspiracy just because I do not care for your Judge Wannamaker. No matter what you think of me. I'm not the only person with skeletons in their closet. Maybe you should look a little closer at some of your so-called friends."

With that, he swaggered toward the courthouse and left me adrift in a sea of suspicion.

Three scones, two laps around The Quad, and one cell phone purchase later, I walked into the sterile marble lobby of the industrial complex where *The Bugle* and several other news outlets lived. The goal was to gain access to *The Bugle's* sole investigative reporter, Mike Slocum, and share my concerns about Ms. Freddie's and Mr. Stevenson's deaths.

I'd Googled Mike the moment I got my replacement phone and found he was an even-handed journalist who seemed ahead of the curve when it came to the dirty dealings in Bickerton. More importantly, he had no personal ties to the deceased and no obvious motive that would keep him from hearing me out. After the one-sided conversation with Harriston earlier that morning, a civil exchange of facts was what I craved.

I approached the information kiosk in the center of the lobby and found the same amber-haired receptionist I'd encountered on my visit with Ashton. The hour was too early for lunch, but she gazed at her computer with the same steely concentration she'd given her cheese curls throughout my last visit.

I leaned across the counter to get her attention. She didn't look up.

"Excuse me, miss," I said to the crown of her head. "My name is Victoria Justice. I'm here to see Mike Slocum. I have some information I'd like to share."

"Tip line's over there." She raised a hefty arm to point at a white phone on the wall by the restrooms. "If you want to talk to Mr. Slocum, dial star eight two five five." Her voice was so flat, I wondered if she was animatronic. "If he likes your story, he'll come down."

I followed her instructions and found myself on the phone with the reporter.

"Hello. Mr. Slocum? My name is Victoria Justice, and I'd like to talk to you about—"

"Why does that name sound familiar?"

"Well, we met the other day when I dropped off the Langley Mulligan trial transcript, and my mother just got elected mayor so you might have seen me at—"

"No, no. Well, yes and yes, but you're the one...aw, man, I could kick myself for not recognizing your name when you came by before." His voice pitched upward in excitement. "You're the one from Tuesday morning—from when we were trying to set up interviews outside the courthouse. You're the woman the crowd wrangler told us about. You discovered the murdered judge, right?"

"That's correct." The words tasted bitter on my tongue, and I hated him asking the question as if it were a celebrated mark of distinction—though I hoped the recognition garnered me a receptive audience.

"Tell the receptionist I'm letting you up. Take the elevator to the third floor. I'll be there when you arrive."

I did what I was told.

"What's on your mind, Ms. Justice?" Mike said as the elevator slid open to reveal his gangly form.

"I'd like to share some information about the deaths of Judge Wannamaker and DAG Stevenson. The festival may have been a setup—"

"Ha. That's the word of the day. Everybody in town's been calling and claiming they saw strange things during the festival."

"What kind of strange things?"

"Not so fast. You're on my time. I get to ask the questions." He stayed polite, but his raspy voice was firm. "Now, I love a good tall tale, but why come to me? Why not go to the police?"

"I've already talked to the police. I told them I think the deaths are related and Stevenson was murdered too, but the detective in charge won't listen."

He breathed heavily for several heartbeats. When I'd almost given up on a reply, he cleared his throat. "What makes you think Stevenson was murdered?"

I stepped away from the elevator, deeper into the cramped waiting room of *The Bugle*, but he placed a sinewy arm in my path as if to suggest I couldn't go farther until I'd earned the right.

"Stevenson's suicide letter confesses to the judge's murder," I stammered, "but I think it's all a cover-up for the real killer—well, I guess I should start by saying, there is a suicide letter, and I read it. I don't know if the police have released that information yet but—"

"Yeah, yeah. We already know about the note and the confession." He stood firm but used his hands to wave away my words. "Some city councilman is running his mouth all over town about finding it. He even managed to snap a picture on his cell. WSYS will beat us to press on that with their noon broadcast, but we got the scoop. The info is already up on our website. What else you got?"

I told him my theory about Stevenson's signature, showed him the PDF of the receipt from Cake & Kettle, and explained the real killer may very well be one of the people in court at the time of Langley Mulligan's trial.

With that, Mike led me to his cubicle.

"Sorry to break it you," he said over his shoulder as he rounded the grungy tabletop that was his desk. "The Wannamaker investigation is basically closed."

"What? Seriously? If that's true, why did you put me through—"

"I wanted to hear your story. Helps to verify my other sources. Don't take it personally. Sit down."

I plopped into the canvas chair wedged between his desk and the padded wall of his miniscule workspace. Ringing telephones and the voices of other reporters clamored from all directions.

"Wannamaker's official cause of death," he sorted through the papers on his desk, "murder via traumatic asphyxia caused by aggressive thoracic compression. The cops are following through with the idea that Stevenson killed the judge and hung himself. The way I hear it, he's the only solid lead they had."

"If the details of the suicide letter are hitting the street, everyone in town is going to know about the confession. They're going to think it's real."

"Maybe it is. The bathroom where they found Judge Wannamaker held no fingerprints. All they found was some suspicious talc, which could have come from latex gloves used by the killer. And word is, surveillance footage puts Stevenson near the murder." Mike opened his laptop. "But then again, maybe the note is a hoax.

Without any witnesses to the murder itself, the killer could be anyone."

"That's exactly my point," I said. "Especially since, as far as the cops know, Beau Harriston was the last person seen with the murder weapon and at least three other people were near the crime scene. Shouldn't that be enough to keep the investigation open?"

"Maybe. But when a government official is murdered, a quick confession trumps all that." Mike's boyishly round face crumpled into a series of distressed grooves. "Of course, the cops can't make the official declaration about Stevenson's suicide or his role as the killer until they receive a complete autopsy to rule out foul play."

Mike stopped to type a few commands on his keyboard. "My source at the ME's office says results are still pending, but initial findings indicate Stevenson's neck as the sole point of trauma. No scratches. No defensive or offensive marks. It could be just a matter of days before the cops close both cases."

"In other words, I just wasted ten minutes of your time?" My voice was so small I surprised myself.

"Nah. I wouldn't have let you up here if I didn't agree with you on a gut level. With the suicide note in circulation, I think your side of the story might be worth exploring. I mean, a confession that gets the judge's murder solved in the most public way possible—before an investigation can really even begin? All of it comes off as a little too convenient, if you know what I mean." He leaned back. "Talk to me about what else you think you know, and I'll decide what's worth following up on."

"I'm happy to share." I clasped my hands. "But the

signature and a brief conversation with Stevenson before his death are all I have, and I don't—" I thought about my run-ins with Langley and Chance. "I don't want to be accused of making stuff up. I've already had enough trouble this week."

"Don't worry. You're an anonymous source. We'll stick with the facts. With a little more investigation, I'll ask my editor if he'd consider this for print with the slant that maybe..." He narrowed his dark eyes and the ebony skin around them crinkled, "...the state police are rushing through both investigations because of the political ties and the public display."

That sounded reasonable to me. Definitely the conclusion I'd come to thus far.

"I'm curious though," he grinned wide like a hungry cartoon shark, "just between you and me, if Stevenson isn't the killer, then who? Talk me through the players. What's the angle?"

I considered the events of the last three days: the missing drugs, Ms. Freddie's body on the bathroom floor, Maggie's cynicism about the murder, Ashton's obsession with Chance, Phyllis's questionable alliances, the Mulligans' duplicity, Harriston's evasiveness, and the hours I'd spent the night before poring through audio. A long, exasperated breath escaped my lips.

"That depends. How much time have you got?"

TWENTY-SIX

AFTER SPENDING PART of the morning and most of the afternoon swapping theories with Mike Slocum, I walked into the house around 4:00 and found my mother on the sectional in the family room. Logs crackled in the fireplace, and the savory aroma of pot roast wafted through the air. Piles of pictures and old photo albums covered the coffee table and the carpet around her feet.

I sat beside her and picked up a tattered black-and-white photograph. Teenaged versions of Ma and Ms. Freddie smiled out at me. They posed cheek-to-cheek with their arms around each other. Both women held a sheet of paper toward the camera with their free hand.

"That was the day we both found out we'd been accepted to Howard University. First in our families to go to college, and we got to do it together." Her voice tapered off, and tears lodged in the lines of her sienna skin. "This is the longest we've been apart in almost forty years."

I studied the picture. Their big brown eyes brimmed with hope and anticipation, futures stretched out before them. Now, a tragedy had separated them forever. One look at the camaraderie between them made me realize what I had to do. I had to tell Ma the truth—or at least what I believed to be the truth about her friend's killer.

"Ma," I didn't dare look up from the picture, "I don't

know if you've been watching the news today, but there have been some developments—"

"I know, Angel. I heard about Stevenson's suicide note…and the confession." She tilted her head toward the dormant television above the mantel. "That's all they can talk about. As if the murder itself wasn't enough… now this scandal. And the police are refusing to comment. It's like everyone's forgotten a woman's life and legacy lies at the heart of all this."

"I haven't forgotten." I put down the picture and grasped her hand. "Ma, nobody expected things to end like this, but I want you to know I don't think Stevenson killed—"

"No. Don't." She snatched her hand away. "I can't talk about that right now. We have the funeral in a couple of days. I'd rather focus on Freddie." She reached for the picture I'd set aside. "Russell asked me to put together a slide show for the wake. I may be biased, but I think this one is perfect. Help me pick out a few more, would you?"

"Sure thing." I reached over and wiped a tear from her chin.

"Oh, I love this one." She plucked a faded color photo of Ms. Freddie and Mr. Russell wearing Panama hats and boarding a massive ship from the folds of an old high school yearbook piled atop the clutter. "A bunch of us went on a Caribbean cruise for their twentieth wedding anniversary. My gosh, the two of them were quite the pair. They met when she was in law school— I'd come back here to teach by then, but he was all she could write about. She couldn't wait to bring him home to meet everyone. And when they finally came to town, he proposed. Swore he'd follow her to the ends of the earth."

She turned away from me, perhaps hiding newly formed tears.

"They've had their ups and downs," she sniffled, "but he'd still do anything for her."

"How's he doing?" My hand rested on her knee.

"Not so good." She picked up a thick, red album. "I couldn't get him on the phone this morning, so I went over and let myself in with the spare key. He was sitting at the kitchen table staring out the window with the phone in his hand. I could hear the dial tone from the front door. Come to find out Grace had just called and told him the police had taken down the crime scene tape, and he could go pick up what he wanted from Freddie's office. I guess the thought of going through personal items just broke him. God knows the only thing she loved more than him was her work."

"Gosh, that's awful. You know, he said the same thing when I caught him moping outside of Cooper's during your victory party."

"Oh, really?" She frowned and slid three photos from the album's plastic pages. "Well, I'm glad you were there to talk him through the rough patch. Did you tell him about that recommendation letter she left you? I bet he'd love a chance to read it. Seeing something she wrote might stir some fond memories."

"No. I forgot, but I guess I should have." My skin prickled as I recalled the conversation. "We mostly talked about Harriston and his rivalry with Ms. Freddie. Mr. Russell seems to think Harriston has something to do with his wife's death, and I agree, despite what the news says."

"I told you, now is not the time to talk about that." She closed the album with a thud, and her expression turned to frost. "We need to focus on Freddie—on trying to preserve her memory."

"That's what I'm doing, Ma." My voice cracked as part of a tacit plea for her to stay calm. "I'm just talking through it, trying to make sense of it. Hasn't Mr. Russell mentioned any of his suspicions to you?"

"No…" Her gaze avoided mine. She leaned over and put the album back on the table. "But he didn't have to after I witnessed Harriston make a fool of himself at the candidates' luncheon yesterday. I don't know how that man managed to get in there, but he practically kissed the governor's ring and washed the man's feet. Jesus himself couldn't have gotten a better reception. I always knew Harriston wanted Freddie's job, but I never imagined how far he'd stoop."

"I did, and I went to talk to him about it today."

"You *what*?" She straightened and looked over at me, her eyes wide. "You went to Harriston's office? You shouldn't have done that. Stirring the pot is not going to change—"

"Ma, please, relax. Nothing happened. He wouldn't talk to me. He spent half the time accusing Mr. Russell of harassing him and the other half bringing up his pedigree. He basically implied Ms. Freddie's appointment was due to her gender and the color of her skin."

Ma closed her eyes for a moment. When her voice emerged, the words were slow and low. "There's a reason Freddie was the only female Superior Court judge of color this state has ever seen, and it had nothing to do with affirmative action. Harriston may be from old stock, but Freddie put in the work."

Ma reached down to shuffle through the photos piled around her feet and pulled out a large newspaper clipping. She thrust the page toward me. "Read her obituary There's stuff in there that even I didn't know."

I took the paper and scanned its contents. The article consumed most of the page and had a photo insert of Ms. Freddie wearing her black judge's robe, with her dark hair pulled back in a tight bun. Her signature pearls rested peacefully along her neckline, and her patented iron stare completed the image of the woman I remembered.

"Freddie has always been the first at everything," Ma said. "First in her college class, first in her law school class, first woman to preside over the Delaware Bar Association—did you know she's licensed to practice in three states? She taught legal terminology at Del State, ethics at U Del, contributed essays to several books on the legal profession, and that's just what I can remember. Freddie is the one whose last name should have been 'justice.'"

I grinned at that, and the moment of levity erased the tension between us.

Ma sat back and pulled me toward her so my head rested on her shoulder. "Let it lie, Angel. I know in your eyes Harriston disrespected Freddie, but leave it alone. Harriston isn't worth the trouble. Let the authorities do their job."

"But what if his involvement is more significant than we think?"

She tugged at a strand of hair and wound it around her finger. I sensed her debating whether to use her motherly authority to shut down the conversation or give in to my concerns.

"Let the authorities do their job. If Harriston played a role in any of this, his ego will sink him in due time."

I lifted my head, ready to pounce on her comment, but she quieted me with a squeeze of my shoulders.

"Trust me," she said. "His ego got the best of him the last time he tried to screw Freddie over. Back in the day, she was the only prosecutor who could shut him down, so he did his best to avoid her—couldn't afford to have her destroy his precious win-loss record. When that didn't work, he wooed her to join his firm. In his efforts to avoid going up against the best, he played himself. Within a year, Freddie's judicial nomination was front-page news. And as the saying goes, 'You reap what you sow.'"

TWENTY-SEVEN

I WOKE UP early the next morning, too fidgety to sleep late and take advantage of my time off. The previous day's heart-to-heart with my mother only managed to make me more distrustful of Harriston and the suspicious circumstances surrounding Ms. Freddie's murder.

My main concern, however, was I'd made it to Friday, the day Grace agreed to go over the surveillance footage. We planned to meet at 5:00 that evening—after hours for the courthouse—but I intentionally arrived twenty minutes late to avoid running into any coworkers who'd undoubtedly have questions or condolences regarding my role as a prominent figure in the week's tragic events.

When I reached the bailiffs' suite, I extended my arm to knock, only to miss my target as Grace ripped open the door.

"Where the heck have you been?" She hustled me inside. "Get the lead out. I don't want to explain to folks why you're hanging around here so late. Nobody needs to know I'm giving you access to this stuff."

I followed Grace through the maze of desks that occupied the outer reaches of the office. The bailiffs, like the court reporters, shared a space, but since there were six of them and only three of us, their office was twice as big and three-times as plush. Grace was the head bailiff, as well as the courthouse's chief security officer, so she had a genuine office space all to herself at the back of the suite—replete with glass windows that overlooked the bullpen where the other bailiffs toiled. The whole setup reminded me of the squad rooms I'd seen on *NYPD Blue*.

"Let me get out of this uniform, then we'll set you up." She crossed through the doorframe to her inner sanctum.

Part workspace and part command center, Grace's office was a juxtaposition of two worlds. On one side, she struggled to contain an explosion of printouts and paperwork. On the other, she ruled over a console with monitoring equipment that loomed menacingly along the wall. I sat in a wooden chair on the border between realms, peeled off my coat, and mentally ticked through the list of the footage I hoped to review.

Meanwhile, Grace reached for the duffle bag that hung from a hook behind her door. The movement revealed a second slightly more casual bailiff uniform that someone had placed on a hanger and covered in plastic.

"Uh, short-sleeved duds are the typical evening attire for ambitious yet fashion-forward bailiffs on the go?"

"Oh yes, girl, so comfortable," she said in a vampish voice as she played along. "You know the state spares no expense and uses only the finest polyesters this side of the nineteen seventies."

We both doubled over with laughter, and the tension of my tardiness melted away.

"Geez, don't even get me started," Grace said in her normal voice. "That hot mess is our summer get-up, and this little number is what we wear the rest of the year."

She twirled like a runway model so I could get the

full effect of the long-sleeved white shirt and basic black tie that hung on her athletic forty-something frame.

"I just got a bunch of that stuff back from the company that cleans everything for us." She set her duffle on the desk and rummaged through it. "What's the plan for tonight, and why so urgent?"

While Grace methodically removed the gun, radio, mace, Taser, and handcuffs from her duty belt, I outlined the events of the previous forty-eight hours. I told her about the encounter with Chance and Phyllis in the alley behind Cake & Kettle, described the recent confrontation with Harriston, and explained my mistrust of Ashton based on the revelations from the audio and his apparent willingness to lie for his own gain. Then we discussed how it all related to what I hoped to see on the tape.

"Basically, you want to figure out who in that group had the greatest access to the judge before she died." Grace unbuttoned her uniform top to reveal a white T-shirt underneath.

"Exactly. I also need to know what happened to the murder weapon. Harriston claims he set it down somewhere, but I have my doubts. Also, Ashton—"

"You keep calling him by his first name. How close did you guys get over the last few days?"

I shook my head and let a thick curtain of tendrils mask my embarrassment. The corporal had grown on me more than I cared to admit, but I hadn't spoken to him since reviewing the transcript. "Do we really have time for that?" I whined. "I thought I had to 'get the lead out.' What happened to all that hustle you greeted me with at the door?"

Grace responded to my defensiveness with the sly cluck of her tongue.

I ignored her mocking. "*Corporal* Ashton North never made it clear what he did after he stepped down from the jury box. He said he went looking for Phyllis, but that could mean anything, now that we know she's somehow entangled with the Mulligans."

"Well, we know Phyllis went back to chambers with me at the top of the recess so that should be pretty easy to find on the video." Grace pulled a set of keys and a pair of rubber gloves from the pocket of her polyester pants, which she slid off and replaced with a baggy pair of mom jeans. "Tracking North once he leaves the courtroom may be more difficult if he didn't give you his whereabouts, but it's all doable. Let's get to it."

She plopped into a rolling chair and wheeled herself over to the monitoring console, where eight tiny televisions sat stacked on top of each other. From her vantage point, she could see into each of the courtrooms, the lobby and other public areas, the hallways and offices throughout the personnel unit, and the parking lot. Each of the monitors rotated through a series of images—some of them too quickly for me to process. Grace typed a series of passwords into a computer I assumed linked up with the system.

"Keep your eyes on the computer monitor." She beckoned me to draw my chair closer. "Don't worry about the TVs. Those are live. Remember, we've got no sound here, so watch carefully. I'm going to pull up footage from Monday." She clicked open files. "The copy I made for Detective Daniels contained all the courtroom and personnel footage before, during, and after the time of the murder. But I imagine you want to stick with what happened during the trial recess, right?"

"Not necessarily. I'm willing to go where the trail leads us."

"Okay." She rolled her chair backward and grabbed a stack of papers from her desk. "These keycard time-stamps might help. We can get a clear line on where most of the employees were during the murder—although, I suppose someone could have loaned out their keycard, effectively rendering the readouts inaccurate." She froze for a moment and chuckled. "Which reminds me, even though Maggie's out of here in a couple of days to take that job with Old Beau, I modified her key-card to the lowest possible access. I wish I could have seen her face when she discovered the change."

After we indulged in a little merriment at Maggie's expense, Grace fired up the system and searched for the moments prior to recess.

"Try looking for the sidebar when we were all up on the bench," I said. "That's probably somewhere around eleven a.m."

Grace zipped through a kaleidoscope of images.

"There!" I pointed at the center of the monitor as she slowed to the 11:19 a.m. timestamp.

The image showed a distant but distinct image of Stevenson slapping his striped indigo tie down onto Wannamaker's desk.

"Can you click ahead thirty seconds or so?" I asked.

She complied. The footage showed Harriston pick up the tie and stuff it into his right-side suit jacket pocket as he walked toward the counsel's table, where Stevenson sulked. Seconds prior to arriving at his destination, Grace collided with him. She'd been standing against the wall near defense counsel's table during the side-bar, but she crossed into Harriston's path on her way toward the bench.

They appeared to exchange words. She attempted to walk away, but he motioned her back. She seemed nervous or upset at his gesture because she tugged at the cuff of her sleeves and was slow to return. He reached into his breast pocket and gave her a business card. Then he moved over to the prosecutor's table with Stevenson as she headed in the opposite direction.

I turned to Grace. "What happened there? When we talked about this at Cooper's, you said he was rude and rammed into you. Looks like you crashed into him."

"I guess I was a little thrown off." She ran a hand across her brow. "That man gives me the creeps. Nothing he says seems genuine, and he's intent on stirring up trouble wherever he goes."

I couldn't argue with her there. "Well, can you change angles or get closer? I want to watch for the tie."

"Closer? No, but…." Grace hit some keys, and the computer opened a second video window beside the first—the original angle from Harriston's front, and a second angle at his back.

"He definitely still has the tie in his pocket," Grace said.

From the rear angle, we could see that when Harriston reached the prosecutor table, he once again put his right hand into the side pocket where he'd stored the tie.

"Keep continuous play on both angles," I said, "but slow it down if you can. I want to make sure we see what happens when Harriston removes his hand from that pocket."

She did what I asked, and the images ticked by at a

slug's pace for over fifteen minutes. I didn't dare take my gaze away from the screen. As the two men wrapped up their conversation, Harriston shifted his posture to shake palms with Stevenson, but his hand came out of the jacket completely empty.

No tie.

"I knew it. I knew it. He never gave it back to Stevenson." I drummed my hands on the wooden surface of the console to celebrate my minor victory. "Yesterday, he told me he probably put the tie on one of the counsel's tables, but he didn't. He must still have it there." My voice became squeaky with excitement.

"Or he gave it away to someone else later on," Grace said.

"What's that supposed to mean?" My excitement curdled. "I thought you said he was up to something."

"Of course he is. But let's get real. That doesn't prove anything. Who's to say Stevenson didn't ask for his tie back later then kill the judge just like everybody's been saying? That's all I'm getting at."

"Are you seriously considering—" I let it go. I couldn't afford to get into an argument when I was relying on her to run the show. "Can we at least stay here until Harriston leaves the courtroom? I want to see how far this thing goes."

"If you insist, but I don't have all night." She reset the video to normal speed and returned to a single angle so we had one large view of the courtroom.

I kept a sharp eye on Harriston, but I also noted the order people left the courtroom in so I could string that info together with what allegedly unfolded in the other areas of the courthouse.

While Harriston finished his plea negotiations with

Stevenson, Grace and Phyllis left through the judges'
door at the front of the courtroom to speak with Wannamaker in chambers.

No tie.

Harriston then walked the few feet to defense counsel's table and leaned over the edge to speak with his
client while Stevenson spoke with Maggie. Grace reentered the courtroom through the judges' door. She
released the jurors from the jury room and left with
them out the main doors.

No tie.

A few minutes after that, Corporal North stood up
from the witness stand to leave the courtroom. He
slowed as he reached defense counsel's table and put
on his campaign hat. As North did so, Harriston took
a seat beside his client.

No tie.

Not long after North departed, Maggie and Stevenson followed the corporal's path. They exited through
the main doors at the rear of the courtroom to go check
the evidence closet and have coffee at Maggie's desk.
Harriston still sat at counsel's table with his client.

No tie.

At that point, only three people remained in the
courtroom—Harriston, Langley, and me. Through gritted teeth, I watched the confrontation with Langley un-
fold while Harriston stood by. The video version of me
fled out the judges' door at the front of the courtroom.
A few beats later, Langley vanished through the side
door to holding, courtesy of a few beefy guards.

No tie.

For a moment, Harriston stood alone in the center of
the courtroom. The empty counsels' tables, jury box,

and judge's bench surrounded him like a silent set of witnesses. Grace and I crouched forward in our seats, our noses less than a foot from her computer monitor. But before Harriston moved from the spot, Maggie's buxom figure sashayed into the space. Within a few minutes, the pair escaped into the jury room.

So did our chances of finding the tie.

I grabbed the arm Grace used to control the mouse. "Can we see in there where they went? Is there surveillance?"

"No cameras in the jury room." Grace pursed her lips and gave me a schoolmarmish look that highlighted my folly.

Of course not. In my excitement, I'd forgotten the sanctity of jury deliberations made it immoral and unlawful for the courthouse to have cameras in the jury room.

Grace moved the mouse to click closed the browser window containing the video.

"No. Wait," I pleaded. "I want to see how long they're in there. Is there any way they could have left the jury room without being spotted by the cameras?"

"No. They'd have to come out the way they went in, and the cameras in the courtroom are the best coverage in the building. You want me to scroll through until we see them?"

"Do it."

The counter increased by eight minutes before a figure appeared on the screen.

"Is that them?" I asked.

"No." Grace slowed the footage. "That's me doing a sweep of the courtroom, not too long after I got back from throwing Dodd, North, and Stevenson out of the kitchen on a noise complaint."

We watched her roam through the galley and up to the jury box where she straightened chairs until something caused her to stop. She reached for the walkie-talkie mic attached to the shoulder of her short-sleeve shirt.

"I got a distress call from one of the clerks about a second disturbance in the kitchen," she said. "This time screams—"

"Screams coming from me," I whispered.

My mind receded from the room and latched onto the gruesome image of the purple tie twisted around Ms. Freddie's neck. Her double strand of pearls broken and strewn across her lifeless form.

"Are you still with me?" Grace gripped my shoulder and forced me to meet her eyes. "They were in the jury room a little over thirteen minutes. I think you need to let this go. Harriston couldn't have committed the murder. He never left the courtroom, and they didn't come out of the jury room until after the body was discovered."

I pushed my chair away from the console and stood. The room had grown hot—tight.

I needed to get my bearings.

Breathe.

Gather my thoughts.

I gripped the back of the chair and closed my eyes but still felt Grace watching me.

The pressure of the revelation pressed down on me. We'd both seen Harriston with the tie. Where had it gone? How did it get into the personnel area if Harriston never left the courtroom? And if Harriston and Maggie didn't have a hand in its transport, the only suspects left were Phyllis, Ashton, and…Stevenson.

Had I been wrong about this whole thing? Was it really possible Stevenson murdered the judge and killed himself?

"Hey, Victoria. I think we should stop here. Call it a night."

"No." I opened my eyes and swallowed the emotion that had settled at the back of my throat. "If this is how things are going to play out, I want to see it all. Take me back. Let's go through the steps." I pointed at the keycard log she'd left on the console between us. "Pinpoint Ms. Freddie's location. I want to see everywhere she went during the recess up until the moment of her death."

I sat back down and braced myself for what we would find.

TWENTY-EIGHT

THE KEYCARD LOG revealed that Ms. Freddie swiped out of the courtroom at 11:27 a.m. With a few clicks of the mouse, we glimpsed the back of her black robe moving down the judges' private hallway toward chambers. She used her pass to gain entry to the secluded office suite and dropped out of sight.

Grace consulted her spreadsheet and fast-forwarded the video ten minutes to the point of the judge's next card swipe. Soon, we observed Judge Wannamaker emerge from chambers with Phyllis right behind her.

"Wait a second." I placed a hand on Grace's arm and cued her to pause the video. "That's it. That's all you've got?"

"Yeah. We're not going to be able to see much because we don't have cameras in chambers—just like there aren't cameras in here or the jury room—you know, for ethical reasons. And, before you ask, we don't have cameras in the kitchen either. That one is a matter of employee privacy since that acts as a break room. And obviously, there's no camera footage in the—"

"Bathroom." I finished the sentence for her. I bit the inside of my jaw out of frustration, but I couldn't give up in the face of a few obstacles. I had to keep pushing. If not for me, then for Ma and Ms. Freddie.

"If Phyllis is with Ms. Freddie," I placed a finger on

the screen, "that means we're past the point where you took Phyllis back to chambers."

"Right. Wannamaker didn't want me hanging around. She sent me to dismiss the jury. I did notice, though, before I left, they seemed to know each other—outside of work, I mean. Their greetings were informal, familiar."

"Hmm. Yeah. Phyllis mentioned that to me."

Grace scrunched her eyebrows together in a confused expression.

"When I was making my transcript rounds with Ashton, we ran into Phyllis on the street. She mentioned she had a history with Ms. Freddie and that she wasn't a fan. I should have pressed her about it." I placed both hands on my temples. "Okay. Show me the rest."

Grace restarted the video, and we watched as Phyllis and Ms. Freddie traveled along the judges' private corridor from chambers toward the kitchen. The judge was still in her robe, but Phyllis had taken off her gray suit jacket and draped it over her arm. When they reached the kitchen door at the end of the secluded hall, Ms. Freddie pulled out her keycard and swiped the two of them inside.

"Where to next?" Grace consulted her paperwork. "The last keycard timestamp I have for the judge is at eleven forty-three a.m. on the egress side of the personnel area double doors—hold up. That can't be right."

"Maybe it is. I remember Detective Daniels saying Phyllis left the kitchen through the personnel area, which means Ms. Freddie had to swipe her out. Do you have camera views of the kitchen doors on the personnel side?"

"For sure." Grace typed, clicked, and scrolled until we arrived at our target time and location.

Sure enough, the camera captured Phyllis in profile as she stepped backward out of the kitchen, as if deep in conversation with someone still inside. Seconds later, Judge Wannamaker walked out and faced Phyllis. Both women sliced the air with their hands, strained looks on what we could see of their faces. After a couple of minutes, they both turned abruptly and marched toward the camera. Phyllis stepped out of frame while the judge spun around and retreated into the kitchen.

"Pause it." I turned to Grace. "Did you catch that look on Ms. Freddie's face?"

"Yeah." Grace pointed at the monitor. "Right before the judge stepped back into the kitchen, she gave that iron glare she's so good at."

"I'm pretty sure they were arguing. Phyllis half-admitted as much when I ran into her the other day." I wrung my hands. "Can you get a different angle on that hall so we can see more of the double doors? A different vantage point might help us determine what was going on, especially since that's the only door back there that requires a keycard."

Grace went through a set of keyboard commands and conjured up a wide shot of the personnel hall. Based on what we could see, the archway to the criminal clerks' office sat in the middle of our view on the left-hand side, with the kitchen's archway directly across the hall on the right. Our viewpoint ended at the double doors that separated the personnel area from the public lobby of the courthouse.

We replayed the scene with the new angle. This time we could see that when Phyllis attempted to leave through the double doors, the bulky figure of Corporal Ashton North blocked her path as the judge returned to the kitchen.

"How'd he get in the mix?" Grace asked.

"I told you earlier. He went looking for Phyllis. He wanted to confront her about some tampering we found on the drug evidence envelopes. When I first asked him about this, I had a hard time believing this is where he found her. I guess he wasn't lying."

"Do you think the judge was really staring at him?"

"Who knows—"

I didn't get a chance to answer because Maggie came onto the screen. She sashayed out of the clerk's office and down the hall toward the double doors, where Phyllis and Ashton stood. She carried a manila file folder pressed to her bosom and lingered with the duo for several beats.

"What do you think?" Grace's index finger hovered over the scroll wheel of the mouse.

"Relax. If everyone's telling the truth, we should see Stevenson next."

As if on cue, the young attorney burst through the clerk's office archway with a cell phone pressed to his ear. I knew, from my conversation with Maggie, he'd come from her desk. He made a beeline for the kitchen, but I had plenty of time to notice the full suit he'd worn in court was now just a pair of slacks and a dress shirt.

Still no tie in sight.

Stevenson's hunched shoulders suggested anger, and the scarlet hue of his skin confirmed it. He crossed through the doorway to the kitchen, apparently unnoticed by the trio at the end of the hall.

Grace made a tut-tut sound with her tongue when

we'd lost sight of him. "Geez. Without footage for the kitchen, what's our next move?"

"Let's keep track of how long Stevenson and the judge are in there alone. Can't be too long because Ashton said Maggie was being an annoying flirt and he and Phyllis ditched her by going into the kitchen. Let's see if he continues to be a man of his word."

My gaze followed the blink and flash of the time-stamp located at the bottom of the video. As the seconds morphed into minutes, I found myself willing the threesome to move as if their departure for the kitchen would change the inevitable.

As the minutes multiplied, Grace squirmed beside me. I knew what was on her mind even before the gentle nudge of her husky voice broke my focus on the clock.

"This gives Stevenson plenty of time to kill the judge," she whispered.

She was right. Six minutes and thirty-three seconds passed before Ashton and Phyllis joined Stevenson and Ms. Freddie in the kitchen.

I gaped at the video as Maggie exited the double doors and left the hall empty. "Everybody made it sound like it was only a few seconds. Six—nearly seven minutes? Stevenson was in there alone with Ms. Freddie for seven minutes?"

Grace rolled her chair back from the desk and leveled her gaze at me. Her mouth curved downward as if the act of forming words caused her physical pain. "I'm here because I want to help…" her sentence came out slowly, "but I think things are pretty clear—"

"What's clear? That Stevenson's the killer?" I let the shrillness of the question bounce between us and dared her to reply. "You really think he would just walk out of the bathroom after killing the judge and engage in conversation with North and Phyllis as if the murder never happened? That's insidious."

"Who are you kidding?" She titled her head to the side and stared at me like she'd never seen me before. "That's exactly what could have happened...it's the perfect diversion."

"I don't buy it." I couldn't. Not like this. I mentally groped through every conversation I'd had with the young attorney. "Stevenson insisted there was no one in the kitchen when he arrived. We talked about it in his office the day before he died. This can't be right."

"Well, then, he was lying. What else could it be? Because we sure as heck can't see what's going on in there." She sucked her teeth, and the timbre of her voice became grave. "We have to assume the worst—and, based on all the rumors flying around town about Stevenson's confession, this is a safe bet."

I shook my head and hoped it would jar loose some ideas. "What about Phyllis or Ashton? One of them could have committed the crime and had the other cover for—"

"But they arrived *after* Stevenson." She rolled her eyes and let her body go limp in the chair, as if she was tired of pointing out the obvious. "At the very least, he'd still have to be in on the whole thing. In which case, that makes him guilty. Or worse, he witnessed a murder and didn't say anything."

"Maybe that's really what got him killed." I rocked forward on the edge of my seat, not quite sure how else to express the agitation I was feeling. "Maybe they forced him into silence and he couldn't handle the pressure. The only thing we know for sure is they were all in the kitchen with the judge."

As I poured out those final thoughts, Grace's brow furrowed and her eyes grew distant. She never left her chair, but I could tell I'd lost her.

"I don't want to argue with you." She dipped her head toward the computer's clock. "Look, it's quarter to seven. Let's call it quits. The only reason you're pressing this is because you think you owe it to Wannamaker— but this guilt thing isn't your burden to carry. It's the killer's." Her face softened, and she stood. "Give me a second. I'll walk out with you."

Grace trotted off to the restroom located in the outer office. While she was gone, a notion hit me. What if the judge wasn't in the kitchen alone when Stevenson arrived? We'd only watched the side of the kitchen that faced the personnel area. The kitchen also had a door that opened onto the judges' private corridor. Only a limited number of people with high-grade keycards could access that special hall. Hadn't Grace herself suggested someone could have borrowed another person's card to move through the courthouse? If someone accessed the judges' hallway prior to or during the time of the murder, we'd have an additional suspect for our dwindling list.

When Grace returned, I broke it down for her. She didn't seem amused but agreed to check the keycard log and set up the footage.

"Satisfied?" she asked after we'd reviewed several minutes of video that showed nothing but the dingy blue industrial carpet in the judges' hallway.

According to the keycard timestamps, no one used

that door to enter the kitchen prior to Ms. Freddie's arrival and no one used it after she'd entered.

"I won't be satisfied until I get some answers." The room began to swim as my eyes filled with tears.

I rose from my chair. I had to get out. Reconsider my options.

"I need to see the kitchen before I leave—and chambers," I demanded. "Can you get me in there? I must see everything."

"I don't know why you want to torture yourself with this." Grace avoided my gaze.

"Because her life mattered to me."

Why didn't anyone get that? This was no longer about guilt. This was about vengeance.

TWENTY-NINE

EVEN THOUGH I didn't have keycard access, the judges' chambers was a place I visited frequently. Not just to chat with Ms. Freddie, although that happened more than I'd dared to admit, but also to take down the verbatim record during office conferences, to speak with the law clerks and secretaries about filings, and to read back snippets of argument or testimony for the other judges. I'd started my professional training in chambers as an intern and eventually launched my career there when I took my oath as an official court reporter. My heart swelled with pride whenever I walked into that office suite.

But as I walked in with Grace that night, dread gripped my chest like a vise.

The apprehension grew as we cut through the reception area, waded through the secretarial pool, glided past the conference room, and drifted beyond mounds of paperwork toward Ms. Freddie's office at the rear of the judges' private area.

Grace unlatched the dead bolt on Ms. Freddie's door and turned the metal knob.

"Wait." I placed my hand on top of hers. "Give me a few minutes alone, okay?"

Grace stepped aside. "I'll be waiting right out here. Five minutes max and leave the door open."

I agreed and pushed open the office door. It didn't look any different than I remembered, but the stale air of the sealed room reminded me of what was lost. The antique parlor chair behind her hand-carved mahogany Victorian writing table sat empty, and the broad bay window acted as a dramatic backdrop to the desolate scene. Matching end tables with stained glass lamps flanked the delicate desk, and a trio of velveteen wing-back chairs completed the grandeur.

With no time to waste, I slipped into the seat of honor behind her desk and hoped to retrace the moments before her murder. The tabletop looked normal on my initial in-spection, but, upon further perusal, three things stood out.

First, Langley's criminal file was open on the desk. I didn't have time to read everything, but I flipped through each page and scanned the text dotted with several orange Post-it notes. They marked Langley's significant brushes with the law and Ashton's name as the investigating officer. Her detentions were numer-ous, but the actual convictions boiled down to a DUI the year before and the underage drinking charge she received our senior year of high school.

Second, the four framed photographs of friends and family that Ms. Freddie normally kept on display at the front of her desk sat in a jumbled cluster off to the side. The largest picture frame had been placed faced down. When I flipped that one over, I discovered someone had ripped the picture out. Curled edges of torn photo paper were still stuck in the frame. By my count, the miss-ing photo had to be the picture of Mr. Russell. A quick look around confirmed it, I found a dapper picture of him crumpled in the wastebasket.

Third, the yellow notepad by her phone held a mes-sage written in Ms. Freddie's hand that read, *11/3 Yaris—misconduct and complaints of false arrest*. Yaris was the name of the President Judge of the Delaware Superior Court system. During the trial recess, Ms. Freddie had left the bench to seek his advice on the pending fallout from the missing evidence in Langley's case.

I slumped over the desk and rubbed my eyes.

Where did these pieces fit?

"It's getting late." Grace appeared at the door wearing her motorcycle jacket. "We should move to the kitchen if that's still your plan. You can stay in there as long as you want, but I don't feel comfortable letting you hang out here. If one of the judges or their clerks return to do some late-night research, we'll have a lot of explaining to do—and I'm already bending a ton of rules."

"Fair enough." Reluctantly, I stood from behind Ms. Freddie's desk.

Grace locked up. I followed her back through chambers and out along the judges' private corridor that ran behind the courtrooms. The special hall was the fastest route to the kitchen.

As we moved along the stark white passageway, a giant camera eye beamed down on us from the far end of the hall and mocked my lack of productivity. I'd walked into the courthouse thinking I'd leave with some answers—only to realize I wasn't asking the right questions. I glanced at Grace and wondered if she could sense my defeat.

"Thanks for this." I called to her back as she stepped ahead. "I know I asked a lot, and I didn't mean to take advantage. I thought I had it all figured out."

"Don't sweat it. I'm sorry I gave you a hard time. I just don't want to see you get worked up only to be disappointed later."

We stopped at the end of the hall, where one door led to the antechamber of the employees' entrance off the parking lot and the other door led to the kitchen. My card didn't access the judges' special entrance to the kitchen, so Grace swiped hers to unlock it.

She held open the door and used her free arm to pull me into a half hug. "No hard feelings? We're okay, right?"

"We're okay." I pressed my back against the jamb as she finished her farewell.

"I'm going to head out. Be safe, and don't stress." She threw up a hand and moved toward the employees' door.

"Where are you off to? Hot date?"

"Is it still a date if you go straight to dessert?" She clucked her tongue a couple times at that, winked, and let herself out.

When she was gone, I lingered in the doorway of the vacant kitchen, not sure how to approach the task ahead. As morbid as it might have been to request a visit to the crime scene, I needed to see everything in order to piece together Ms. Freddie's final moments.

But as I summoned the courage to close the door and move into the kitchen, something struck me as unusual about the corridor where Grace and I had loitered during our conversation—we'd been standing *underneath* the two pieces of surveillance equipment mounted for the hall.

The cameras in the judges' corridor weren't like the countless dome fixtures discreetly nestled in the ceiling tiles throughout the courthouse. These two cameras were exposed CCTV-type units mounted overhead on a base with a rigid line of sight. One pointed over my shoulder and down the hallway toward chambers. The other hung to my right and pointed at the exit Grace had used to depart.

Where I stood by the kitchen door was a total blind spot.

THIRTY

A BLIND SPOT.

The angle of the area was small but noticeable to the observant. If a person stopped in the right place by the kitchen door, he could enter the judge's hall then disappear from the cameras.

The realization sent prickly flares of anxiety across my skin.

I stumbled into the kitchen and fumbled for my cell phone. I needed to call Grace. Someone could have been hiding in the hall at the time of the murder. Maybe even someone who didn't work in the courthouse.

I leaned against the Formica counter for support and waited for Grace to pick up. My gut clenched at her likely response. She'd undoubtedly dismiss me and claim anyone lurking in the hall would need a keycard to enter or exit the kitchen, which would log his presence and position. And yet, I couldn't take comfort in her confidence or those safeguards. The blind spot opened up too many questions regarding the accuracy of the footage I'd seen. And if someone stole an all-access keycard, that person might have the ability to slip in and out of the courthouse relatively unnoticed.

"What are *you* doing here?" said a voice from behind.

I whirled around to find Maggie emerging from the stunted alcove that led to the unisex bathroom off the kitchen—the one where Ms. Freddie was killed. I gnawed at the inside of my jaw and tasted blood. The scene of the judge's murder was open to public use and that set my teeth on edge.

Maggie ignored my glare and ran a lazy hand over her obnoxious blond bouffant.

I unclenched my jaw and ended the call on my cell. Grace had failed to pick up, but Maggie was a suitable replacement—she certainly had a lot to answer for.

"What am I doing here?" I struggled to maintain a civil volume. "I work here. What are *you* doing here so late? Aren't you supposed to be at Harriston's or something?"

"Believe you me, darlin', I'm more than ready to fade off into the sunset." She walked over to the coffeepot and poured herself a cup. Her lazy southern drawl was silky sweet. "But, I've still got to finish my two weeks."

"What are you working on tonight?" I asked.

"What do you care?" She rolled her eyes and sipped from her mug. "You know, some of us have real jobs that don't give us the luxury of taking a week off." And with that, she sashayed out of the kitchen toward the clerk's office across the hall.

I followed her. "You didn't answer the question."

"Neither did you." She didn't look back.

We reached her impeccably organized workspace, and she settled into her seat as if it were a throne. Her station sat in the center of a vast row of desks, where the clerks normally reigned over the hubbub of phones, faxes, and felony allegations. But in the immense silence of the vacant office, her terse reply sounded like a challenge.

"Come on, Maggs. You put on a good performance, but you can be straight with me. Both of us know you're not the overachieving type. What are you really doing here so late? You working on something for Harriston?"

She ignored my feeble attempt at comradery and slid a thick file from the stack dominating the center of her desk, leaving me standing there awaiting a verdict.

After several ticks of the wall clock had slashed my patience to smithereens, she said, "Isn't your office down the hall?"

"Look," I growled, "I'm going to be honest. I spent the last couple of hours going through surveillance footage with Grace, hoping to wrap my head around what happened to Ms. Freddie. We saw you getting cozy with Harriston during the trial recess. You spent several minutes in the jury room alone with—"

"Worried we were conspiring against you?" She flipped the pages of her file. "He was offering me my new job—"

"Fine, if that's how you want to play it. But don't you think people—like, maybe, those who work for the press—might find it weird that mere minutes before your little clandestine meeting, a bunch of drugs go missing, a trial falls apart, and a judge loses her life?"

She looked up from her work and stared at me through narrowed eyes darkened by thick lines of mascara. "Are you trying to intimidate me?"

"Of course not." I batted my lashes, my voice like honey. She didn't hold the patent for southern charm. "All I'm asking is that we stop playing games. Help me make sense of this."

"Make sense of what?" Maggie's chubby cheeks formed a devilish smile. "You know dang well I've got nothing to do with Wannamaker's death, and I'm tired of you harassing me about it. You need to calm down.

You're making yourself look like a fool. Between finding the judge and being on stage during Stevenson's suicide, don't you think you've hogged enough spotlight for one week?"

"Are you serious? I didn't ask for any of this. I want the truth. You're the one who leaked my name to the press."

"Me? Get off it, Victoria. Stop playing innocent. They already knew you'd be coming in with a security escort. You leaked that fact and everything else because you're desperate to be the center of attention." She rose slowly and leaned over the desk. "First, you have Grace corral that media circus around the courthouse. Then you disappear from work to run around town blaming good people like Mr. Harriston and me. Now you want to play the martyr and the hero. I see you for what you are, and I'm sick of it."

"All right." I bit the inside of my jaw again in a vain effort to stop what came out of my mouth next. "You want to talk about playing the martyr? What about you and this sudden alliance with Harriston? Is he really your boss, or are the two of you more than friends?"

"How did you get so arrogant? Mr. Harriston is a businessman—"

"Or, better yet," an image of Mr. Russell's crumpled photo flashed in my mind, "what about you and Russell Wannamaker? Isn't that the real reason you lost your job in chambers? How long have you been his mistress? Eight? Nine? Ten years?"

The crack of the slap that followed was so loud and fierce that, at first, I didn't realize she'd hit me. All I knew was the room reeled and I staggered. Pain seared through my right eye. My vision exploded into a series of gray dots. I clutched my face and the skin grew hot.

"Let me stop you right there." Her sweet voice turned to poison. And when my sight returned, she stood in front of me, with her chin stuck out in that haughty way a person did when they wanted to show you they had nothing to hide. "Everyone's so quick to give me a bad reputation, but the truth of the matter is I've never lied, and I've owned up to everything I've ever done. I'm not the first cheater this courthouse has seen, so don't be so quick to jump to conclusions—"

Ring! Ring! Ring!

The petulant blare of Maggie's office line cut through her tirade, but neither of us turned to look at the phone.

"I didn't get my job with Mr. Harriston by sleeping around," Maggie shouted over the noise, "and I wouldn't go work for him if I was having an affair with Russell Wannamaker since those two hate each other more than we do."

Without taking her eyes off me, she picked up the screaming telephone. "Hello. No, I'm done here. Just got to get some trash out of my office and I'll be right over."

After Maggie dismissed me from her office, I stood in the deserted parking lot, the shock of the encounter still stinging my face. The only thing that had kept me from retaliating was the nagging awareness that calling her an adulterer had crossed a line. Was her reaction an indicator of innocence or a well-timed red herring?

Regardless, the surveillance footage seemed to put Maggie and Harriston in the clear—except for the question of the tie.

That damn tie.

If Harriston held on to it, how did it migrate to the

bathroom and become a murder weapon? And if he got rid of it or gave it to Maggie, when did he have time to make the switch? He never left the courtroom, and she was hunkered in the jury room with him when the murder took place.

As far as I could tell, the only—living—viable suspects were Phyllis and Ashton, neither of whom appeared to have had any interaction with Harriston or the tie, but both of whom were in the kitchen at the same time as Ms. Freddie and both of whom had reason to want her dead.

In particular, Phyllis. Her unexplained association with the mysterious Chance placed a dark twist on what was already a tenuous relationship with Ms. Freddie. The two women obviously engaged in an argument mere steps away from the crime scene. A crime scene that Phyllis later reentered with Ashton—a man who I now suspected due to his apparent willingness to lie whenever it suited his best interests.

Not to mention, Ashton had his own warped connection with Chance, as well as a personal grievance against Ms. Freddie based on rulings she'd made in his partner's murder case.

Of course, the biggest question of all was what happened in the kitchen when Ms. Freddie was seemingly alone with Stevenson during that seven-minute span? The thought of what could have unfolded made me shiver.

I pulled the collar of my wool coat tighter around my neck. The night had grown frigid, and I'd walked outside without my hat and gloves. I looked at my numbed fingers. They still clasped the keycard I'd used to exit the building. That was when it occurred to me that maybe the *judge's* keycard was the answer.

Before Stevenson died, he'd claimed he never saw the judge in the kitchen. Was it possible Ms. Freddie exited the space before he arrived? After all, there was a blind spot in the judges' hallway where someone would have the perfect opportunity to ambush her without witnesses.

I shook my head and shoved my hands into the pockets of my wool coat. Something about that idea seemed off. The keycard log marked Phyllis's aborted departure through the personnel doors as Ms. Freddie's last card swipe. For an ambush to work, the judge would've needed to use her card one more time to exit the kitchen and move into the judges' hallway. Therefore, whoever killed her had to have already been in the kitchen.

I breathed out a heavy sigh and let it condense into a thick mist that rose and disappeared into the onyx sky above. Since the problem and the chilly temperature had gotten the best of me, I made a dash for the Mustang and slipped inside.

Prior to Ms. Freddie's murder, I'd sat in my car and listened to Stevenson, Ashton, and Phyllis as they argued about the judge. Now, the attorney was dead, the cop was under suspension, and the chemist was without a lab.

As I started the engine, the simplicity of that parallel should have provided all the answers I needed, but I still couldn't bring myself to believe Stevenson could commit murder.

THIRTY-ONE

I WOKE UP Saturday morning to the sound of my mother's scream. She was in the middle of a self-contained rant.

"Where's my white suit? Oh, no. Don't tell me I sent that suit to the cleaners. I can't show up to the church as a Kappa in crème."

Her frustration caused me to poke my head from under the comforter. I checked the time, 8:13 a.m.

Ms. Freddie's funeral wasn't set to start until 11:00 a.m. But based on the various concerns that floated in from the room next door, my mother intended to leave a lot earlier.

Apparently, the Kappa Mu sorority—where Ma served as the local chapter president—had agreed to gather at the church by 9:00 a.m. for the final viewing. They planned to use the extra time to conduct their revered "Kappa Beyond the Veil" ceremony, reserved for sisters who'd passed on.

Before I could duck back under the covers, Ma stepped into the open doorway of my room. Her hair was in a tidy bun and her makeup was immaculate, but she wasn't wearing anything except a bra and a girdle. "Have you seen my white—why aren't you up yet? I thought you were going with me to the church—hold on, I wore that white suit on Election Day, didn't I?"

I slowly sat up against the headboard and shrugged. All hope for sleep was lost.

"Shoot. That means it *is* at the cleaners. And I don't have time to pick it up if I'm supposed to coordinate—" She pursed her lips when she noticed I hadn't moved from the bed. "I hope you showered last night because we need to be out of here in fifteen minutes."

I hadn't showered. In fact, I hadn't intended on going—mainly because I didn't share Ma's eagerness to perpetuate the status quo. To attend the funeral was to accept Ms. Freddie's death, and I couldn't accept her death until I understood why she died. I started to sink back into the recesses of my blanketed hideaway when Ma stepped into the room and yanked the comforter from my bed.

"No moping today. This is a celebration of life, not a reminder of what we've lost. Help me find something to wear."

With the reluctant enthusiasm of the condemned, I climbed out of bed and helped her select an ivory sweater set to replace the missing suit. Fifteen minutes after that, we were both dressed and headed toward the funeral site in Ma's Buick.

I sat in the passenger seat and leaned my head against the window as we entered The Quad. The whole ride should have taken less than five minutes, but we found ourselves at a standstill on Bickerton's roundabout. Cars jammed the roadway. Pedestrians weaved through traffic. Police officers tried to unblock intersections. The town square overflowed with people en route to the viewing, so we parked on the side of the road near the fountain and joined the foot traffic southbound toward Wesdale United Methodist Church.

By the time we squeezed our way into the sanctuary, Ma was fuming again. We were twenty minutes behind schedule and our progress ground to a halt as people leaned in with hugs that transitioned into condolences and morphed into questions about her mayoral bid and the festival tragedy.

"We should have left an hour earlier and been the first ones here." She dodged the massive frame of City Councilman Iverson and made an aggressive lunge toward the front of the church. "I don't know how the sorority expects me to preside over this ceremony and deal with everything else. Do me a favor, Angel. Save three pews for the Kappa Mu's and watch our coats."

I nodded and waded beside her through the stream of overly perfumed bodies. She'd yet to notice I wasn't speaking. My silence, however, wasn't because I was upset with her or because she'd forced me to come. I just wasn't sure how I felt about the authenticity of mourning or even honoring someone in the middle of such a spectacle.

Bass-heavy gospel music flowed through the sound system. Gaudy floral arrangements stuffed with musty red roses lined the aisles, and the photos Ma had selected for the slide show flashed on a widescreen above the altar.

As we approached the front of the sanctuary, I caught a glimpse of Ms. Freddie's pearl-white casket. I was still too far away to see her face, but part of me imagined the iron stare she'd give everyone for making such a fuss over her and her achievements. The work she did for the community was a natural extension of her personality, not a technique for winning friends and spreading her influence.

Thinking of her made me smile, but I couldn't walk up to the casket. I couldn't bring myself to face a lifeless Ms. Freddie yet again. What I wanted more than anything was to remember the passionate woman whose fascination for the law was so infectious it inspired me to change my life. I wanted to tell her how much she meant to me and I was still fighting for her, but all I could do was sag onto the nearest pew and sob.

"Excuse me, everyone. Please, excuse me." My mother stood behind a microphone in the pulpit. "Could we turn off the music, please?" She cleared her throat and the music dropped out. "Thank you. The family appreciates all of you coming out today to pay your respects to The Honorable Frederica Scott Wannamaker. Let me assure you, the viewing will continue right up to the start of the service. But, at this time, we ask everyone who isn't a member of the Kappa Mu sorority to please remain seated for the next five minutes so the members can engage in a special song and prayer to honor our beloved sister."

As people took their seats, the sisters emerged all dressed in white. Some held sprigs of holly. Others held long, white candles. Two by two, they proceeded up the center and along the outer aisles until their presence circled the casket and the perimeter of the sanctuary.

An elderly woman's voice rang out a cappella in a call and response that caused the sisters to sway in unison. I didn't recognize the song that unfolded, but those who did filled the room with joy and praise.

Ma, who'd been singing and swaying in the pulpit, stopped abruptly and stomped her way over to the foot of the casket. At first, I thought she was simply paying her respects, but then I saw her grab the arm of a pale woman with freckles.

The woman, dressed in a tailored white suit, towered over my mother. She resisted when Ma attempted to drag her away from the ceremony toward a door at the side of the room. Not sure what was happening, I stood up for a better look and noticed the willowy female was Phyllis.

With a few nudges and pardons, I climbed over the young couple who'd piled onto the pew next to me and flew down the center aisle just as the two women disappeared into the side door.

When I caught up with them, they stood in the middle of a tiny hallway arguing in hushed tones.

"You had no right to stand up there with us," Ma said.

"You had no right to embarrass me like that," Phyllis replied. "Doesn't the fifteen years I was a member of this sorority count for anything?"

"No. If you want to pay your respects to Freddie, that's understandable. You certainly owe her your career. But do it on your own time, not ours. We made your status perfectly clear when we voted to revoke your membership."

"That was decades ago. I paid my price."

"Ma," I asked, "is everything all right?"

She held up a finger for me to wait. Her voice grew cold as she shook her head at Phyllis. "I don't think you did. Not the price God intended. Freddie put her reputation on the line for you when most people would have let you rot. Don't get indignant because the sorority let you go when she told the membership board the truth. She could have told the whole town and then where would you be?"

Phyllis was silent.

Ma looked over at me and cupped my cheek in her hand. "Everything's fine. Just reminding Ms. Dodd non-members are to remain seated." She cut a sharp look up at Phyllis and stepped toward the door to the sanctuary. "You coming back inside, Angel?"

"No, I—"

Out of the corner of my eye, I caught Phyllis turn and lumber toward the fire exit at the end of the hall. I waved for Ma to move on without me then scurried after the chemist.

"Ms. Dodd, wait."

She didn't respond.

"Phyllis," I called to her back. "I saw you with Chance. You were with him when he threw me into the dumpster."

"You saw *what*?" She paused with her hand on the knob to the exit. I couldn't see her face.

"I know the two of you were together during the Post-Election Festival. Are you his supplier? Did you help him switch the drugs for Langley's trial?" My head buzzed with dozens of questions, and each one caused my voice to tremble. "Is that what this whole thing has been about? Was it all just a ruse to get Ms. Freddie off the bench so you could have her killed? I know you were arguing with her before she died."

"No, it's not like that. It's not like that at all," Phyllis whispered. "Frederica and I were friends once. I would never hurt her. She tried to warn me."

Phyllis turned around. Heavy lines etched into her pale, freckled skin. Her eyes brimmed with tears. "We fought because Chance blackmailed me for access to the Controlled Substance Lab."

THIRTY-TWO

"BLACKMAIL? ARE YOU saying Ms. Freddie knew about you and Chance?" I asked.

"Of course not," Phyllis said. "She would have reported everything. No. When the drugs went missing at trial, she assumed I was drinking again and accused me of being a liability—that I made the error and tried to cover it up by shifting the blame to DAG Stevenson and Corporal North. She tried to warn me that the Department of Justice would demand an investigation into my conduct. But, I fought her because I didn't want her to think I was an alcoholic, and I couldn't afford to tell her about Chance."

"Why? That was your opportunity. If Chance blackmailed you, you could have gotten him arrested for threatening a government official, evidence tampering, or worse."

"It wasn't that simple. Chance threatened my family. He knew about my past." She crumpled against the exit door and let her body slide to the floor. Her words dissolved into an incoherent mix of weepy sniffles. "Don't ask me how. He just knew. Maybe he heard it from the sorority. Maybe he pieced it together from snippets I let slip at AA. Maybe he got ahold of my records. I don't know. I just—don't know."

"Slow down." I crouched on the floor beside her. "None of that explains why you helped him throw me into a dumpster. The lab is under investigation. You're out of a job. Why are you still helping him?"

"What else am I supposed to do? Exposing Chance means exposing myself. I don't want my family to get hurt. I want to have a career again. If people around here knew I'd almost been convicted of manslaughter, I'd never get another—"

"Did you say 'manslaughter'?" I rose from my crouch and took several steps back.

"Vehicular manslaughter. An accident. Frederica helped make it go away—got the blood alcohol tests thrown out on a technicality and had the charges expunged from my record—you know what? Forget it. Just ask your mother. She seems to think she's an expert."

The horror must have translated onto my face because she wiped her eyes and scrambled to her feet. Her demeanor sobered, and she held out her palms as if to suggest she held no more secrets. "The point is, everybody turned their back on me when they thought I had a drinking problem. I can't let that happen again."

"Instead of finally doing the right thing, you let a known drug dealer use your lab as his personal supply closet?" I tried to keep my voice devoid of judgment, but I failed.

"You've got it all wrong. He was just some guy from AA until he turned on me. When the agreement started, he was only supposed to take the items marked for destruction…for his recreational use. I had no idea he was dealing until it was too late, and I definitely didn't know he'd switched the drugs for Langley's trial—that's the truth. I found out the same moment as everyone else. I would have stopped him if I'd known. Any signs of tampering would have been on me and gotten the lab shut down—did get the lab shut down."

"Phyllis, do you hear yourself? These are crimes. Pure and simple. You need to go to the police. Langley got away with a felony, and Chance is dangerous. He hurt me. He threatened you. What's to stop him from doing something worse to someone else? The authorities need to be involved. If you don't go, I will."

"Why?" Her voice was so soft she might have been speaking to herself. "The damage is done. I'm already under investigation for criminal misconduct and evidence tampering. If I can just ride out the storm, I can protect my family. I might be able to find work—"

"Phyllis, listen to me. This is bigger than your career. Did it ever cross your mind that maybe *Chance* killed Judge Wannamaker?"

"Of course. Why do you think I'm here?" She threw her arms out wide, and frustration crept into her voice. "But he's a ghost, and I don't have any proof that doesn't implicate me."

"Well, did you see Chance or anyone else leave or enter the kitchen when you first walked in there with the judge or when you went in there later with Corporal North?"

"I don't remember. I was too upset. The whole situation felt like I was caught in a lie I didn't even know I'd told. It was all I could do to stay sane."

"Can you tell me about the last moment you saw Ms. Freddie alive?"

"When I walked into her office," Phyllis closed her eyes and rubbed her temples, "she was on the phone with President Judge Yaris, talking about the missing drugs and the possibility of false arrest. She finished her call and invited me to the kitchen for tea. We argued, and she kicked me out. That's the last I saw of her—that's all I can tell you. I'm sorry. I really am. For everything. If I'd known that day would lead to this, I would have—" Her voice cracked and tears began to flow.

The singing in the sanctuary ceased and bass-heavy gospel music drifted in through the wood of the hallway door. The musical equivalent of the proverbial bell.

"Go to the police," I said.

"I'll try." Phyllis pulled herself together and opened the exit door. The morning sunlight rushed in and formed a halo around her as she turned. "You ought to know that wallet chain Chance wears is an access card to the Controlled Substance lab. I don't know what good it will do him now the lab is shut down, but I figure someone needs to know the truth in case he gets to me before I get to tell my side of the story."

THIRTY-THREE

MY RETURN TO the sanctuary was like entering another world. The Kappa Mu's reverent voices were gone and the atmosphere had become more casual. A few folks hugged each other and chatted quietly while others stood in line to view the body.

When I crossed the threshold, Ma seized my arm. Her face held a mix of concern and anger. "What were you doing in there? Why didn't you follow me out?"

"Take it easy, Ma. I just wanted to talk to Ms. Dodd alone."

I hated being dismissive. She deserved to know what was going on, but since I hadn't told her about my encounter with Chance and Phyllis in the alley, I needed to keep my response brief. "Phyllis was in the courthouse the day Ms. Freddie died. She was one of the last people to see her alive."

"Oh, my gosh." Ma squeezed my hand. "Is that why she was so determined to stand with us? I feel terrible."

"Don't. You did what you thought was right, and she was only up there out of guilt. Nothing good ever comes out of feeling guilty."

I should know since I deliberately failed to tell my overprotective mother the truth about Phyllis's confession. "How much longer before the funeral?"

"Less than an hour." Ma pulled at the belt string of my black wraparound dress and adjusted it so the bow aligned with the center of my waist. "I think you should go say something to Mr. Russell before you mentally check out again." She winked. "Don't think I didn't notice."

I found Mr. Russell at the back of the church by one of the stained-glass windows. He chewed on the end of his unlit pipe and patted at his suit pockets like he'd lost something. Grace stood across from him, holding his Fedora in one hand while she adjusted his tie with the other. They seemed absorbed in their conversation, but Mr. Russell's dark bloodshot eyes caught me as I approached.

"Let me guess." He removed the pipe from his lips. "Your mother sent you over to check on me."

I started to reply, but Grace broke their huddle and pulled me into a hug. She looked almost youthful in her velour jumpsuit, her Peter Pan haircut curled for the occasion. The smell of sweet tobacco engulfed our exchange to the point where I wasn't sure if the smell was coming from her, the hat she was holding, Mr. Russell, or all three.

"I've been looking all over for you," Grace said when we parted. "Sorry I missed your call last night. Figured I'd catch up with you here."

"Let me give you ladies some privacy." Mr. Russell took his hat from Grace.

"No. Stay. What I wanted to talk with her about concerns you too—or Ms. Freddie rather." I gripped the nearest pew and forged ahead. "I found a blind spot in the judges' hallway last night. Right outside the kitchen."

"But that's impossible," Grace said. "That hallway has two cameras."

"What is she talking about?" Mr. Russell turned to Grace.

"She's saying that there's a flaw in the surveillance system at the courthouse."

"We overlooked something," I added. "Ms. Freddie could have been ambushed by someone who wasn't even supposed to be in the courthouse."

"No." Mr. Russell exhaled. His body deflated, and he sank onto a pew.

I shouldn't have sprung the information on him, but he needed to know, especially if he'd in any way resigned to the theory of Stevenson's confession and suicide note.

He looked at Grace. "Could it be true? I've always suspected the police weren't telling me everything."

Grace widened her eyes and scanned the crowded sanctuary. I'd put her on the spot, and she seemed desperate to escape. "I just don't think anyone would be hiding in the judges' hallway. It's not possible. That was the first question Detective Daniels asked when he started this investigation, and the governor's security team audited all of our surveillance equipment while he was here for the festival. Everything checked out. Besides, anyone accessing that hallway, seen or unseen, would need a keycard to get in and out."

"What if someone used a keycard that isn't on your system? The Controlled Substance Lab uses the same type of keycard locks. I saw it myself, and Phyllis practically confirmed it. What if she used her card or gave a card to someone like Chance Mulligan?"

"Langley's husband? That wouldn't work. He'd need a keycard specific to the courthouse and one with full access like Wannamaker's or Maggie's, before I downgraded her."

"Maggie, right. I talked to her last night and she

was—" I recalled her slap "—evasive. Maybe she let Phyllis or Corporal North borrow her card. They both spent time talking to her right before the murder, and I don't know what to think about either of them at this point."

I glanced over at Mr. Russell, whose eyes seemed determined to keep pace with our conversation. He inclined his head in a way that encouraged me to continue. He had his own suspicions in that he didn't trust Detective Daniels to follow through on anything beyond the courthouse employee theory—so I made my final plea with his silent blessing.

"Look, Grace, I know we went through some of the footage last night, but I need you to check again. Go back through the logs and go look at the camera setup. I know what I saw. When I stood by the kitchen door, the cameras were pointed nowhere near me."

"Okay." She sighed and backed away from us. "I'll go right after the funeral, but I'm telling you…it's just not possible."

When she'd melted into the crowd, I sat beside Mr. Russell. His seventy-year-old face showed every bit of its age.

"I'm sorry about that. I just don't believe—" I pressed my lips together to hold back the tears. "Everyone I talk to has a different story about what happened."

"It's all right. I understand. You want answers. So do I." He put the unlit pipe back in his mouth and began to chew. "That thing they're reporting about Stevenson is too perfect. No motive. I don't know much about that corporal, but Freddie never did trust Phyllis, and all that stuff you said about Maggie makes sense. She could be awfully reckless sometimes. Freddie always complained about her letting people into chambers and leaving confidential information lying around."

I slowly turned my head and gaped at Mr. Russell. His face was in profile to me as he surveyed the altar where his wife's casket sat surrounded by flowers, candles, and well-wishers. But as I examined the weathered lines of his tired expression, I couldn't tell if his words were absentminded musings or if he'd intentionally confessed something that would tie my hunches together.

I took a chance but treaded lightly. "Did you know Maggie well?"

"Not really." His eyes remained on the parade of mourners. "I've just seen her around town."

"You've stayed in touch with Maggie?"

He chuckled. "Oh, no. I just remember she was a constant headache for Freddie. Heck, there was a period when she'd come home and talk about nothing but that damn secretary. I think she thought Maggie was causing her grief on purpose."

"Was Maggie deliberately causing trouble?"

His brow furrowed. He slipped the pipe into his jacket pocket and spoke wearily. "I doubt it. Maggie was social. Freddie was all business. I finally told Freddie to get herself a new secretary. Why do you ask?"

"Well, you said the other day that Ms. Freddie's work was a strain on your relationship and—" I hesitated because I was about to break the promise I'd made to my mother about the suspicions of an affair. "I was in your wife's office yesterday, and I noticed she'd removed one of your pictures. I thought maybe the two of you had an argument before she died. Maybe one about Maggie, since I saw you getting friendly with her at the festival."

If it were possible to do a double take with just one's

eyes, he accomplished the feat like a pro. "You don't actually expect me to take that statement seriously, do you?"

I studied him. I felt terrible for thinking about him being in a relationship with Maggie and even worse for implying it aloud, but watching him squirm indicated he was hiding something. I'd seen it too many times in the courtroom. Rapid eye movement, blinking, and avoiding eye contact were all signs the witness had something to say but couldn't afford to incriminate himself.

"No, of course not. I never should have suggested it. I'm sorry. That was rude." I wasn't going to press it. I'd seen enough. The man had just lost his wife. I didn't need to rob him of his dignity too.

"It really was, young lady." He stood, adjusted his suit jacket, and put on his hat. "I'm not in a relationship with Maggie. Never have been. Now, I know this whole thing has shattered everyone's beliefs, but you should definitely know me better than that. I can honestly tell you I truly loved my wife, and I would never do anything to hurt her."

"I know," I whispered.

Then he wedged himself into the crowd and vanished.

I didn't doubt he loved Ms. Freddie, but he laid his response on too thick. I'd always been wary of people who used a ton of "-ly" words as a bridge to sincerity. If a person is "actually," "honestly," or "truly" on the verge of "really" telling the truth, they don't need to qualify what's being said with a bunch of adverbs.

Mr. Russell had used all of those sticky little words. Something wasn't right.

On the other hand, maybe by telling me nothing, he was telling me everything.

The rest of the hour between the viewing and the service passed quickly and without much fanfare. My mother had taken up the duty of reserving three pews for the Kappa Mu's. When the organ music began to signify the start of the funeral, I stood beside her and her sisters as the Wannamaker family marched down the aisle to the front of the sanctuary.

When the music stopped, I sat down and closed my eyes. The events of the viewing had drained my energy, and I couldn't bear to speak with another person.

"Man, this place is packed," said a male voice.

A hand nudged me, and my eyes flew open. Mike Slocum squeezed his skinny body into the pew beside me and fanned himself like he'd been running. He had a program whose cover had the picture from Ms. Freddie's obituary, and he wore a cheap-looking gray suit that hung loose on his gangly frame.

"What are you doing here?" I whispered.

"I'm fairly sure the whole town is here." He pulled a pen, notebook, and mini-recorder from the inside pocket of his jacket. "As a dedicated journalist, I couldn't afford to stay home."

Ma looked over at the two of us talking and bared her teeth. Mike mimed a military salute in reply.

I covered my mouth and hissed a response. "I thought you only did investigative reporting."

"Too true. So here's your hard-hitting news flash: I got a call from my source at the medical examiner's office this morning. The toxicology report from Stevenson's autopsy revealed the presence of phenacyl chloride. He also exhibited signs of bronchial spasms and a mild cardiac arrest."

"What does that mean for my theory about his suicide being a cover-up?"

"It means your theory has legs, and I've got some digging to do." He opened his little notebook and pointed at the inky scrawl inside. "Phenacyl chloride is the aerosol equivalent of tear gas—most commonly found in police-issued riot control products like mace. Someone could have used a chemical element or some other method of submission to force Stevenson into the noose."

Just as Mike finished, the minister asked us all to bow our heads in prayer. Thrilled my theory finally had scientific proof, I couldn't wait for more answers.

I grabbed Mike's pen and wrote, "What about the cops? Are they keeping the judge's case open now Stevenson's suicide is in question?"

He scribbled back, "Judge's case officially closed. Stevenson's autopsy evidence deemed inconclusive. Chemical quantities inconsequential. Death declared suicide via acute asphyxiation."

I stared at his note until the church said, "Amen."

With a soloist taking the podium, I leaned in to Mike's ear. "How much time until the cops make an official announcement?"

He responded with a series of tickly, hot breaths on my cheek. "I imagine all the news outlets got the press release a half hour ago. That's when I heard. The only reason you haven't heard anything yet is because most of the media and law enforcement communities are in this room instead of at their desks."

I looked around. He was right. In addition to the

dozens of uniformed police officers, a few judges from neighboring counties, several local politicians, and the press corps who covered the festival occupied a large portion of the sanctuary. As I continued to scan the room, I noticed Maggie and Harriston two rows back. My neck stiffened.

"What?" Mike turned to look in the direction of my frown.

Ma, probably frustrated by our constant movement, reached over and slapped my thigh. A man behind us cleared his throat. Mike settled back into his space.

I leaned into him. "Remember when you told me someone at the courthouse gave my name to the press as the person who found the judge?" I inclined my head in Maggie's direction. "Is that who you were talking about?"

"No."

"*No*? Are you sure?"

"I'm sure," he whispered without taking a second look. "Not that I should have admitted as much. Smart reporters don't reveal sources—although, I am curious why it matters. The truth is that it *was* you, right?"

Indeed, that was the truth, but no one should have known about my role in finding Ms. Freddie. And if it wasn't Maggie, how did everyone find out?

Once the eulogy began, Mike clammed up, and I forced myself to focus on the ceremony. Ms. Freddie had been a member of Wesdale United Methodist Church and the Kappa Mu sorority for over forty years so, after the minister finished his remarks, almost everyone in the community stood up and shared their memories.

When it was my turn to make the slow march up

the aisle toward the pulpit, my legs wobbled. The room grew hot—humid as all eyes turned to me and the massive podium that dwarfed my petite frame. I gripped the sharp wooden edges for support, startled at the nasally pop of my voice over the microphone.

"Ms. Freddie was a second mother to me. She taught me to work twice as hard as everyone else because she knew the outside world would see the color of my skin as a disadvantage—a disadvantage that, by its very nature, made me stronger. That fierce determination—*her* fierce determination—acts as my beacon for what's right…" I turned my head toward the casket and studied the ebony face that rested within. "I miss you, Ms. Freddie, and I promise to make you proud."

I drifted back to my seat. My head hung low, prepared to block out the world for a while—that was, until I found myself wrapped inside the strong arms of Mr. Russell, who met me halfway down the aisle. The nutty-sweet aroma of his tobacco engulfed me as he pressed his head against mine and whispered, "You have, my dear. You have."

We parted, and he brushed past me on his way to the podium. The room buzzed for a moment as people murmured their shock. Mr. Russell rarely spoke in public—he preferred to let his wife do the talking—but the words he chose to grace us with sent a ripple of goose pimples across my flesh. They were so pointed I wondered if they were in response to our earlier conversation.

"Freddie was my everything. Brilliant, smart, funny…one of a kind. No one could ever replace her… whoever took her life must have been jealous of that."

THIRTY-FOUR

THE MODEST CEMETERY next to Wesdale United Methodist Church had probably never seen so many living souls. What felt like hundreds of people—what probably *was* hundreds of people—gathered around the tiny burial site and shivered in the cold to watch Ms. Freddie's pearlescent casket disappear into the earth.

"Heavenly Father, grant Frederica grace," recited the portly minister as the interment drew to a close, "that as she faces the mystery of death, she may see the light of eternity."

Was the mystery of death as painful as having to say goodbye?

My eyes refused to focus on the scene in front of me, so I concentrated on everything else—the pale blue of the noonday sky, the crisp white of the minister's collar, and the wall of black that surrounded me as people pressed forward to place flowers at the foot of the open grave.

I spotted Corporal Ashton North towering over the crowd. His mammoth, unyielding frame blocked the gravel path back to the church, and a mass of retreating mourners parted around him like the Red Sea.

Ashton met my gaze with a wistful smile. He'd dressed respectably in an expensive-looking black suit and a tweed overcoat clearly custom cut for his broad shoulders. He'd even shaved for the occasion. Gone was the copper-colored stubble that had marred his sharp jawline during the festival where we argued over what to do about Chance…and where Ashton's willingness to exaggerate the truth raised a ton of dark questions about his character. Questions that grew murky when coupled with his proximity to both of the town's recent deaths.

I stopped in front of him.

"I'd hoped to run into you."

I swallowed hard. "I'm surprised to see you here."

"Well, maybe if you returned my calls…" The up-turned curve of his lips faltered a little. "When I didn't hear from you, I started to worry—especially after everything that happened on stage at the festival. I wanted to know you were all right."

"I'm fine, other than having to deal with everything…" I looked around for Ma, who milled among the tombstones with some of her sorority sisters.

She waved for me to join them.

"Can we talk later? This isn't the best time."

"Yeah. Sure, sure. I just thought I'd hear from you after Stevenson's confession. I thought you'd be happy—satisfied. I mean, you'd feel avenged… I guess those aren't the right words." He shoved his hands into his pockets and shifted his weight from foot to foot. "But, I think you know what I'm trying to say."

"I do."

"I'm sorry for your loss."

"Thanks." I checked his face for sincerity.

Did he really believe Stevenson killed Ms. Freddie and himself, or was Ashton covering for his own mis-deeds?

Maybe I could call his bluff. Ma would have to wait.

"The tough part about Stevenson's confession," I

crafted each word with purpose, "is he confronted me in Cake & Kettle just before he died. If I'd known then what I know now…you didn't happen to see him at the festival, did you? You know, after I left you standing by the bandstand?"

"No. I didn't see any sign of Stevenson until…" He shook his head "…until it was too late. I was still standing by Trooper McIntyre's barricade waiting for you when everything went sideways. People rushing the stage. Pure chaos. I'm still trying to piece it together."

"Did you see anyone else in that area around the bandstand before the chaos? Anyone we might know? Like Phyllis? Maggie? Harriston?"

"Of course not. McIntyre didn't even want *me* waiting in that area. I almost had to fight her on it. Everyone I saw go through her barricade was supposed to be there." He raised his brow. "Why? Is everything okay? Is there something you're not telling me?"

I feigned a shiver and pretended to recheck the buttons on my coat. Ashton and I hadn't spoken since I'd developed the theory Stevenson's death was a cover-up, and I sensed it wasn't wise to share that revelation, at least not until I was sure of his intentions.

"Not at all. There's nothing to tell." I made a clunky effort to change the subject. "I simply wondered who else might have seen what happened. I can't understand how Stevenson managed to fool all of us. Weren't you in the courthouse kitchen with him at one point? That had to be around the time of Ms. Freddie's murder. Do you remember seeing anything suspicious?"

"Hard to say. I was pissed at him, and he was so busy screaming his head off—first at someone on his cell and then at Phyllis and me. The bailiff couldn't get his loud mouth out of there fast enough. The second he went nuclear, she materialized out of thin air. He refused to leave and acted like he owned the place."

"Really? Is that all you saw?"

"Pretty much."

"Nothing that would indicate someone else was in—"

"What's with the twenty questions?" He crossed his arms and took a step back. "Am I missing something here? I thought we were on the same team."

"We are."

"Then talk to me, not at me." His blue eyes seemed to plead with me, and I ransacked my brain for something I could say to pacify him when a trio of uniformed police officers crunched past us on the gravel path. Ashton gave them a curt nod, and I decided to share the one piece of information that concerned him most.

"Chance blackmailed Phyllis. You were right. She told me he's been getting drugs from the Controlled Substance Lab, and he has employee access to the building. She also suspects him of switching the evidence in Langley's case, but she claims she doesn't have any proof."

"And you believe her, even after she helped Chance toss you into a dumpster?"

"Well—yeah. She said he forced her to do it. Threatened her family." I licked my lips and considered whether I let the blackmail overshadow Phyllis's role as a suspect. "You don't think I should believe her?"

"No, it's just…" Ashton bowed his head as if something was troubling him.

I thought he would be happy to hear the news. Wouldn't proof of Chance's involvement in the evidence tampering get him reinstated twice as fast as any paperwork they might dig up at the troop?

After a minute of silence, Ashton said, "If Chance had access to the lab and switched the evidence, he's been manipulating everyone the entire time. Problem is, Chance isn't the type to leave loose ends. I can't imagine he'd let anybody outside his circle have knowledge of his comings and goings. He wouldn't risk it—couldn't risk it. Unless..."

"Unless what?" I demanded.

Ashton stared out at the dozens of grave makers, unable or unwilling to answer.

I gripped his elbow. "Unless what?"

Ashton clenched his jaw and started to walk down the path away from the church.

I edged along beside him and clung to his arm. "Wait. Tell me what's going on."

"I'm sorry you had to be the messenger. But it sounds like Chance wanted someone to know what he was up to—wanted to make sure I'd find out so he'd have a real excuse to come after me." Ashton wrenched my hand from his arm and spoke without looking back. "But I'm ready for him. I just need the gun from my truck."

He broke into a run.

THIRTY-FIVE

"FRIEND OF yours?" Ma called.

She strolled over as Ashton's hulking figure shot past the final tombstone and disappeared over the horizon.

As odd as that sight might have been to her, the strangest aspect of the moment was the question at hand: was Ashton a friend or a foe? He seemed harmless, but his cryptic reaction to the news about Chance left no doubt he was capable of murder.

"C'mon," she said when I didn't reply. "They're having a repast for family and friends in the church basement. Let's get some food."

"I don't think I can eat right now, Ma. I've had enough socializing for one day. Can we just get out of here?"

She wrapped an arm around my waist. "You did good today, Angel. What you said about Freddie was beautiful. Now, I know it was hard seeing her in a way that's different from what you remember, but don't punish yourself. Freddie lived a magnificent life, and you helped her by being a part of it." Ma hugged me against her side and let out a loud sigh. "Take the Buick. I'll see if one of the Kappa Mu's can drop me off at the house."

She pulled the keys from the pocket of her faux fur and held them out.

"Thanks for understanding." I reached for the collection of metal.

"Not so fast." Ma snatched the key ring from my grasp. "You're not going after that man, are you?"

"No, Ma," I groaned. "He's not that kind of friend."

"Good." She relinquished the keys and cupped my chin. "Women who chase are easily replaced. Remember that."

I closed my eyes and stifled the urge to gripe. I loved my mother, but she'd always be a helicopter parent. I cringed to think what she'd say if she knew what I suspected of Ashton.

Keys in hand, I cut through the cemetery and trudged along the sidewalk toward the center of town. The three-block hike had seemed easy earlier that day—all the people, noise, foot traffic, and gridlock had kept my mind away from the elements. Alone, the journey felt like capital punishment. Wind whipped through my curls, lashed at my cheeks, and nipped at my ears. I clutched the collar of my coat and ducked my head to no avail. The frosty air seemed determined to rob my skin of feeling, despite the redeeming rays of the afternoon sun.

By the time I reached The Quad, I was desperate for shelter. Ma's Buick sat just beyond the meditation garden and fountain that adorned the hub of the roundabout. I dashed into the street. My vision locked on the wall of evergreens that separated me from my destination. I was only a few feet from them when I noticed a flash of red among the hedgerows.

Splash.

I stopped mid-stride, one foot planted on the roadway, the other on the pathway in front of the meditation garden's entrance. While it wasn't unusual for people to stop inside the garden—toss a penny into the water for good luck—there was something peculiar about that red. Something familiar. Familiar enough to send prickles along my numbed skin.

I held my breath and studied the foliage. I needed to get a read on what I'd seen. I didn't want to overreact.

Seconds passed.

I exhaled.

Nothing. No movement.

I glanced over my shoulder to calculate an alternate route. Parked cars lined the street, but, otherwise, the area behind me was deserted. I could walk the perimeter of The Quad instead of going through—

Swish. Swish. Swish.

A second flash of red—no, orange—captured my peripheral vision.

I snapped my head back to the garden, and a flood of recognition washed over me.

The orange flash was the badly dyed hair of Langley Dean Mulligan, who emerged from the trees with blood dripping from her hands.

THIRTY-SIX

"WHAT UP, SOOTY?" Langley had dropped her affected vocal fry, so the question sounded as if she was as shocked to see me as I was to see her. Her ruddy skin had gone deathly pale, her face a twisted collage of fear and confusion. She wore a puffy pink down coat covered in blotches of red so large and distinct I would have described the garment as scarlet if I hadn't already identified the substance as blood.

I stumbled backward into the street. "Don't call me by that B.S. nickname," I shouted, "and stay back."

I brandished Ma's car key between my knuckles like a corkscrew and crouched low, never taking my eyes off her hands. My limbs primed to strike.

"No, no. Please. Don't—wait. I meant—I need your help. You're one of them—law enforcement. You work at the courthouse. They'll believe you."

She waved both palms in a beseeching manner then froze when I gestured toward the blood.

"This is not what you think. I couldn't wash it off—there's so much. They wouldn't get clean. I didn't—it's not like that. My husband is dead—he's been shot—that bastard corporal took things too far."

"Corporal?" I relaxed my stance. "Are you talking about Ashton? He wouldn't have—"

"Wouldn't have done this?" She spread her red fingers wide. Her eyes flared, and her frazzled voice grew firm. "I saw that bastard standing over my husband's dead body—right before he ran off like a freaking coward. That cop stalked us all week. When Chance didn't come home this morning, I tracked his phone, and the app led me here. Your boy toy Ashton has my husband stuffed in the back of his truck."

Langley lifted her arm and pointed a bloody fingertip toward a big-wheeled Ford F-150—Ashton's wannabe monster truck—parked two cars away from where I stood. I couldn't see anything unusual about the vehicle from my angle, but the simple gesture made her body fold inward like a small child who'd taken a punch to the gut.

I remained motionless, but my thoughts moved at warp speed. I didn't trust Langley. This had to be another cruel joke where I suffered while she watched. And yet, her story caused a seed of terror to form in my stomach. Ashton was obsessed with the Mulligans. He'd left the funeral to find a gun, and he was the only person in town with multiple motives for murder. My conscience urged me to run, but the muscles in my legs refused to react and every tendon strained under the tension of indecision.

Finally, my voice reemerged. "I—I'm calling the police." I fumbled for my cell.

"Please. My cell got wet. Call for help. That's all I need—but don't call the State Police. They'll cover for him. Call the local guys." Her lips twisted into a sneer. "They might be less likely to side with a dirty cop."

"I don't know what's going on between you and Ashton," my fingers hovered over the smartphone's screen, "but don't act like some smug little victim. You attacked me in court. Chance attacked me at the festival. Don't you dare think I'm calling the cops to help you or your husband. I'm calling because Chance tampered with the drug evidence at trial. Harriston might have gotten your charges dismissed, but that doesn't change the fact both of you sell drugs."

Langley cackled. The same maniacal sound I remembered from our youth. She'd asked for help then mocked my efforts, despite what was right. I didn't need another scandal. I'd worked too hard to make a decent life for myself. With half the roadway between us, I could simply run back to the church and forget everything I'd seen. Surely, if Ashton shot Chance, someone heard the sound and had already called the cops. Maybe this moment was my opportunity for retribution—to do nothing and let Langley suffer her own fate.

I returned the phone to my coat pocket and backed away. "Call the cops yourself. I'm not your patsy."

"This isn't about me and you." The last of her laughter dissipated. "I need your help because I haven't done anything wrong. North planted drugs and cash on me to rattle Chance. You were at the trial. Didn't you think it was weird for a cop to set up a stakeout in front of Cooper's in the middle of the day? That bastard wasn't looking for drunks. The bar wasn't even open." She inched toward me, her voice frenetic. "He was looking for an arrest. He knew my routine. He'd been following me. I didn't know Chance sold drugs—I didn't even know about the evidence switch until after the trial. I swear. And by then, nobody was going to believe I wasn't involved."

"You're lying."

"You say that because I've given you a thousand reasons to hate me—and I'm sorry for that."

A scornful snort escaped my throat.

"For real. Please. This isn't about us." Her eyes filled with tears. "Don't you get it? That cop thought my husband would sacrifice himself to save me but instead, Chance chose to expose that hypocrite for what he is: a dirty cop turned murderer."

"You had to be involved. You had to at least know Chance sold drugs—you covered for him a few years ago during the shootout with Ashton's partner, Natalie Knowles. You had to have known."

"I covered for him?" Her voice cracked, and her breath grew heavy with frustration. "Did you read that in my file somewhere, or did you hear that from your homeboy North? Because I just met Chance last year. We've only been married six months."

I opened my mouth to challenge her but opted for silence. I wasn't sure what was real. My mind drifted to Ashton's trial testimony and his voice on the AudioSync—*The AudioSync!* What had he said during his conversation with Maggie? *Those drugs were specifically picked out for her.* As in, picked out to frame her? Ashton's off-the-record comment seemed to give credence to Langley's claim.

My brain pressed the idea further, this wasn't the only time I'd run across the notion of a setup. Hadn't Chance warned me about a "frame-up" during my attack, and hadn't I seen the words "complaints of false arrest" on a notepad near Langley's file in chambers? Could they both have been referencing to Ashton? My mouth went dry.

"That cop wanted to punish Chance with an eye for an eye," Langley said. "North lost a partner, so he wanted to make sure Chance lost something too. Go look in the bed of that truck if you don't believe me, but you've got to help me. We're running out of time. The cops will listen to you."

I pushed aside my growing anxiety and edged over to the big-wheeled monstrosity. My makeshift key weapon at the ready. I had to know the truth.

Careful to keep one eye on Langley, I let the other eye scan the area surrounding the pickup. Ashton had parked flush with the curb adjacent to the meditation garden, so I approached the rear profile of the vehicle from a street-side vantage point. I noticed the tailgate was open and the truck bed cover was askew. I'd have to get closer to look inside. On a deep inhalation, I stepped in front of the car parked at the pickup's rear bumper and steeled myself for an ambush.

But no ambush came…none except the sour metallic smell of death.

Inside the truck bed, Chance laid sprawled on his back in a puddle of blood so thick his jeans and flannel shirt looked like they'd been plastered on his body. Three gunshot wounds marked the center of his torso. A nasty gash split open his temple, and his legs sat twisted to the side, as if someone had shoved them in to make sure he'd fit, his wallet chain tangled alongside.

Everything Langley had said was true.

I reached into my pocket for the phone but stopped short at the sight of some items scattered at Chance's feet: a cell, a box of latex gloves, a coil of thick rope, two cans of mace, and a courthouse keycard… Frederica Wannamaker's courthouse keycard.

I stared at the tiny piece of rectangular plastic, which contained the judge's picture, and only one thought echoed through my mind.

Run.

THIRTY-SEVEN

I GRABBED LANGLEY'S ARM, careful to avoid her bloody hands, and dragged her toward the secluded meditation garden. We had to get out of sight. If Ashton came back before we contacted the police, we were as dead as Chance.

As dead as Stevenson.

As dead as Ms. Freddie.

The presence of Ms. Freddie's keycard in Ashton's truck put everything into perspective.

Ashton's obsession was to capture Chance. He wanted the drug dealer brought to justice. He needed to avenge his partner, and he resented Ms. Freddie for failing to make that happen.

That much I could account for firsthand.

But what I didn't count on—what none of us could— was that when Chance tampered with the drug evidence to set Langley free, he touched a nerve in Ashton that must have broken the officer's spirit…and sent the corporal on a killing spree.

Ashton was the only person unaccounted for prior to the judge's murder, and he was one of the last people to see her alive. What if he stole the judge's keycard before she left the bench? He certainly lingered in the witness box long enough to have done it.

What if he stole Stevenson's tie from one of the counsel tables? I remember him stopping by at least one of them on his way out of the courtroom, and Ashton definitely hated Stevenson enough to frame him for murder.

What if after Ashton entered the kitchen, he lied about how and when Grace escorted him out of the courthouse? He could have lingered in the surveillance video blind spot just long enough to double back and kill Ms. Freddie then spark an argument in the parking lot with Phyllis and Stevenson to create an alibi.

What if Ashton used his skills as a state trooper to create a second crime scene that would suggest Stevenson killed himself while also providing a neat suicide note confession to close the Wannamaker case? He was undoubtedly in the proper position to have created such a display and athletic enough to orchestrate the hanging.

But the final murder, Chance's shooting, was all my doing…at least in motivation. I'd confirmed Ashton's worst fear: that his nemesis had not only outfoxed him, but done so in a manner that threatened to destroy him.

That fear pushed Ashton to take the law into his own hands.

Knowledge of that fear put Langley and me in danger.

Ma's Buick was about a hundred yards away on the other side of the roundabout. If we could get there, we'd have shelter. Better yet, we could drive to the police.

"This way," I hooked Langley's arm with mine. We needed to get on the move, and we were safer if we worked together.

I stabbed at the home button on my cell. My hands shook so much I could barely tap the screen.

The insides of my chest twisted as we entered the garden and approached the fountain.

Almost halfway there.

My thumb dialed 9-1-1. I placed the phone against my ear and prayed for a connection.

I could see the tail of the Buick up ahead—just on the other side of the trees. We were going to make it.

"You've reached nine-one-one. What's your emergency?"

"I'd like to report a—"

My voice hitched. Words failed. Breath evaporated from my throat.

Ashton stepped onto the sidewalk about twenty feet in front of us. His body eclipsed my view of the Buick… and our closest chance of escape.

Langley and I stopped and huddled together.

He stared at us for a second, shoved his hand into his coat, and opened his mouth to speak. His features pulled upward in astonishment. The words never came, though. His expression simply flat-lined, and his hand emerged holding a big, black gun.

"Duck!" Langley rammed her shoulder into my sternum.

The sheer force of her strike propelled me sideways and knocked the wind out of me. The phone slipped from my grasp. My legs buckled. My body crumpled. Gravity pulled me toward the ground, but the ground wasn't there.

The only thing there was the fountain, and I toppled headfirst into the water.

THIRTY-EIGHT

THE FRIGID LIQUID bit into my flesh. Branded me. Bound me. Smothered me beneath its depths as the gauzy fabric of my dress and the heavy folds of my coat tangled around me, my body immobile—mouth open in a futile scream against the watery shroud.

Icy liquid slipped down my throat and set fire to my windpipe.

A spasm clenched my neck. I couldn't breathe.

Sharp white flashes blinded me as the invading liquid shut down my senses.

All I had left were my thoughts.

The fountain was only three feet deep, but a person could die in far less. Less water than it took to fill a sink or a toilet…like the one where Ms. Freddie died. A picture of her mutilated form—twisted and broken—slashed through the panic that tethered me in place. I couldn't let things end like this. Ms. Freddie would have expected more of me. She would have wanted me to fight.

Rise above and forge your own path.

The words from her recommendation letter drifted into my brain. I focused on them. Repeated them over and over until I had the courage to move. To rise up.

I thrust my face through the water's surface and emerged to a cruel wind that raked across my drenched skin, but I didn't care. I sucked up a greedy mouthful of arctic air and prayed it was enough to assuage the fire in my throat. To reignite my ability to breathe. Rich oxygen filled my lungs. I heaved and sputtered until a series of coughs cleared my airway.

I rose to my feet. I'd made it.

I was alive and free.

Or so I thought.

Ashton appeared above me, his angular jawline devoid of humor. He stood a few feet from the fountain. Gun still drawn. But he didn't have it pointed at me. He aimed at someone or something over my shoulder.

"Ashton, please—"

"Don't move." His voice was so deadly serious it robbed me of my newly found breath.

My eyes searched his for some indication of what he wanted from me, but his gaze never wavered from the area over my shoulder. He'd directed his command at whatever was going on behind me.

I twisted my neck and caught the familiar sight of Langley's unkempt orange hair. Only this time, she didn't greet me with a haughty remark. She floated face down in the fountain. Her arms spread wide in surrender. Blood seeped from a gunshot wound in her back and transformed her pink and scarlet coat into a morose shade of burgundy.

"Langley," I whispered as I turned toward her body.

I reached for her shoulders, lifted her face out of the water, and flipped her over. Freezing liquid sloshed beneath the line of my breasts, and I fought the urge to faint as my phobia resurfaced. I called her name once more, but the only response came from the fountain as droplets continued to trickle overhead.

"He killed her, Victoria," said a voice. "He killed them all."

A shadow loomed over me, and my panic doubled.

Someone else was in the garden.

I pulled my focus away from Langley and squinted into the sun. "*Grace?*"

She stood in silhouette at the opposite end of the fountain, with a gun pointed in Ashton's direction. And thanks to my position in the water, I found myself in the middle of their standoff.

"He's a killer," Grace repeated. "I heard three shots when I was coming out of the courthouse and caught him dumping a body into his truck. By the time I ran over here, he'd taken aim on another victim." She lifted her chin to indicate Langley, but her gun remained steady. "He would have shot you, too, if I hadn't shown up."

"Don't listen to her," Ashton hollered from behind me. "I didn't kill anyone. She's trying to manipulate you—use you as leverage so she can shoot me. I don't know what's going on here, but you've got to understand. I didn't do any of this. All I've been trying to do is warn you and protect you. I would never hurt you. I drew my gun because that Grace woman fired on you. And if Langley hadn't pushed you into the fountain, you'd both be dead."

I lowered my gaze toward Langley's unblinking stare and forced myself to examine her dull silver eyes. The truth was I hated Langley for the chaos she'd brought into my life, but no one deserved to die like this, not even her. I couldn't be sure who'd made what sacrifice, but I could make sure I didn't suffer the same fate—not while I could still fend for myself.

I'd lost my cell phone to the fountain, but I could still get out of this mess alive if I focused. Pins and needles plagued my limbs as I stood in the frigid water, but I willed my hands to grope through the wet folds of my coat until I found Ma's car keys—a weapon and a means of escape rolled into one.

"Why should I believe you?" I turned my head to the side and addressed Ashton in profile. I couldn't bear to face him head-on. The truth of his betrayal cut me to the bone. "When you left the funeral, you said you were getting your gun and going after Chance. Next thing I know, I see his dead body in the back of your truck." I shuddered. "Langley told me everything. She said you lied about her involvement in your partner's death. She said you planted drugs on her and falsified her arrest. All you've done is lie. Why should I trust you now?"

"I didn't kill Chance Mulligan." Ashton's words came out as a roar. "Someone planted his body in the back of my truck. The tailgate was open when I got there and when I pulled back the cover, he was already dead."

"Why didn't you call the police? Why run?"

"Because I was being framed. I got scared. Look, I may have fudged a few things about Langley's involvement in my partner's murder as a way to gain your trust and bent a few rules to get her arrested, but it was for the greater good. I had to flush Chance out. He was dealing, plain and simple—we both know that for a fact." He raised an eyebrow. "But I would never kill anyone. You've gotta believe me. Trust me on that."

"Save it, buddy," Grace said. "He's stalling, Victoria. You heard him. He's admitted he's a criminal. Let's get out of here while we still can."

"But what about—" I said.

"I've got you covered. Now move." She jerked her head as if to hurry me out of the fountain but otherwise continued to grip the handle of her gun with both hands.

I closed my eyes in a vain effort to catch my breath and comply. If I wanted to get out of this alive, I had to make smart decisions—and the smart call was to go with Grace. She was the person I could trust. I glanced at Langley's limp form bobbing along the water's surface then waded to the side and flopped over the concrete lip of the fountain, my limbs numb and useless from their submergence.

"Good," Grace said, "now get behind me."

"Victoria, wait," Ashton said as I moved into position behind my friend. "I rescued you when Chance attacked. I stood by you. I thought we were partners."

"Partners?" The word lodged in my airway and made it hard to swallow. "You used me. We stopped being partners the minute it became clear you murdered Judge Wannamaker—framed Stevenson, too, the way I figure it. You've been lying from the very beginning."

"No, no. You've got it all wrong. Why would I kill Wannamaker or Stevenson in the most public ways possible? Whoever killed them was either *trying* to get caught or knew they could remove every trace of evidence. Under the circumstances," he tightened his grip on his firearm, "I'll admit my wrongdoings with the Mulligans, but that's as far as this goes. I'm not a murderer."

"What about that stuff in your truck? You have the judge's keycard, all that rope, rubber gloves, and—"

"I have no idea what you're talking about." Ashton lifted one shoulder in a half-shrug but kept his aim firm.

"Anything you saw must have been planted there along with the body."

"How do you expect me just to take your word for it? You're the only person that's been around for every murder."

"No." He shook his head and edged closer. "That's not true."

"Hold it right there!" Grace ordered. "I will shoot."

"Victoria," he said, "she's playing us both. She wants this to turn into a bloodbath. You have to trust me."

I shivered and bit back a curse. No need to aggravate the situation with vulgarities. We stood staring at each other in tense silence. Grace and me across the fountain from Ashton, both camps with guns expertly drawn. Grace carried a sidearm for her work in the courthouse, but I'd never seen her use it. If this came to a showdown, would she have the marksmanship to take on a state trooper? And if she didn't, would I have the courage and the energy to fight after another near-death experience?

I gripped the car keys in my coat pocket and stepped out from behind Grace's rigid frame. I was sick of arguing. I was sick of the manipulation and the lies. I was sick of being the victim. No more. Not today.

"If you want me to trust you," I said to Ashton, "drop your weapon."

"Not until she drops hers."

"What kind of idiot do you think I am?" Grace quipped.

"The crazy kind," replied Ashton. "Ladies first—"

A loud smack followed by a moan and a splash cut the tension. My eyes zeroed in on Ashton's face for fear he'd fired his gun. A wrinkle of confusion tarnished his forehead as if he couldn't understand what was happening. His eyes shifted toward the sound—a flit of his pupils away from me toward the fountain—for an instant. And in that millisecond, the source of the noise became clear.

Langley.

Her torso twisted and thrashed against the water. Eyes rolled back in her head like she was having a seizure. I started to move toward her, but Grace blocked my path with her back.

Crack! Crack! Crack!

Gunfire.

Grace aimed three quick shots at Ashton, who'd lowered his guard in response to Langley's convulsions.

I flinched and covered my head. The earsplitting blasts echoed through the wall of trees that surrounded the garden and planted a sharp ringing sensation in my skull.

Ashton jerked backward with the impact of each bullet. Their momentum contorted his frame and forced him to teeter on his heels. His chest deflated, and his gun hand fell limp. Color drained from his face. A mangled grunt escaped his mouth. He tumbled to the ground in a slow arc and collapsed onto his side.

THIRTY-NINE

THE WHOLE SEQUENCE of events flashed by in an adrenaline-filled instant. I cowered against Grace's back, unable to control the pounding in my chest. She'd shot him. She'd actually fired her weapon and won.

Thank heavens.

While I was grateful to have escaped the moment alive, taking Ashton down so brutally seemed...wrong. He'd almost agreed to surrender. If he was a stone-cold killer on the verge of getting caught, wouldn't he have gone down guns blazing? Perhaps I'd seen too many action flicks, but a cornered bulldog had nothing to lose. Ashton, however, begged us to give him the benefit of the doubt and let us take the lead.

I shook off the thought. Grace still had her gun in hand, arms outstretched toward Ashton's form. I felt the taut lines of her muscles as each fiber prepared to pounce. My insides were just the opposite—twitchy and out of control. I clamped a hand over my mouth to suppress a dry heave.

"Do you have your phone?" I murmured once my stomach recovered. "We should go for help. Langley needs medical attention. I'm freezing, and Ashton should be detained." I grabbed Grace's shoulder to get her attention.

She whirled around on me but lowered her gun seconds before catching me in its sights. Clearly, her nerves were as frazzled as mine and her thoughts still on the threat.

"Sorry. No, I don't. We should stay here anyway." She pushed back the waistline of her coat.

She wore her bailiff's duty belt over her funeral attire. As she clipped her gun into its holster, I noticed the mace pouch sat unsnapped and empty. A rubber glove stuffed in its place.

"The gunfire is bound to attract attention, despite the foliage," Grace said, "and we need to get our story straight before we talk to the authorities."

"What about Langley?"

"What about her?" She glanced over at the sunken figure in the fountain. "Nothing we can do. She's dead. Let the boys in blue handle it, and thank your lucky stars she gave you that shove."

I winced. Lucky stars? Had Langley really pushed me out of the way of a bullet? I had a hard time believing that, given her track record. But if so, whose bullet? The panic attack from the fountain left me a bit muddled, but Ashton never directed his aim at me, even though he had plenty of opportunities and doing so would have given him an advantage. Grace, on the other hand, had just barely avoided placing me at the end of her barrel—by accident, of course.

Goose pimples sprouted along my neck as the wind took its toll on me and my wet clothes.

Something was wrong. I could sense it.

"You look like crap," Grace said. "Are you going to make it? I need you with me on this. We can use that blind spot theory of yours to pin this whole string of murders on North. Prime some surveillance footage to back up the rest. But it all starts here with the self-defense. You got it?"

She glared at me, and I froze.

At the funeral, Grace couldn't dismiss my theories fast enough. Now she not only believed me but also wanted to work with me on sharing the story with the police.

What had changed? Well, mainly, Ashton was dead, which made him the perfect fall guy.

My thoughts went into hyperdrive but got stuck on the last point Ashton made before he died—why kill so many people in such a public way? Why leave corpses in a bathroom, on a stage, or in your own truck when you could take them into one of the dozens of woodland areas, sand dunes, or farmlands around town and make the bodies disappear until spring—that was, unless you gained something by letting everyone see the deaths.

Even though Ashton had motive to kill Ms. Freddie, Stevenson, and the Mulligans, he gained nothing from letting everyone know about it…except the risk of arrest. Grace, however, benefited quite a bit, including plausible deniability—and, in this particular moment, the opportunity to look like a hero for defeating the bad guy and cleaning up the town. But why would Grace want to kill Ms. Freddie?

Then everything began to crystalize. Grace had full access to the courthouse and could have ambushed Ms. Freddie at any time. Grace had the power to doctor the keycard logs and the surveillance video: a video she doesn't appear on except to establish an alibi that showed her being called to the scene of the initial crime. Grace was in uniform the day of the festival and could have used her state employee status to gain access to the areas needed to stage Stevenson's hanging. Grace shot Chance and planted the mace, gloves, and rope in Ashton's truck. And, of course, Grace shot Langley because she missed me when Langley knocked me into the fountain.

Grace was the mastermind behind it all.

Rage swept over me. Ashton was completely innocent, and she'd shot him. I thought of the hard lines of anguish on his face when she'd pulled the trigger. He'd pleaded for trust. I should have listened to him. His blood was on my hands.

"Self-defense," Grace repeated. "You got it?" This time her hand hovered over her holster as she spoke.

I squared my shoulders. This wasn't my Grace—the devoted friend I loved. This Grace betrayed me and lied. This Grace had killed four people, maybe more. And she'd kill me too if given another opportunity. I had to protect myself by any means necessary.

I pulled the keys from my pocket with the edges set like the claws of a wolverine and lunged at her.

FORTY

BOTH OF MY arms slashed at the air in front of Grace's face. The claws in my right hand found purchase in the fleshy part of her cheek. She shrieked as I scraped the metal across her skin. I reinforced the punishment with a punch that connected with her neck. She staggered backward along the garden's cement path to avoid my reach, but I charged forward, determined to keep her off balance.

I was younger and faster than Grace, with the element of surprise on my side, but she was taller and more experienced. When the retreat failed to shake me, she quickly changed tactics and hopped laterally like a boxer. But rather than meet me blow for blow with blocks and counterpunches, she defended her position with a series of push kicks—the third of which landed square in my stomach. The power from her leg doubled me over and knocked the breath from my lungs. I dropped the keys and fell to my knees.

Seeing me down and winded, she whipped her weapon from its holster and stretched her arm toward me. With a step forward, she pressed the muzzle against my brow, still hot from where she'd recently fired.

"If you'd just left well enough alone, Victoria, no one else would have died. You're too smart for your own good. This was supposed to be about Frederica Wannamaker getting what she deserves." Grace's voice grew low. "Sorry it's come to this."

"Sorry because you're about to shoot, or sorry because you killed the only person who cared more about me than my own mother?"

"Cut the sentimental crap." Grace shoved the gun deeper into my skin until the muzzle seared my flesh and my head tipped backward. "That soulless dilettante cared about nothing but her career. I strangled her because she didn't deserve a bullet, but don't think I have a problem putting two in you."

"Are you insane?" I hoped the question would stop her.

Her finger rested on the trigger, and I wasn't ready to die.

"You've left a trail of bodies so long a blind person could stumble upon the truth. No way you'll walk away from this."

"That's wishful thinking, Victoria," she chuckled. "The cops believed exactly what I wanted when I put that suicide note together for Stevenson's hanging. Getting him into that noose was a bit of a trick, but a little mace and lot of Tasering go a long way." She patted her duty belt. "People love a scapegoat, and that would have been the simplest solution to everyone's problem if you'd kept your mouth—"

"You mean *your* problem," I hissed through gritted teeth. "If your solution was so perfect, why bring Ashton into this—or the Mulligans?"

"That was your idea. I was prepared to let the suicide-confession thing ride, but you pegged North for the killer after we watched the surveillance footage. You wouldn't buy the Stevenson theory, even after I said he could have been hiding in the bathroom with her while other people entered the kitchen—which is exactly what I was doing." She wagged a chastising finger at me and placed it back under the hand that held her gun. "I gave you the scenario you wanted: North goes on a grudge-inspired killing spree that started with the judge and ended with the execution of his most elusive suspect."

A tingle creeped up my spine as she told her tale with a cold and calculated confidence. She'd been three steps ahead of me the entire time and held no qualms about hurting me. Maybe if I could figure out why she was so eager to shut me down, I could reason with her, try to stall until people from the funeral flooded The Quad. That was my only chance.

"You left the funeral, shot Chance, and stashed his body in the back of Ashton's truck along with those supplies?"

"A woman's work is never done." She smirked. "Based on everything you told me about the corporal's obsession with the Mulligans, framing your buddy seemed more believable than pinning things on Stevenson and, let's face it, the festival stunt was a bit risky with the whole town watching. But this—*this* let your imagination and the abundance of evidence do all the work."

"What about Phyllis? What does she have to do with all this?"

"Not a goddam thing. She and North were too busy arguing with Stevenson to see me come out of the bathroom after having snapped that bitch's neck." Grace leaned over to meet my glare, and her voice grew oddly cheerful. "Although, I suppose I should thank Phyllis... and Langley. Killing Wannamaker in the courthouse was a lightbulb moment that might not have happened without the chaos of the trial. I mean, I'd always planned to kill her, but this made it seem fated. Stevenson became the ideal fall guy with all that douchery he tossed around. Nipping the tie from Harriston's pocket was easy, thanks to the camera angles and a little sleight of hand. I had the perfect murder weapon and pawn to seal the deal for everyone. Except you."

Gun be damned. The desire to scream and scratch her eyes out thrummed through my body. I clenched my fists and sat on my heels so I wouldn't be tempted. She'd basically confessed to killing people for sport. No way I'd let things end like this.

I owed it to Ms. Freddie and Ashton…

…and to Langley and Chance…

…to outwit her…

…or die trying.

"Why?" I squealed. "Why did you do it? Why Ms. Freddie?"

"Because she wouldn't let him go." Grace's voice came out ragged. Desperate. "It's been ten years—TEN! Even once she suspected the affair, she wouldn't let him go. Held him by the short hairs and treated him like trash. Afraid a separation would sully her image in the political community and ruin her delusional ambitions. Everything was about *her*. Russell was never going to escape. The only way we were going to be together was if I got rid of her."

This is personal.

How had I been so blind? Grace, not Maggie, was having an affair with Mr. Russell. Meanwhile, Grace watched me—no, encouraged me—to ridicule Maggie for breaking up a marriage and left me to falsely accuse Mr. Russell of lying when she knew I had faulty information. But then, why didn't Mr. Russell tell me about Grace when he had the chance?

"Maybe you got this all wrong," I pleaded in a futile attempt to reason with her. "Maybe he didn't want to leave his wife. What makes you think you had the right to interfere?"

"Who are you to talk about rights? What do you know about marriage?"

Grace removed the gun from my forehead and slapped me across the jaw with it. Blood exploded in my mouth, and my neck snapped to the side. The momentum carried me to the ground, where I curled into a ball. A white-hot searing sensation raged behind my eyes. I lost sight of her as my vision clouded into a series of dark splotches.

"Russell needed to be avenged!" she shrieked. "He wasn't happy. He needs a woman who treats him with respect. He deserves someone who is going to put his needs first. She never intended to do that. She never wanted a family. She never supported his dreams. But I can give him what he wants. I can give him happiness."

I swallowed a mouthful of bloody saliva. That was as much as I dared move for fear she'd pull me up from the ground and strike me again. Fighting the dull throb that reverberated through my skull, I pieced together a final question. The most important one of all. "Is Mr. Russell in on this? He knows you killed his wife?"

"No, no." Her voice was a whisper. "I never told him—I'd lose him, but he's not stupid. You heard him at the funeral. I'm sure he suspects."

I opened my eyes and peered up at her. "You're crazy

if you think he'll ignore his instincts and continue to love—"

"If that thought makes you feel better, so be it." She reached down, grabbed me by the hair, and pulled so I rose shakily to my feet. "This whole self-defense scenario will be a much tougher sell without you, but I'll manage. Walk."

She pressed the gun into my side and pulled me toward the fountain.

"No!" I went limp to add resistance. I couldn't let her throw me back inside.

"Walk!" she commanded and yanked my head so hard she must have pulled out a handful of hair.

I limped along beside her as she maneuvered me to the opposite side of the fountain, where Ashton lay in a heap.

"Get down on your knees and don't move." She deposited me about five feet from Ashton's body. I was almost too ashamed to look at him. I'd let him down. He lay on his side, his face obscured.

Forgive me.

Two words I wished I'd uttered much sooner.

"The way I figure it," Grace seemed satisfied with my position, "North shot you and Chance."

She crouched beside Ashton but kept her gaze on me. She then placed her gun on the ground while she slipped on one of the rubber gloves from her duty belt. When she finished, she picked up Ashton's gun with the gloved hand and her own gun with the bare one.

"Now, forensics may ding me for shooting Langley, but I'll just have to say she got caught in the crossfire during the standoff with North. My shot was from the back, so his should be…"

She stood, lifted Ashton's gun, pointed it at the fountain, and fired one round into Langley's chest. The loud crack of the gunshot startled me into closing my eyes for a second. And when I opened them, the half of Langley's body that had been floating above water had slipped below the surface.

"His should be from the front." She smiled at me. "Now your turn."

She pivoted to face me head-on and took aim with Ashton's gun.

A nervous heat scorched my skin. All hope evaporated. This was it. This was the end, but I wouldn't give her the satisfaction of witnessing my defeat. I thrust my chin and chest upward in an act of resistance. "All these dead bodies out in the open—you can't win."

"Watch me."

FORTY-ONE

I BRACED MYSELF for gunfire, but I wasn't ready for what I saw.

Ashton's bloody torso rose from the ground like a zombie in search of flesh.

A scream erupted from my throat.

Grace twisted at the waist, presumably to follow my line of sight, when Ashton half tackled, half flopped onto her back. As his weight crashed into her body, she stumbled forward and her hands flew out, but the two weapons prevented her from bracing herself against the trip and flounder that followed. She belly-flopped onto the ground, and her chin hit the earth with a teeth-chattering smack. Her ungloved hand popped open at impact. Her gun clattered across the cement and skidded to a halt between us.

I didn't hesitate.

I lunged for the firearm. This was my only chance. The black casing sat less than a yard away from me, but the gun hadn't fallen far enough from her grasp for me to have the upper hand for long.

Besides, she had a second gun.

I completed my lunge, stretched open my palm, and placed my hand down to find we'd reached the gun at the same time. My hand on top of hers. She laughed, and I cringed as I caught sight of the blood in her mouth. With the other gun still in play, it was game over.

But Ashton, sweet Ashton, who had clearly lost too much blood to engage in a real fight, used his massive body weight to hold Grace down so she couldn't lift the gloved hand that held the other gun—his gun. The move bought me just enough time to snatch the weapon from her grasp.

I squeezed the molded nylon grip and scrambled to my feet, gun extended before me with one hand cupped under the other. It was much lighter than I'd imagined. Tons of guns came through the courtroom as evidence, but I'd never picked one up before, and I wasn't sure what to do. But I wasn't going to let Grace know that.

Without thinking too much about it, I did my variation of what I'd seen dozens of times at the courthouse when an inmate got unruly. I rushed forward, rammed my knee into her neck, and pressed the gun to the crown of her head.

"You lose."

Grace stiffened but said nothing and remained still.

I groped around on the ground until I felt the other gun. I didn't want to take my sights off her until I was sure I had both weapons. When I found the second firearm, I pried it from her fingers and tossed it toward the fountain. Then I glanced over at the corporal.

"I'm sorry, Ashton. I should have trusted you, but I'm going to get us out of this."

He simply swallowed in response. His face was ashen. The line of his mouth was taut, and he clenched his jaw against the pain. Blood was everywhere. A big plume of the dark liquid decorated the shoulder of his coat, but I couldn't see all his injuries due to his prone position atop Grace's back. All I could do was hope the wounds wouldn't bleed out before I could get help.

"Do you have your cell on you?" I asked.

"Coat pocket." His voice was barely audible.

I kept the gun and my sights fixed on Grace while I used my free hand to blindly prod through his coat.

With a working phone finally in my grasp, I made the call.

"Nine-one-one. What's your emergency?"

"There's been a murder on The Quad. We have the killer—and the officer in pursuit is down."

I reached for Ashton's hand and held it to my heart.

FORTY-TWO

LIGHT SHIMMERED ACROSS the water as the sun rose over the Delaware Bay. A flock of seabirds glided along the horizon and slipped from view in a graceful dive. Ashton and I had parked at the back of the vacant lot outside the Cape May-Lewes Ferry Terminal. Both of us sat on the hood of his F-150 and watched the hazy gray sky blossom into shades of orange, yellow, and gold. Tourist season didn't start for another month, so we basked in the serenity and solitude. My aquaphobia was still a work in progress, but, after the recent ordeal with Langley—how she'd used water to save rather than punish, how she'd given her life for mine—I decided to finally address the issue that had haunted me for a decade.

Even still, I was nowhere near ready for a ferry ride, although Ashton hoped to help me work up to it. He believed a breathtaking moment could be empowering once we learned to appreciate the strength and beauty of those things that could make or break us.

A lesson he apparently desired to reinforce in himself as much as impart because we'd been meeting every Sunday since the conclusion of his plea negotiations three weeks ago.

"What's that Tolkien quote you came up with last week?" Ashton asked. "You can only come to the morning through the shadows?"

"Something like that. Though, I take it from your

answer things aren't going well with your probation officer."

The corners of Ashton's mouth twitched as if to censor his words. "It's been tough. Being on the other side of things, you know? I mean, I want to make up for what I did…" He looked at his hands and started picking at the cuticles. "I know the ends don't justify themselves. I get that. I made bad choices that I regret. But now, most people will only see me as a criminal, and that's the part of this I can't stand." He looked over at me and used a hand to hood his face against the sun. "My probation officer seems cool, though. If he's got a problem with me, he doesn't show it. I'm talking more about the guys I'm leaving behind at the troop…"

He leaned into me, and I wrapped an arm around his massive shoulders.

While Ashton had spent two months in the hospital recovering from surgery, he'd confessed to the wrongful arrest of Langley Mulligan. Even though the cocaine and cash he claimed to have seized from her were 100 percent real at the time of submission into evidence, he'd actually siphoned the items from a raid overseen by the Drug Task Force earlier in the year and claimed to have found them in Langley's car when he detained her.

At his plea hearing, Ashton faced three misdemeanors and four felony counts for official misconduct, evidence tampering, perjury, and filing a false instrument. Each of the felony charges carried up to four years in prison, and the misdemeanors a max sentence of a year each. But due to Ashton's cooperation with the investigation and his heroism in solving Ms. Freddie's murder, the judge gave him three years probation, a $3,500 fine, and 100 hours community service.

While some might consider me weak for allowing Ashton to take credit for my footwork, I found solace in the ability to come to his rescue. After all, I owed him my life. Deep down he was a good man. He'd simply been put in a desperate situation due to the loss of a mentor—a feeling I could understand.

"You'll find another job," I gave his shoulders a squeeze, "and people will come around."

"Will they? Your mom sure hasn't. That look she gives me when I pick you up—" He shuddered.

"Ma is a work in progress. Measure the world by her standards, and you'll always come up short. Let's just say she's been coping with a lot."

An understatement of epic proportions.

The truth behind Ms. Freddie's murder put Ma in mad dog mode, and Ashton was at the top of her list due to his proximity. She considered him a liar on par with Phyllis, who succumbed to similar charges of criminal misconduct and evidence tampering because of her failure to tell authorities about Chance's access to the Controlled Substance Lab. The fallout of which became a political nightmare, due to the millions of dollars spent revamping the CSL and adopting new coding procedures.

But when Ma wasn't cursing Ashton or Phyllis, she was on the attack against Mr. Russell, who ultimately confessed to the decade-long affair with Grace. So Ma felt as if she'd lost two of her oldest friends instead of one.

Determined to school Grace on the price of duplicity, Ma used her newfound political connections to convince a member of Delaware's House of Representatives to propose a bill to reinstate the death penalty. Whether the endeavor succeeded was out of Ma's hands, but she wanted Grace to believe freedom would never be an option.

"Hey, hey there. You still with me?" Ashton waved a hand in front of my eyes and pointed at the glowing circle on the horizon. "We've got to make this visit official with some fun facts. Ready?"

"Aye, Captain." I sat up a little straighter and folded my legs into lotus pose to prepare for our little ritual.

"Did you know our bay supports the world's largest freshwater port system, acts as home to the world's largest population of horseshoe crabs, and boasts the second-highest concentration of shorebirds in North America?"

"Is that last one a crack at my Scrappy the Seabird days?"

"Not even close," he tilted his head toward me and smiled, "but I bet you were adorable in that costume."

Heat seared my cheeks, and I wasn't sure if it was a latent reaction to my past or a sign of hope for the future. I leaned my head on his shoulder—the way people did when there was a history of things better left unsaid—and enjoyed the dawn of a new day. We'd agreed to make a fresh start with each other based on a newfound trust.

And that was enough for now.

* * * * *

ABOUT THE AUTHOR

ANDREA J. JOHNSON is a writer and editor whose expertise lies in traditional mysteries and romance. She holds an M.F.A. in Writing Popular Fiction from Seton Hill University and a copyediting certification from UC San Diego. Her craft essays have appeared on several websites such as LitReactor, DIY MFA, Submittable, and Funds for Writers. She also writes entertainment articles for the women's lifestyle website Popsugar.

To learn more about Andrea's work, visit ajthenovelist.com or follow @ajthenovelist on Twitter.

Get 4 FREE REWARDS!

We'll send you 2 FREE Books plus 2 FREE Mystery Gifts.

Harlequin Romantic Suspense books are heart-racing page-turners with unexpected plot twists and irresistible chemistry that will keep you guessing to the very end.

FREE Value Over **$20**

YES! Please send me 2 FREE Harlequin Romantic Suspense novels and my 2 FREE gifts (gifts are worth about $10 retail). After receiving them, if I don't wish to receive any more books, I can return the shipping statement marked "cancel." If I don't cancel, I will receive 4 brand-new novels every month and be billed just $4.99 per book in the U.S. or $5.74 per book in Canada. That's a savings of at least 13% off the cover price! It's quite a bargain! Shipping and handling is just 50¢ per book in the U.S. and $1.25 per book in Canada.* I understand that accepting the 2 free books and gifts places me under no obligation to buy anything. I can always return a shipment and cancel at any time. The free books and gifts are mine to keep no matter what I decide.

240/340 HDN GNMZ

Name (please print)

Address   Apt. #

City   State/Province   Zip/Postal Code

Email: Please check this box ☐ if you would like to receive newsletters and promotional emails from Harlequin Enterprises ULC and its affiliates. You can unsubscribe anytime.

Mail to the **Harlequin Reader Service:**
IN U.S.A.: P.O. Box 1341, Buffalo, NY 14240-8531
IN CANADA: P.O. Box 603, Fort Erie, Ontario L2A 5X3

Want to try 2 free books from another series? Call 1-800-873-8635 or visit www.ReaderService.com.

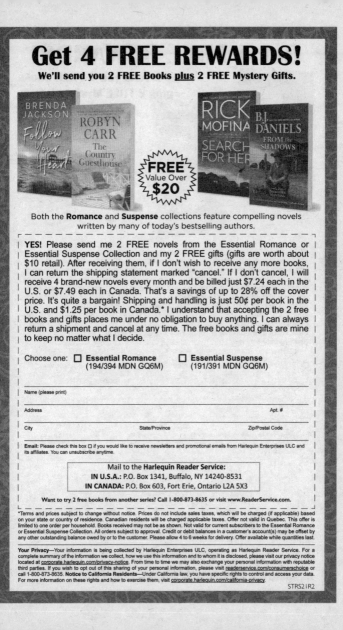

Visit
ReaderService.com
Today!

As a valued member of the Harlequin Reader Service, you'll find these benefits and more at ReaderService.com:

- Try 2 free books from any series
- Access risk-free special offers
- View your account history & manage payments
- Browse the latest Bonus Bucks catalog

Don't miss out!

If you want to stay up-to-date on the latest at the Harlequin Reader Service and enjoy more content, make sure you've signed up for our monthly News & Notes email newsletter. Sign up online at ReaderService.com or by calling Customer Service at 1-800-873-8635.